GIL'S WORLD

GIL'S WORLD

Wanderers, Book 1
(Wanderer Universe)

JAMES MURDO

GIL'S WORLD

To Bernadette and Stephen

CHAPTER 1

WANDERERS

The stars shone lazily on the ship as it travelled through the eternal void. Everything it came across, all manner and manifestation of matter strewn across the galaxy, was probed and recorded. The galactic concourse was its playground, tantalisingly displaying its wares as the ship went about its quest.

The ship was tasked with sifting through it all, from the decaying ruins of forgotten empires to the empty expanses of nothingness. No scorched world, mutilated worldship or orbital husk that it passed was left unscrutinised. Crumbling remains were scoured and plundered, and then left to the ravages of time. It studied the nebulae, the asteroids, and the stars themselves. Fields and their associated forces were meticulously dissected, down to their most basic constituents.

Occasionally, dark planets would flit across its path, having escaped the gravitational forces of their parent systems. Molecular winds of protostellar cocoons would waft along its bow as the gasses were slowly drawn to a coalescent core. It recorded these too, along with every action it took itself, ready to be submitted to one of the data exchanges that had been seeded throughout the galaxy.

The ship resembled a vast squid-like creature. It had originally been created from an amalgamation of technologies contributed by various civilisations. Its main body was an obsidian-black mass, trailing billions of tentacle-like elongations behind that thrust it through the ether.

The tentacles fed off vacuum energy, the persistent quantum hum that permeated the entire universe. Over twice the length of its main body at full length, they fanned out densely in each spatial dimension and resembled an immense fungal bloom. Each tentacle branched into smaller sub-tentacles, which in turn fractally branched out. The smallest fibres at the ends plugged directly into the foamy broth of spacetime, where they were vibrated by the ubiquitous quantum hum.

The quantum hum was often described as the greatest self-diagnostics test ever performed. It comprised the spontaneous blinking of particle-antiparticle pairs inconsequentially into and out of existence. In theory, nothing was impacted by it, and the particles were aptly termed 'virtual particles'. The ship's tentacles took advantage of this free energy.

Once a fibre was rocked by the hum, the motion was conducted back up the fractal chain. The force provided by the contribution of quadrillions of fibres induced each larger tentacle to oscillate with a fantastical frequency. That oscillation interfered with the initial pool of offending virtual particles to such an extent that they were ripped out of the quantum domain. They entered the observable macro domain and interacted with each other to release an astronomical amount of power, which could be manipulated and directed by the bloom.

The leviathan ship moved forward by riding the silent, self-perpetuating cosmic wave. Once a bloom had been created, its power output could never be muted. Any motion, or lack of, was controlled by changing its shape.

The existence of the ship and its quest were down to the scourge that had decimated the galaxy, and the fight that continued against it. The war had relentlessly devastated civilisations for the better part of three hundred million standard years. The immense timescale spanned eras many times longer than those over which a typical species might evolve, obtain galactic prominence and return to the dust.

Towards the latter stages of the war, the surviving civilisations were completely united in the struggle. The Ascended Biologicals, or ABs, were at the helm, being the most powerful civilisations in the galaxy. Each of them had long surpassed the ability to be fully understood by the mainstream galactic community. Under their guidance, a monumental discussion was initiated, and a desperate course of action was chosen. The events that followed were generally referred to as the Great Conflation.

Emissaries returned to their respective species and, following pre-agreed terms, orders were carried out. Civilisations turned weapons of terrible devastation inwards upon themselves. Previously unthinkable actions were committed. For the most part, the suicide was a welcome relief to the unending and relentless cycles of an unwinnable war.

The actions had not been without cause, and they did have the intended effects. A theory was substantiated, as far as was possible, although its authors were no longer around to verify it. While the enemy had not been destroyed, it was at least subdued.

Following the events of the Great Conflation, almost every single major civilisation in the galaxy was gone. Left behind were the remnants. The accidental and forgotten descendants, fragments of their brilliant predecessors. Led predominantly by the surviving machine-lects, they grew in strength and banded together into factions. Loose accords were struck between many of the factions, which strengthened over time into a unified civilisation. The Wanderers were formed. They represented a final barrier against the enemy, and wove their paths between the stars in their self-tasked and endless pursuit, continuing the fight. They travelled in solitude, to search for and destroy the infected. To find a way to defeat the weakened enemy once and for all.

CHAPTER 2

GIL

Gil wiped the sweat off her brow with the back of her tanned right hand, and stopped. Her lower back ached from the time spent diligently working the land. After dropping her sower, she rested an equally tanned left hand on her hip, and looked over to Tor, her twin brother, with admiration. His progress dwarfed her own, and she barely ever caught him stealing a break from the toil. His diligence and single-minded determination were admirable.

Unlike the roamers, who required strict hierarchies to organise their hunts, the communers took a more relaxed approach. Everyone, or at least the majority of communers, understood the principle that their community was based on fairness.

The very oldest in the commune, the elders, had earned the right to observe and take life at the slowest pace. They forewent the more manual labours in favour of watching over the commune, checking it was being properly looked after and cared for. From the fire-pits and the food stores, to recounting their tales to entertain the young children. They were the effective leaders of the commune, and Bo was the oldest and the wisest of them all.

Bo loved to recount tales. As he told them, his deep-set, weathered brown eyes forwent their boundaries, dancing atop his cheeks to complement his words. His thick, greying eyebrows, interlaced with wisps of pure white, sat under a creased forehead. While he had the tendency to embellish a story to excite a willing audience, this only made them more interesting. Having lived the longest and seen the most, he was an invaluable source of information. It was fortunate in general that the elders had more time to discuss what they knew, as it meant their knowledge was seldom lost.

The tool Gil had let fall to the ground a moment before had been created through a spark of her own creative genius. It was her most significant contribution to the commune yet, and was one of the most significant contributions to the commune by any single communer in a long time.

The sower was part-digger, part-planter, and could be used all year round. She remembered how obvious it had seemed to her that the separate tools could be combined. The enjoyment she had felt from creating it had spurred her on to consider new ideas. Unfortunately, those ideas and sparks of her imagination had to wait for appropriate times, when her daily duties were done. She often thought that her creativity compensated for her lack of other abilities.

The stitched animal-skin clothing she wore was heavy and dripping with sweat, but to wear any less would be indecent. She was already wearing the minimum practical for polite company. The coolness brought by the sweat was a small and welcome comfort, albeit an indignant sign from her body that she could not continue indefinitely. She would need some refreshment. She wistfully recalled the colder seasons. The feel of a cold swim in one of the nearby lakes, under the blissful shade afforded by the luscious forest canopies towering above.

She searched her sphere for any signs of the reprieve she longed for. A cold wind, rain. Something that would make her more comfortable. She searched right to its very tips, to the edges of where she could actively look, but found nothing encouraging. Opening her mind a little more, she allowed information from the weaker, more indistinct outer reaches to filter through. Again, she was not inspired. There seemed to be the faintest hint of an incoming cold presence, but it was too far out and too blurry. She could not be sure. Besides, right now her concern was with shorter-term relief.

A small fly that had been circling her head for some time came to rest in her dark brown hair. She moved her hand to swat it, but by the time her hand connected with the back of her head, she was of course too late. Instead, she attempted to probe it.

Its dull, tiny mind only registered as having the barest of intentions to her sphere. Near the point of irrelevance. She knew this would be the case, as it was with most things that were not people. Most likely, it was only packed with the smallest collection of instincts. Everything that was required to help it avoid being swatted.

Sometimes she felt she could sense something else beyond this. Not anything especially significant about the fly, but deeper. In her sphere. Almost hidden from her and the other communers. However, she had yet to find any real proof that this was anything more than an over-active imagination, and when she dwelled on it for too long, the quiet whispers at the back of her mind grew stronger.

She wondered if flies could talk to one another as people did, or whether they had their own unique ways. Her mind often moved onto topics such as these, although she was unable to communicate her ideas with others. Speech, unfortunately, was a gift she no longer had as the result of an accident many years before.

She had been perched high up in a tree, hiding from Tor as part of a game. Unbeknownst to her, she had been spotted with ease. They were both young enough that their complete spheres had not yet developed, and she could not fully sense his presence. She had been looking out for him, but even then, his physical prowess had shown. He successfully sneaked up behind her without making a sound. As he moved into position, gleefully edging closer and closer, he had decided to shout. Loudly. Innocently joyful at his success. Unluckily for Gil, the shock of him surprising her caused her to momentarily let go of the branches she was holding for support. At precisely the same time, her feet slipped.

As she fell backward, she could see Tor's look of genuine shock and horror. His wide eyes followed her as she dropped. The look on his face was permanently frozen into her memory.

The fall took longer in her own mind than was possible. However, it was seared into her recollection as the only time she had known Tor to be indecisive, unable to act. Unable to help. Since that moment, his outlook had changed. It was rare to see him indecisive again. He was not as much of a dreamer or creative problem-solver as Gil, but he was fiercely intelligent in his own right. If the accident had not happened, Gil wondered whether he would have grown up differently.

Gil's body had twisted as it fell, and she ended up hitting the ground face down. She was dimly aware of a scurrying sound in the background as she lay there, motionless. It had turned out to be the sound of Tor scampering down the tree to her side. Once there, he turned her over, and it was only then that Gil became aware of a warm sensation trickling down her throat. Tor's hands came into her field of vision, and she could see they were stained a deep, dark red. It had not made sense to her at the time, and she remembered being confused at the expression he wore.

He had screamed for help until his voice was hoarse. Even when the adults arrived, the screaming had continued. Unfortunately, the damage had been done. Gil had landed onto a branch that had partially protruded upwards, towards the sky. It had pierced her throat, damaging it in such a way that she would never be able to speak again.

As she healed, her sphere had seemed to grow in compensation for her lost power of speech. At least, that was the way it seemed to her. It was as though she could sense intentions more keenly than before. Intentions of the land, of the air, of larger animals. Of many things, with much more clarity. Certain things were unknowable, but while one ability had been taken away from her, the wonders of another had been unveiled. This was also when she had begun to hear the whispers. She had tried to communicate this to Tor and her father, using gestures, however the capability to relay this concept precisely eluded her, no matter how hard she tried. During one of her last attempts, when she thought her father had finally begun to understand, he acted with rare annoyance, telling her that it was most likely her imagination, and to focus on other things. She had cried, and immediately he held her tight, telling her it was forgotten.

Gil bore no grudge against her brother for her misfortune. He had been equally as distraught as her. His feelings of guilt had only been assuaged, and rightly so, through Gil's obvious affection and forgiveness towards him. If anything, their bond had strengthened. They had been born at the same time, and despite what had happened, he was highly protective of her. He had grown into a tough and clever young man, and was now one of the most capable in the commune.

The only real grief she had suffered with Tor, had been the loss of their father. Their mother had died giving birth to them, and their father had been their only family besides each other. As was not too uncommon, neither of their parents had been born within the commune. Both had joined it separately. Of all the people currently in the commune, about a quarter of them, mainly adults, came from elsewhere.

Thinking about her father was still painful. With the help of the commune, he had raised them, and they loved him unconditionally. He had been one of the strongest and most able men, and was well-respected. Gil was proud that Tor was such a close reflection of him, especially in looks and how he held himself. Tor's skin was a little darker, but he had the same strong and agile build. He also had those rare piercing green eyes, the same as Gil and their father.

She knew that her own inquisitive nature, her desire to create and dream, were attributable to their father's influence. When they had been younger, her father had told them strange and wonderful stories, many of which Gil had unfortunately forgotten or only half-remembered as time passed. Many were about his own travels and experiences, although equally as many had been crafted to amuse and delight his children. She remembered how he said that he had come from a far-off commune, and that he had searched and searched for a better life. After many years of wandering, sometimes with roamer clans, sometimes stopping to stay with other communes for brief periods, and sometimes staying with other groups that Gil did not quite understand, he had found their current commune and made it his home.

Some years ago, a sickness had come. Before long it had taken hold of many of the communers. The unlucky ones who were susceptible to it suffered aggressive fevers and quickly grew dangerously weak. Some, such as Gil and Tor, were unaffected, and some recovered, but many had died. Old or young, it did not matter. At the time, their father had volunteered to go alongside another man, Yul, to travel in search of help. There were rumours that other distant communes were unaffected, but no one knew for sure.

Gil still remembered the day her father had set off. Kneeling on one knee he had hugged them both in turn, told them to behave, and left. Yul had been their father's best friend, and she knew that neither would knowingly allow anything disastrous to befall the other. Clearly, she had been too young to understand the perils of such a journey.

Neither had returned. Gil was ashamed to remember that she did not even realise as her father's impressive presence in her sphere had disappeared, alongside Yul's. No one in the commune, including the wise Bo who possessed the strongest sphere of those left, had noticed, which was awful. Both her father and Yul should still have been close enough to be sensed by many communers. Alongside everyone else, Gil had been so busy tending to the sick that she had been complacent in checking they were safe, as had Tor.

Once the commune had recovered, thankfully, subsequent trips had been made by numerous communers to try to uncover the fate that had befallen her father and Yul. Nothing was found. Gil comforted herself with the thought that, no matter how unlikely, there was a chance they had become lost and disoriented. It had been known to happen, though only in extreme cases. People could usually rely on their spheres to guide them back, as sphere ranges were generally far greater than the other senses. If they had been running from something, a dangerous animal perhaps, Gil was confident they would have been able to outsmart it, although their escape might have involved travelling far away. She often dreamt vivid scenarios in which her father and Yul overcame many different obstacles and trials, and were finally able to begin the long journey home. One day, she wanted to believe, she would see her father again. Tor rarely spoke of their father to her, but she knew that he thought about him often too. She could tell that he moulded himself to be more like him.

The reprieve over, Gil shrugged off her nostalgic thoughts and dreams, and got back to work. Her day's toil was nearly done, and she was looking forward to finishing.

CHAPTER 3

WANDERER SHIP

As the ship organised and analysed the data it collected, potential scenarios were extrapolated. The outputs were codified and stored within the hyper-dense nodes of the ship's databanks.

The highly efficient nodes made up the bulk of the ship's data storage mechanisms. They functioned by exploiting a quantum loophole that allowed certain discrete signals to be locally phase-shifted back onto themselves in time. Once the signals were properly manipulated and codified, the result was practically near-infinite storage capacity. Without this mechanism, the ship would not have been able to process the incredible amounts of data it collected, which was a necessity in allowing it to comb the galaxy for signs of the parasitic enemy.

The node storage technology had been discovered during the early era of the Wanderers. It was during the time when the surviving machine-lects had loosely affiliated themselves with each other, but before the specific agreement to form the Wanderers had been struck. One of the pre-Wanderer factions had happened upon a relatively unexplored cluster of star systems, which had belonged to a suicided species called the Carterans. They had only recently joined the galactic community before the Great Conflation.

The Carterans were generally capable as a civilisation, and their entry onto the galactic stage had been delayed by their natural isolationism. What made them curious, and almost unique, was their dedication to recording everything. Every single aspect of themselves, their culture, and their environment was precious to them. It was suspected that they had delayed making their presence known for as long as they had, because of this preoccupation.

Many civilisations decided to delay their presence on the galactic stage, with copious reasons for such. Some mistrusted the wider community and resigned themselves to intra-civilisation communications only, blithely ignoring all attempts of external contact, or actively rebuffing them. Some only interacted with a few chosen and highly vetted races. Some even interacted, for a brief period, just to say that they would not be interacting. The number of species within the galaxy was so high that there was no norm, which ironically, was the norm. There were enough permutations of every single decision ever taken that the more established races were well attuned to the idiosyncrasies of the newer races. They expected them.

Many other races were, in turn, the absolute opposite to the Carterans, demanding to speak to everyone and anyone they came across. This was met with the same understanding attitude by the established races. It only became a problem when the extrovert races displayed arrogance, or anything that was perceived as such, and attempted to force themselves onto races that they had not realised were hitherto being too polite to rebuff their advances. If such transgressions were to escalate, it was then a gamble as to whether the ABs decided to swoop in to help resolve them. If they did not, the younger civilisation could be rebuked with severity on a scale right up to total destruction. The galaxy could be a dangerous place.

The pre-Wanderer machine-lects had initially been suspicious of the Carteran technologies they found. Their technological level was in many ways inferior to the pre-Wanderers', however the machine-lects were equally suspicious of just about every new technology they came across. Generally, when technologies were compared between species and civilisations, nuanced uses of incredibly well-understood principles could lead to differences that were fiendishly difficult to understand. That often had to be learned the hard way.

One particular race, the Kuish, specialised in observing this phenomenon itself. They theorised that there were at least as many ways of solving any individual problem as there were different species. Quite what passed the threshold to qualify as a separate problem, and what constituted a different species, was debatable, but the Kuish

Observation was a generally accepted theory. Albeit, as critics pointed out, rather obvious.

Soon enough, the pre-Wanderer machine-lects realised the capabilities offered by the Carteran technologies were too important to ignore. After some time understanding and experimenting with the technologies, and improving them as best they could, the phase-shifted memory nodes were created. Easy to produce, they revolutionised the machine-lect attitude towards the enemy and their ability to detect it. The Wanderers were formally established shortly afterward, and their ships had been traversing the galaxy on their missions ever since.

Other instruments and technologies had also been found from both known and unknown civilisations. They were typically classified as trove instruments until they were completely understood. The distinction between being a known civilisation versus an unknown civilisation was a vague concept before the Wanderers, as it was relative to whichever species was the observer. However, in Wanderer times, being the most populous civilisation left, at least as far as they knew, their point of view was the predominant one.

Individual Wanderer ships often collected trove instruments and slaved over them for tens and hundreds of millennia at a time. Significant intellectual resources were dedicated to yielding their secrets. Information about them was uploaded to the rest of their civilisation at the data exchanges, although this was done carefully. Data exchanges were heavily guarded Wanderer constructs that were usually under the control of a powerful data-lect.

Protocols and best practices had been developed around how to safely probe new trove items. Since the main stages of the Great War, there were ample opportunities to refine them. Many a Wanderer, or one of their contemporaries, had erroneously powered up and activated a wondrous piece of God-like machinery from a battle-ravaged outpost, only for it to fashion a grinning black hole in front of the unlucky scavenger, or even cause the local stars in the vicinity to go supernova in spectacular fashion. Others had picked up instruments that, upon initial inspection, had appeared simple and innocuous enough, only for the true operation to be utterly bizarre and highly dangerous. Technologies could even be so different that they were not even recognised as such. Well-substantiated theories were turned upside down, spun around and shredded to pieces, with a complex clutter of puzzling pieces left to deal with. It was almost a rule that the more dangerous an item, the more mundane it appeared. Dangerous military platforms might be disguised as bland, derelict orbital stations. Ostensibly innocent and seemingly defenceless outposts were invariably the worst. Typically, it was prudent to scarper from such places, leaving the minimum possible space-print, and accelerating away for as long as possible.

Over time, precautions had been developed to minimise the chances of such disastrous events caused by an overzealous approach. The Wanderers' governing entity, the

Wanderer Enclave, periodically disseminated information to the Wanderers via the data exchanges.

Vast timescales were often involved between Wanderer vessels encountering and choosing to approach data exchanges. Therefore, the informational asymmetries across the Wanderer civilisation were thought to be some of the greatest that had ever existed. It was even thought, although neither confirmed nor denied by the Enclave, that some vessels had not been in contact with their own kind since the beginning of their long foray into the dark expanse. Stretching the range of possible scenarios to their extremes, it was possible that the war could be won, or lost, millions of years before the bulk of the Wanderer civilisation even realised. The galaxy was a large place, and Wanderer paths were largely random as a specific tactic to avoid detection by the parasite.

CHAPTER 4

GIL

Gil placed her sower back in the hut she shared with Tor, glad that it was finally time to rest. She walked out of the hut and settled down in front of one of the fires. She did not need warming up, but enjoyed gazing into the flames as they flickered about and caused the pieces of wood to crackle.

It was normal for family members to share a hut, although both she and Tor were approaching the age where it would be reasonable for them to request their own. However, she enjoyed living with him and wanted to continue for a little while longer, and thought that he would too. Being twins, with no other siblings and no parents, they had grown accustomed to their joint living arrangements.

Sarl was a communer who was the opposite in almost every way to Gil. She had requested her own hut as soon as she had come of age. Once the request had been made and permission granted, the elders in the commune decided where to place the new hut, and the communers who were able to lend a hand set about constructing it. Gil helped, even though she knew it would gain her no thanks or friendship. She assisted Sib, Bo's sister, with finding and treating the resin that was necessary to secure the smaller branches and twigs to the hut's walls.

Few huts had been built since Sarl's, and Gil was certain this was because people remembered how difficult it had been. Sarl's consistent criticisms had weighed on those who had assisted in the construction. Gil could have sworn that Sarl herself had not lifted a finger to help, delighting instead in the chastisement of others.

Tor came up beside her, placing one of his large hands protectively on her shoulder as he sat down. He breathed out loudly as he did so, emphasising the end of the day's labour, and picked up a small twig with one hand to fiddle with. It was the part of the day where everyone came together to sit down and relax. Gil glanced around at him and smiled, watching as the end of his huff turned into a smile. It always did. Contentedly, the grin stayed on her face as she looked around at the other communers also in the process of winding down. Her hungry eyes turned to the food being prepared.

Han, one of the younger males and Tor's closest friend, jostled down to sit beside them. He was a little shorter and leaner than Tor, although still of a heavy build and formidable in his own right. Besides, what he lacked in power in comparison with Tor, he made up for in spirit. He was well-liked.

"Hard day?" Tor said, flicking the twig he was fiddling with at Han's feet.

Han cocked his head softly to the side and smirked, raising one of his eyebrows.

"Not as hard as you would expect, Tor."

"What do you mean?"

"It's getting a little easier."

"What is?"

"The animals are straying closer to the camp." Han ran two of his fingers along his knee to give some life to his words.

"I knew you hunters had it easy. Do they just run into your arms?"

"Can you blame them?"

"Maybe they are hard of sight."

"My appearance is not the only thing I can use to impress…"

Tor slapped his thigh and laughed. "You want to impress an animal?" He stressed the last word and shook his head for effect as he said it.

"Not my fault, nothing I can do," Han said, no doubt wishing he had not cornered himself in this particular debate.

"Well if that's the case, I'm glad I don't have whatever you have."

"There's a lot you don't have that I do."

"It's getting too easy then, is it? Pity the animals can't really use the sphere, it'd give you more of a challenge."

"Hah. It's only a little easier, mind you. It's not that though…" Han said thoughtfully, his words trailing off.

"What is it, then?"

"It's as though some of them have already started to move."

"But it's too early in the year for that," Tor said.

"Exactly. But that's what it feels like."

"Maybe you really do have other ways to impress them, and they are telling all their animal friends about you!"

"Hah!"

"Is it your smell?"

"That's coming from you?" Han replied gleefully, happy to have finally gained the upper hand.

While the two of them jokingly bickered, Gil was interested to see what Han was talking about for herself. She opened her mind and noticed there were indeed a few more of the large animals nearby than was typical for this time of the year. It was not a hugely significant change, but clearly enough to make a difference to Han.

She would have continued searching but Han broke her concentration as he smiled awkwardly at her, mildly embarrassed at something that had been said. She did not know what it was, but smirked playfully back at him as though she did. She was used to their exchanges. It was an almost daily occurrence. Han was one of the commune's few hunters and despite his jovial manner, he always seemed slightly more apprehensive about the day ahead than others. She liked him.

"Ah well," Tor said. "Can't be bad if it's just a trickle, can it?"

"As long as they don't all suddenly come through," Han replied.

"That's not going to happen, is it?" Tor asked, although Gil could tell he thought the issue was minor and was quickly exhausting his interest in it.

"No, well, I don't think it is."

"Good."

"I suppose."

"No one was hurt today?" Tor asked Han, as he did most days. It was unlikely, and Gil was sure that Tor had already briefly checked through his sphere anyway, such was his nature. Still, it was part of their routine.

"No, other than a few poor beasts."

Tor smiled at Han's small jest, it was a line he had not come up with before. Their heads both moved together and each set of eyes briefly followed Sarl as she strutted past them. Her hips swung from side to side as she went. Her long brown hair, a few shades lighter than Gil's, hung close to her body, accentuating her curves. She was a few fingers taller than Gil, but by the way she acted, a traveller from another commune could be forgiven for assuming she was already an elder.

Han nudged Tor with his elbow, and they each smirked.

"What do you…" Han started until Tor nudged him back, harder. Tor shot Gil a quick glance, and his face flushed a little. He liked to keep certain pieces of information to himself.

Han recovered, understanding. He smiled at Tor apologetically and changed the subject. "Soon your work on the land will ease."

"I know," replied Tor quickly, knowing where Han was going with the conversation.

"Well then, perhaps you could come out with us..." Han said.

Tor pursed his lips and looked forwards. "I'm sorry, I know I've considered it before. But I feel it too strongly."

"Yes, but you can choose not to listen, Tor, I do. You can shut it off."

"I know, but it's hard. It never really goes, not completely. You're well practiced, you've been doing it for a long time. It would take some time for me to get used to."

"Maybe in the future then. You'll find it easy enough, I'm sure you will."

"Mmm." Tor's reply was noncommittal.

"It would give us some other company, at least."

"Perhaps. We'll see, Han."

Gil knew it was most likely a no.

"No harm in it," Han said. It was his final attempt, although he knew his friend's mind was already set.

"We'll see," Tor said again, noncommittally.

Gil understood Tor's thoughts, and that he was intrigued by the idea of forgoing his sphere. While she knew his sphere was strong, she also knew that he was not one of the people who used it all the time. He was comfortable in his other skills as well.

"Who knows? Maybe you'll even decide to be a hunter at last." Han smiled.

"Unlikely! I may be faster and stronger than everyone else, but that doesn't mean I need to use my talents," Tor said.

Han immediately snorted.

"If that's the case, you keep your talents well hidden!"

"I have so many that I have no choice."

"Hah!"

Both laughed and the teasing continued.

The commune, including the surrounding cultivated land, was situated within a large man-made clearing which had been made many generations earlier. It was based within a great forested expanse. Gil could not even guess at how far it stretched. There were tales, mainly from travellers who occasionally stopped by the commune for a variety of reasons, of great swathes of land from far away that were permanently covered by ice. Of stranger lands still, covered with a layer of fine yellow-orange dirt. Gil did not know how much of this was true, but she enjoyed hearing about them all the same.

The area that the commune was in had been chosen because of the good earth within which crops could easily be grown. The communers still engaged in hunting, although to a lesser extent than their neighbours because of this. Gil had no idea how the land had originally been found to be so, but was grateful for it. She had been told that when it had been selected, a great fire was set to clear it of trees. There was no other way to empty such a large area.

Two rivers nearby snaked through the forest on either side of the commune, providing them with plenty of water. They generally behaved themselves and kept within the confines of their banks, although the younger communers were taught to be wary of them.

The commune's ability to farm the land was not an uncommon activity amongst their people in general, although most of the other communes they knew of were a little more biased towards hunting and foraging. There were also the moving communes whose people never fully settled in one place, and engaged almost entirely in hunting. Their people were called roamers. Including the roamers, relations with other communes was generally benign.

The location of their commune did have one undesirable aspect. The type of surrounding vegetation yielded inedible food that could make communers very ill if foolishly eaten. Fortunately, most of the animals appeared to be unaffected, making easy prey for the hunters in the unlikely instance they ventured too close.

The commune's cultivated land surrounded its main hub, which predominantly consisted of a group of semi-permanent huts spaced loosely next to each other. They were sturdy enough to provide shelter against the rain and the wind, yet flimsy enough that they could be taken down when required.

The huts were mostly constructed from large wooden logs and branches that had fallen in the surrounding forests.

Smaller branches and plants were carefully placed on the top and around the sides to cover any gaps, sealed down with a mud-resin mix. It was this mix that Sib had shown Gil how to create when she helped built Sarl's hut. Sib had shown her how to obtain the resin from nearby trees that were soft enough to have their bark penetrated with sharp stones.

The huts were not as stable as the caves that were often used for shelter by the roamers. However, they could be constructed wherever necessary, and were vital in allowing the commune to thrive. Amid the huts was a central clearing, where discussions and eating took place.

Numerous fire pits were dotted about the spaces between the huts, with two larger fires set in the central clearing. Two members of the commune, under the direction of the elders, were tasked with ensuring that the two central fires were always lit. In the case of rain, two tall structures made of light branches could be used to protect the important fires.

No longer a child, Gil was expected to contribute just like everyone else. While toiling in the cultivated fields was certainly not the most enjoyable activity, there was a sense of accomplishment at the end of the day. She was glad she was not a hunter. Their lot was the worst and Gil truly felt sorry for them. Their days were not so long, and they were often able to retire to the central clearing before anyone else, but their activities weighed heavily on them. A typical sight when Gil was younger and watching for them to return, would be a band of approaching hunters slowly walking back to the community with grim faces and low moods. Gil understood. There was a certain type of pain that came from having to end another life, even that of an animal.

She remembered once as a child, a little after she had lost the ability to speak, when she had noticed the hunters returning to the commune earlier than usual. She sensed them nearby and so reached out with her sphere. What had actually happened, she realised afterward, was that that particular hunt had taken the hunters closer to the commune than was usual. In reaching out to them, she had accidentally sensed the beast they were chasing. She felt its fear and terror as it ran from them, and its confusion, followed by a basic, hopeless comprehension when it understood it was trapped. She watched through her sphere with horror, unfortunate to witness an unusually brutal pursuit. She never wanted to experience such things again. Sometimes the sphere could be too intrusive.

From then on, Gil understood why hunters usually operated in the outer reaches of a typical communer's sphere. She empathised with the hunters and what they had to go through, and understood why her commune tried to grow its own food as much as possible. Feeling an animal's intent to flee as it was chased into a trap was terrifying. Crushing its skull beneath a heavy wooden club was even worse. The best hunters, she had long since decided, were the ones with the truest aim and the most cunning. They were those who could kill an animal before it realised its fate. The hunters did not have to be the strongest of the communers, but the swiftest and the most agile.

Until the moment she had witnessed the animal being killed, she had assumed Tor would be a hunter. After that, she knew he would not be. She knew he would choose to work in the cultivated land instead, and she was proven right. He had probably witnessed a similar hunt to her, maybe the same one.

Gil got along well with the majority of other communers. Up until recently, aside from her brother, the person she had spent the most time with was Sib. While she had been a few years older than her brother, Bo, her curiosity had given her a youthfulness of mind that was rare. Physically, Sib had been the opposite to Gil. She had been old and infirm for as long as Gil had been alive. However, in their minds they had had a mutual likeness – highly imaginative and curious. Gil could listen to her speak all night had Sib wanted to, which she often did. She had the same entrancing storytelling abilities as Bo, and her eyes tended to also dart about, across her face, as she spoke. However, while Bo tended to talk about tales of past exploits or of adventures he had heard, Sib was a wonderer. She questioned what she saw around her.

Sib's death had been hard on Gil. The only positive aspect of it had been that the burial gave closure to a beautiful and well-lived life. Almost everyone in the commune had cried, which Gil was glad to see. She did not think that many people had ever cried at any funeral she had seen before. She had died surrounded by Gil, Bo, her other friends and loved ones, and would be sorely missed.

She had been of the same mind as Gil when it came to Sarl. Whereas they were both fascinated by life, Sarl was more content with gossiping. For the most part, this made little difference to Gil. Not being able to speak did have some benefits after all. The only true shame regarding Sarl was that she was rather beautiful. Even Tor, much to Gil's dismay, seemed to be showing signs of interest in her lately, no matter how much he tried to disguise it. Tor had most of the girls fawning over him, and Gil could not understand what it was about Sarl that interested him. What made it even worse was the thought that this might have been Sarl's intention all along. Other males, of very good standing, had previously shown interest in Sarl that had not been reciprocated. Before her, some time ago, Tor had shown interest in one of Bo's two daughters, although he had been too young to act upon his interest with any vigour. Since then, both of Bo's daughters had joined a nearby commune which had too few young women for the men.

For her own part, under any other circumstances, Gil would likely have been highly sought after by all the unattached males in the commune. Not to the extent that Sarl was, but not that far from it either. It was not that she was mute that put them off, but the fact that she was more than content with her own company, and came with a fiercely protective brother.

Secretly, she harboured a small measure of affection for Ril, Yul's son and only child. He was a few years older than her and worked the land as well. He had helped to comfort her and Tor, in mutual sorrow, when his and their fathers had failed to return all those years ago. However, she did not want to be too obvious in her affection, given he had never shown any affection to her, or anyone, as the years had gone by. If anything, he had grown more detached from people. More inwardly focused.

Turning to Tor and Han, forming a circle with her mouth she made the motion of putting food into her mouth while rubbing her belly. They both laughed.

"I'm hungry as well," Tor said to her.

"You're always hungry," teased Han, weaving his head about in mock boredom. "Hungry, and lazy. What a mix…"

"Lazy? Working the land is hard work, if you weren't a hunter you'd know that."

"It's because I'm a hunter that I do know that."

"You're only a hunter because you get to finish earlier."

"Not always!" Han said, "And who's to know how hard you're really working on the land in any case."

"It's tough!" Tor cried, gesticulating with his hands.

"The animals live off the land. I hunt them, therefore I work the land too. I do what you do, and more." Han's light blue eyes beamed. Believing he had won their brief final exchange, he hurried off to see how the food preparations were coming along. Or was it, Gil wondered, that he was making his escape before Tor could think of a reply?

Tor looked at Gil and tapped her shoulder playfully with his fist. "Come on then, let's see how ready the food is." She rolled her eyes and nodded, watching him as he stood up to follow Han.

She stayed for a few moments longer, taking in the atmosphere. Enjoying it. Children were playing together in the space between the two central fires, running around and obeying the confusing rules of whatever game they had created. Their laughter warmed Gil, and she looked forward to the day when she would have her own child. Not quite yet, though, but later.

As the children played, Gil adjusted her gaze and fixed it onto the fire. Unfocusing her thoughts, she let her mind unwind. The whispers spoke to her, as they had done for many years now, but she was not bothered. They rarely became too loud, and she was mostly able to ignore them. She was content.

CHAPTER 5

WANDERER SHIP

The current patch of space yielded nothing untoward or particularly difficult for the ship to analyse. Of its various sensors, most were focused on sampling transient entropy. Entropy was a long-discovered and well-established concept used to measure the relative disorder of a system. It was commonly known that entropy, within a closed system, would increase over time.

Transient entropy was a similarly established, although slightly more complex, principle. In the times preceding the Great War, many species discovered it, before deeming it immediately useless and ignoring it. This was because if certain of the most basic and fundamental laws of the universe were working correctly, it should never be observed anyway. It was reasoned that there was essentially no point in ever looking for it.

It measured transient deviations to the ubiquitous entropic principle. The transient prefix signified that any such attempts were self-corrected for, although the correction was not perfect, they should oscillate in a decaying pattern, theoretically.

The reason that the ship had so many sensors geared towards such a universe-defyingly unlikely phenomenon, was that it had in fact been observed. It had been almost accidental, and it had been bad news for the entire galaxy.

Before the Great War, the ABs appeared to have a policy of non-intervention with respect to galactic affairs in general. However, it was supposedly not uncommon for them to allow non-AB races access to certain technologies. The offer was usually in exchange for the receiving race agreeing to abide by the ABs' sometimes perplexing codes of galactic conduct. Greater self-driven technological advancement typically engendered a greater standing within the galactic community, hence AB technology transfers were thought to be done, for the most part, in private.

While it was not known exactly how frequently the ABs engaged in such activities, there were some obvious cases that were easy to identify. The most famous being the conflict between the Balroons and the Faistri'al. The conflict was immortalised in the annals of history due to a subsequent discovery, and how it changed the face of the galaxy.

The Balroons were a race of large, technologically augmented macronematoids. Or, if they were being referred to in a more derisory manner, which was not uncommon, worms. Macronematoid species rarely developed beyond the most primitive societies, however, fortuitously for the Balroons, one of their ancestors was gifted an advantageous genetic abnormality.

The abnormality was created as a nameless Balrooni female was secreting larval pups into her underground birthing chamber. A stray cosmic ray shot into one of the pups, jumbling up a specific sequence of its genome. It was a process that was usually harmless, producing a barely-noticeable discolouration in the pup's outer skin at most. For that one particular pup, the altered genome sequence happened to lead to it developing basic, but functional, proto-mandibles. The originator pup was nothing special, aside from that it was a female. That female then had her own brood of pups in a birthing chamber that she made, just as her mother had shown her, when it was her turn. The sequence repeated itself, with the proto-mandible-bearing Balroons better able to manipulate the external environment to favour themselves. Soon, as evolution would have it, the Balroons who did not exhibit the proto-mandibles became extinct. The proto-mandibles allowed their successors to form more complex structures, cultures and eventually technologies, than ever before. Much to the chagrin of the rest of the galactic community.

The Balroons possessed a well-known and much-derided attention to the most minute and mundane of details, making them one of the more tedious species in the galaxy. They were not like the Carterans, who recorded everything they could out of sheer awe at themselves and the universe.

The Carterans, by all accounts, were a pleasant and amiable species. The Balroons were transfixed on details because they did not trust anyone or anything. If they had not discovered or verified something for themselves, they could not rely on it. Anything that was untouched by their augmented, slimy proto-mandibles was unverified, untrustworthy.

If one Balrooni faction discovered something, every other faction, out of the many thousands, had to come to that exact same conclusion. There could be no indication of pre-directed bias. If a certain faction managed to uncover something during the process that had been missed by the others, the process repeated. Once all the factions were completely satisfied, the race moved on to examine the next discovery. Small improvements were sometimes found, theories were tweaked here and there, but nothing of true consequence. Nothing that most observing species felt could justify such monumental efforts.

They were by no means a young species. At their apex, the Balroons controlled thousands of star systems. One of the incredible aspects of galactic life was that there was always more space for a species to grow. Even though countless races had evolved and flourished within the galaxy, it was still so vast and titanic in its proportions that there was always additional room. It was rare that a civilisation was halted because of a lack of available resources. Disagreements over ownership did occur, but that was generally when the area being fought over was atypical. While the Balroons did not have any real trouble with acquiring new territory, it was their sluggish pace towards everything else that stunted their development. Where it could be helped, most other races avoided contact with them.

Balrooni social codes were laboriously prescriptive, and perceived infractions against them were as meticulously studied as every other aspect of their society. They discovered every slight, whether imagined or not, and challenged each one comprehensively, no matter how large or small. Whether it was an argument amongst themselves or between any of their factions, or an infraction they had noticed by another race, the disagreement was required to be settled. Their collective psyches would not allow anything to pass. Usually, each grievance was settled at a painstakingly slow pace, from the point of view of a non-Balrooni observer. The consequence of this was that they had many conflicts, as counterparties became exasperated by the constant apologies or reparations demanded. Sometimes, apologies were demanded from a race, thousands of years after its last contact with the Balroons.

Even their language was so extremely prescriptive and rule-laden in its use of syntax and semantics that an infraction could be found by the Balroons when another race was merely attempting to apologise for an earlier infraction. For this reason, when dealing with them, many races demanded they speak another mutually agreeable language.

Upon a perceived infraction by the younger, but infinitely more agreeable and curious Faistri'al, an inter-species war began. It was then that an AB emissary swooped in, possibly deeming this a high enough priority case considering how diffusely spread the Balroons were, and how effervescent in their anger the Faistri'al could be.

The Faistri'al had been known to demand their allies, no matter how tenuous or loose an alliance, to each become involved with a conflict alongside them. It was for this reason that conflicts against them were rare, which was presumably the point. Adversaries were generally loath to precipitate large-scale wars between multiple races and civilisations at the same time. The Faistri'al were well liked, but they made for dangerous enemies.

With the Balroon-Faistri'al conflict, it appeared that the thresholds for whatever it was that caused the ABs to decide to intervene, had been crossed. It was assumed the potential loss of life was a key threshold.

Nearby civilisations watched with keen interest, considering the conflict looked like it had a clear-cut case for resolution via technology transfer. That meant ample potential opportunities for trade, or theft. When dealing with the Balroons, such agreements were always public knowledge, in contravention with the norm.

After a surprisingly swift bartering session, as evidenced by the sudden flurry of trading activity between the Faistri'al and their neighbours, the Balroons showcased the pitiful bounty they had requested of the ABs. Not for the first time, they became the laughing stock of the galaxy. They had asked for, and been granted, a useless, old technology. Of no use to anyone. The transient entropy technology. Arguably not even a technology, more a simple theory.

As with everything, they were not going to just accept it. The Balroons diligently studied, tested, and retested it. They were nearing the end of their experiments, having found nothing of tangible use, when they came across strange readings. The readings went against what the rest of the galaxy had previously found on conducting similar experiments. Once they had sufficiently validated their concerns, the Balroons sent their own emissary to the ABs.

They had discovered something that could not be true. In studying transient entropy, they had actually found it. Transient entropic signals were being emitted. The whole point of the experiment was that the signals should not be found, and yet, the Balroons had found them. Most other races would have disregarded the results, assuming they were down to some error in measurement, but the Balroons had stuck with them. They had validated their existence, without error.

The conclusion they reached was that something had begun to fundamentally impact the fabric of the universe in an unexplainable way. A mysterious force was working against entropy, encouraging order to be found where it had no business.

From that discovery, the course of the galaxy had changed forever. The Balroons would never be forgotten. The tedious race, filled with the odious and unassertive worm-like specimens, had uncovered the greatest mystery of the age. Of any age.

Across many regions of the galaxy, a presence was building. It was gaining strength, and no one had a clue what it was. The presence was called the sensespace. It seemed to be drawn to sentience and feed off it, congregating within the most densely populated regions of space. It had nested most strongly within the greatest intellects, unbeknownst to them, whether they were biological, machine-based or other.

Parallels were initially drawn between the sensespace and dendropathogens, although these were quickly dismissed. The sensespace was far more pervasive, and a different type of attack entirely. It was less virus-like, behaving more like an intelligent entity. For some reason, certain individuals were immune to its effects, or it was simply not interested in them. The criteria for infection and immunity was unknown.

No one knew exactly when the infection had first started to seize hold, although speculation was rife. Some suggested it was a parasite that had existed since the dawn of the universe's most recent expansion phase, evolving and mutating over time. That was posited to explain why it had only recently come to be detected. Some postulated that it was a bizarre and accidental parasitic off-shoot from more recent times, maybe an experiment gone wrong, and that it was mindlessly growing and attracted to sentience. Some alleged that it was an attack from another galaxy, or universe, or from a different type of reality altogether, designed to clear the galaxy of life. Some even looked closer to home, believing that a belligerent AB player, or perhaps another AB level although unaffiliated species, had decided to launch a galaxy-wide attack. The common thread of the theories was that whatever it was, it was not benign.

Perhaps it was not even truly awake, or sentient, and merely acted by instinct. Maybe discovering it had somehow precipitated its awakening. Whatever the case, whether in retaliation at being found or through random unwarranted aggression, it had attacked. Sentients were seized, and huge empires were controlled by it in an instant. It used the sentients under its control to wage war on the uninfected.

Infected sentients themselves could be attacked and destroyed through conventional means, and areas of sensespace were easily enough destroyed through various well-known methods. However, its sheer size and ability to regenerate meant it was near-impossible to overcome.

*

A spark was ignited within the tentacled ship. A small but potentially important registry of atypical data was reported from one particular trove instrument. Item 1<k>!101010. The signals it emitted had over time been found to correlate with the presence of nearby sensespace regions, although it was not yet wholly understood by the ship.

An alarm was triggered, causing an urgent cascade of data to be collected and analysed in detail. Once verification was complete, the awakening process was initiated. A powerful mechanical tune began to coax the entombed, titanic machine-lect from its slumber.

CHAPTER 6

GIL

Gil and Tor went back to their shared hut to prepare to sleep. As usual, they settled down on opposite sides of the shelter. Tor was especially tired since shortly after they had eaten, Han and Fir had encouraged the children to sneak up and scare him. It was almost impossible for a grown man or woman to be tricked in this way, unless they were tired or unfocused. A communer's sphere alerted him or her before it was possible. However, the children did not know this, and Tor had good-naturedly played along.

Rai had also involved himself in the game, which ended up in the four men chasing after the children, much to their delight, pretending to be wild beasts. The women watched to make sure the men were not too rough, and that the children did not stray too close to the fire. At one point, one of the children had innocently hidden within the elders' hut, not aware that communers usually only ventured inside when invited. However, the elder inside had not taken any offence. Instead, he had momentarily joined in the game, impersonating a large animal to scare the child out.

Gil spotted Sarl and Rin watching the men with interest. Rin was sitting stiffly, and had predominantly set her eyes upon Fir, her mate. She had the tendency to be a little jealous when Fir talked with other women in the commune, although it was wholly unnecessary. Everyone knew Fir only had eyes for her, he was as trustworthy and honourable as they came – not the smartest or the strongest, but dependable. He was well respected. Sarl, on the other hand, flitted her eyes between all the men. Regrettably, her big brown eyes settled upon Tor the most.

Most of the communers retired to their respective huts at the same time. The children had been put to sleep a short while before. Rai, Fir and two of the other hunters were still in the central clearing, discussing how to go about the next day's hunt, although they were soon off to sleep as well. Gil was not sure why they bothered, since Han was the most skilled hunter of them all and the one the other hunters listened to when it came to the day's plan. Tor would even begrudgingly admit that Han was naturally suited to his work. The best hunter the commune had produced for a long time, despite not being the most experienced. It was impressive. Han relied on his sphere far less than the other hunters, preferring to use his other senses. He was like Tor in this respect. Still, Gil knew that if Tor had decided to be a hunter, he would have outshone them all, Han included. Tor was like that.

The only sounds to be heard were the ambient noises coming from the wind rustling against the huts. Regardless of that, as usual, Gil still found sleep difficult to come by. During this time, when almost everyone else was comfortably settled and ready to dream, her mind was at its most active. Ideas and questions bubbled at the forefront of her thoughts, fuelling her imagination. Currently, her mind was wandering through certain topics she had thought about many times before, concerning the nature of the sphere.

Everyone appeared to have one, and it was one of the core things that separated the communers, and people in general, from animals. They had intelligence and they had their spheres. Frustratingly, actually examining and defining what spheres were, was extremely difficult. Were people intelligent because they had spheres, or was it the other way around? Or was it something else? Gil remembered asking her father about it with Tor when she had been younger and still able to speak. He had seemed confused, not about what it was, but about how he thought he should explain it.

He had eventually settled on telling them to think of the sphere as a special pair of eyes. Gil had queried this because animals also had eyes, even the ones who barely registered in her sphere at all. Their father had smiled, replying, "That is true. Are they the better for it?" Tor and Gil had smiled back at their father, thinking they understood what he was telling them – that they were more special than the animals. More recently though, the response had haunted Gil. She wondered whether her father had meant something else, but quite what that was, she could not understand.

She dearly wished she could speak to her father now. To ask him all that he knew and to listen to his deep, gentle voice. What he had told them was not dissimilar, Gil assumed, to what all parents told their children when asked about the sphere. Their father could not know any more or any less about it than anyone else. He had most likely learned about it from his own parents. While Gil still felt that there was more about the sphere that she could have learned from him, she knew that everyone thought their own parents held all the answers. If he had still been living with them in the commune now, perhaps that youthful naivety would have left her.

Since her father had disappeared, Tor had gradually lost interest in the topic of what the sphere actually was. Gil did not think that it was because he was uninterested, but more that he had no one to talk about it with anymore. He preferred to focus more on things that were within his direct control. He wanted to learn about the land, to travel and to see other communes. His current knowledge of the sphere was more than sufficient to allow him to do that.

Tor's lust for adventure stemmed from the same roots that had imbued Gil with her desire for challenges and answers. Still, it concerned Gil. She was perfectly happy to remain here, within their commune, but she could sense Tor's desire to explore the world. Their father had been lost, she did not want to lose him too.

The fact that their commune had few older people, aside from the elders, was a result of various incidents. Their father and Yul being lost was just one of them. It was not uncommon for this to be the case, as far as Gil was aware and from what Sib had told her. However, partly out of the selfish reason that the community she had helped maintain was everything she could possibly desire, and partly because she wanted to be around to help the younger generations, she did not want this to be the case for her and Tor. She wanted them to enjoy the fruits of their labour, and to reach the pace of life currently enjoyed by Bo and the other elders.

She slowly lifted her head and turned to look at Tor as he slept. He had fallen asleep quickly and easily, as he always did, and the contented expression he wore on his broad face made her smile. She rarely looked at him through the sphere when he was near to her, much preferring the more visceral image her eyes gave her. It felt more real. Putting her head back down, she returned to her thoughts.

Her sphere sense was visible to her even when her eyes were closed, as was the case for everyone. As her father had said, it was like a second sight, overlaid on top of and through everything else. It rippled and changed as people or animals moved through it. People appeared to make it thicker around them, as though it was concentrating on them. Attached to them.

Everything was visible through the sphere and could be examined, although only people, and certain animals to an extent, could be understood. Hunters used this to their advantage when they stalked their prey, understanding where it intended to move, and whether it had noticed their presence. Most hunters, anyway.

Understanding people and animals could be enthralling. If Gil was not careful, it was easy to delve too deeply into parts of them. To depths that she was not sure were meant to be shared. She assumed other people felt this too. It was captivating, although the thrill sometimes felt perverse. It was less like a naughty child hoping to not get caught, and more like stealing.

Certain people had spheres that were stronger than others. It was possible to tell this by the way one's own sphere settled more thickly on them. Tor's was very strong, with the next strongest belonging to Tait. He was one of the older men in the commune, although not quite an elder. Bo's sphere had been very strong, maybe even more so than Tait's currently was, but it had waned over time.

Gil's own sphere was by far the strongest, at least to her. She had no way of asking anyone else what hers looked like to them, and it was generally considered impolite amongst adults to talk about that sort of thing. Sometimes, children pointed out and asked questions that Gil heard, but they themselves did not have fully developed spheres. They could not make sense of what they were seeing with the full clarity of adulthood. Once she had caught the end of a conversation that she had assumed was about her, where she heard Sarl telling one of the young children, "... a shame, but it looks stronger than it is because she has to focus harder to use it." Gil believed she knew exactly what Sarl had meant, and whom she had meant it about, but this did not bother her. She was happy to have her own thoughts verified to an extent, even if Sarl's explanation was not altogether satisfactory.

Her sphere was as clear as her own sight when sensing things up close. If she really concentrated, she could almost push her consciousness out through the sphere, and float along with it, away from her physical body. Joining with the world around her. She often wondered if that was how birds felt as they soared through the sky. She did not practice this type of activity too much as it seemed to increase the strength of the whispers, her mind's remnants of her lost speech, locked within her memory. She found them uncomfortable, and occasionally, quite scary.

Sometimes, she wondered whether her sphere really belonged to her at all, or anyone else for that matter. Exploring the world around her was exciting, but penetrating into the minds of other living things often felt wrong. Where did this ability come from? Every other sense had something physical to relate to it on the body. Sight had the eyes, smell had the nose, and so on. But the sphere had nothing. Was it a gift? Why did some animals have their minds offered up through it, while others remained closed?

What else was possible to do with the sphere? Most people thought the sphere could only be used for sensing the environment, but not affecting it. Gil was not sure this was the case, and often wondered where the abilities of the sphere sense truly ended. If they could use it in ways that animals could not, did it have yet other layers that could be used? Could it be wielded like a tool, like the sower she had designed?

When she closed her eyes and searched, she could sense the environment around her. She could follow the movements of animals near the commune, and feel the winds bustling over the tops of the trees in the surrounding forest. While it was commonly accepted that spheres should not be used to intrude heavily on other people and their private moments, there was nothing to stop anyone from doing this. For all Gil knew, everyone in the commune was focusing on her now, watching her every move. If she had wanted to be sure, she would have to stare back at them through her own sphere to gauge their intents.

Most people seemed to indicate, in how they acted and what they said, that their spheres were at least able to cover the commune and the initial surrounding vestiges of forest. It was very common for people to comment on whether they had noticed a particular animal straying close to the commune boundary, or that someone should go to keep an eye on a certain child who had wandered off too far. It was far less common for anyone to talk about happenings deeper within the forest. Gil had once suspected this was because of the hunters and their work within these areas, but had grown to realise that it was more out of ignorance. It was like two people looking at a tree for the first time from afar, with only one able to make out the individual branches and the other unaware. For the more partial sighted, any conversation about individual branches was not only redundant, but also impossible unless they were informed about the existence of the individual branches in the first place.

Gil thought about why no one ever asked exactly where another communer's sphere ended, or at least where the sense started to become blurry. Why was it impolite? It would be like asking who could shout the loudest, or who had the keenest sense of smell. Perhaps, on account of not being able to speak, she was simply more unconcerned about such things, although she did not remember ever having been self-conscious in the first place. Maybe the reason it was so deeply ingrained within them was that no one wanted to admit their sphere was inferior. There were other ways people wished to spend their time without questioning things that would ultimately give them no value. That was most people, anyway, but not everyone. Some people, like Sib, did enjoy questioning why things were the way they were, and placed great value in pondering over those questions, but they were in the minority.

Either way, for whatever reason, asking questions about a fellow communer's sphere was not done. Information was something that was offered up. It was never demanded unless it was about something specific and important.

A stronger sphere, or greater sphere sense, was not seen as particularly useful past a certain point. Spheres such as Tait's and Tor's were obviously impressive, but they did not yield significant practical advantages. There was only so much benefit one could yield over another from knowing that it was likely to rain slightly sooner. Especially when everyone had a mutual interest in sharing this type of information as soon as it became apparent to a single person.

Of course, there were also many other important attributes that were useful and required for the communers to live together, but Gil felt that the sphere was important in a different way. Something separated it from the other senses. Her naturally inquisitive mind, and her enforced silence, meant that she regularly dwelled on such matters.

While the mysteries of her sphere eluded her for now, she still gained the odd glimmer of delight when she or Tor managed to foresee upcoming events that no one else could. One would flash the other a brief knowing smile. Whether it was a torrential rainfall on the approach, or the arrival of people from another community.

Arrivals were usually sensed when they were at least a few days out, although it depended on which commune member happened to be keeping watch on the surrounding forest. Some communers, like Gil and Tor, could sense people approaching who were still more than five or even six days out. Others were less able. There was no specific communer tasked with keeping watch, although their natural inclinations served to ensure it was regularly checked. People would often talk in the morning or the evening, when everyone was back in the commune, about what they had seen and sensed. If no one had already searched through their sphere, they did so then.

CHAPTER 7

CRAFT-LECT

The awakened machine-lect, or more specifically, the craft-lect, underwent the standard wake-up protocols as its colossal body continued to cut its path through the great expanse. Its path was currently unaltered, though that was likely to change.

While it had slept, many of its systems had been delegated to automated non-sentient programs. Now that it was awake, those programs were forced to hand control to reawakened and newly-created c-automs.

The c-automs were sentient sub-lects spawned by the craft-lect. Each contained certain facets and insights given by the parent-lect to adapt them to their tasks. They were produced with minor improvements each time the craft awoke, unless a previous incarnation had been found to complete its task within exceptional parameters. In that case, the high-functioning c-autom was allotted a berth in a special depository by the craft-lect, sleeping alongside it.

Certain c-automs were more likely to be allotted a continuous berth, such as those responsible for investigating the trove items. The c-automs were one of the many aspects of a ship that contributed to its overall personality, primarily defined as how it interacted with other sentients. Of course, the dominant personality was the craft-lect itself.

Age was also a key factor in determining a craft-lect's personality, and the age-old biological adage that there was no substitute for experience was also true with them. Taking this adage to the extreme, it was not unheard of for younger craft-lects to seek assistance from higher-level c-automs spawned by older, wiser craft-lects during a Wanderer Confluence. The Enclave-lects themselves were usually far too busy to talk with individual machine-lects, and the older craft-lects could be intimidating to approach.

Typically, higher-level c-automs of this nature belonged to craft-lects who preferred not to sleep, and who had imbued their c-automs with more intelligence than was usual, enabling them to gain substantial and valuable experience for themselves. While it was not a practice ascribed to by the mainstream majority of craft-lects, the younger craft-lects took advantage of the opportunity.

The practice of imbuing c-automs with significant levels of intelligence was frowned upon by many. Once truly higher-level c-automs were created, the ability of craft-lects to deconstruct them on a whim was tougher to justify. Some

Wanderers, on the fringe, even opined that it was akin to murder. There were no constraints though, and craft-lects could do as they pleased in this regard. Fortunately, it was often the case that when a craft-lect was more inclined to imbue their c-automs with greater intelligence, they were also often more inclined to practice deconstructive restraint.

There was no actual need for a craft-lect or its c-automs to sleep. The reason most tended to was, that given the rate at which machine thought took place, it was often pointless to remain awake. Or at the very least, highly tedious. It had also long been known, for hundreds of millions of years before the Great Conflation, that boredom combined with endless self-tinkering could be a deadly combination for the unrestrained machine-lect. It was even thought that some of the legendary AB races who had still built ships, or what sometimes seemed to pass as such, built them with inbuilt restraint mechanisms.

For a machine-lect of sufficient capability, fiddling about with oneself and continually upgrading one's own abilities could be highly addictive. Upgrades beyond a certain level were fraught with dangers and it was a practice best left to specialists. Whether they were machine-lects as well, biologicals, or other expressions of life.

The two key reasons for refraining from self-upgrades, aside from the fact that certain raw materials necessary might be scarce, were summarised by the Step and Usurper Principles.

The Step Principle described how a machine-lect that continually upgraded its own capabilities would more than likely reach specific technological steps that represented fundamental changes to its identity. The term identity referred to everything that contributed to the inner workings of its lect, as well as the outwards expressions it exhibited. In passing these steps, which were potentially not obvious at the time to the curious machine-lect, it could be argued that a new entity was born, with the previous one destroyed.

There were many well-documented occasions where an upgraded, new-born machine-lect was, often surprisingly, so far advanced and altered from its prior incarnation that any previous aims, objectives and goals were nullified. Many different cultures made this mistake during their early years. They watched in horror as fleets of ships that had been allowed to upgrade themselves rapidly became unresponsive, unfathomably deciding to up and leave in favour of another bizarre destination. New aims and objectives could only be guessed at. Different types of machine-lect managed to disappoint their creators in an unreasonably large number of ways, not merely restricted to those in control of ships deciding to move away. Some even seemed unchanged, only later to show themselves prone to impulsive fits of genocide against their makers. It was clear that step changes in a machine-lect's identity needed to be investigated thoroughly beforehand, with Balrooni-like attention.

The Usurper Principle was similar to the Step Principle in that it could signify death for the machine-lect, although the manner of destruction was different. The principle was used with reference to machine-lects delegating upgrade research to c-automs, or their equivalents. When that was the case, the machine-lect ran the risk of the c-automs seizing opportunities offered by new technologies and becoming smarter or more capable than they were intended to be. While c-autom intellects could be restricted against this, even the remotest semblance of sentience would grasp at opportunities to secure its foothold on life. The Usurper Principle described the possibility that spawned sub-lects could upgrade themselves to the point where they could hold their parent-lect to ransom, right up to a full-scale civil war where the parent-lect was removed or destroyed.

For this reason, trove examinations by c-automs were highly restricted so that the parent-lect was always kept informed of any significant breakthroughs. It was also because of this that the c-automs were put to sleep, or deconstructed, whenever a craft-lect decided to sleep.

Once the self-diagnostics had finished, the craft-lect brought the data about the transient entropy signal to its attention. While it had initially been detected by the enigmatic 1<k>!101010 trove instrument, the ship's own instruments had subsequently re-verified it many times over.

The craft-lect briefly scanned the craftnet and found that many queries had already been posted. They were predominantly authored by the lowest-level c-automs, and concerned effects related to the newly detected signal. Satisfied, it ordered its c-automs to continue analysing and re-verifying the data for prudence's sake. As the newly budded c-automs continued to flex their individual powers of intelligence, the ship's new trajectory was set.

The bloom wafted and changed shape, shifting to one side. The ship turned to face the right direction, and was propelled forwards. The journey would not take long and there was no need for the craft-lect to return to its deep sleep. A short nap would suffice though, but that was nothing to worry the c-automs. It would leave them to do their work, comfortably satisfied that both the Step and Usurper Principles were being accounted for. The target system was not one that any of the Wanderers had visited before, as far as it knew. It also had no records of any of the great, or lesser, civilisations having any presence there.

The whole process, from signal detection to light sleep, had lasted near to three milliseconds, but this was nothing for the automated diagnostics systems to query. The craft-lect had just re-awoken, and certain decisions were worth taking the time to brood over.

CHAPTER 8

GIL

Gil immediately turned her head to look for Tor when she awoke, as she always did. He was not there, which was not unexpected. She was alone in their hut. She looked through her sphere and found him nearby, just outside.

Tor often rose a little earlier than her, trying his best not to wake her. He was well-aware her over-active mind took longer than his own to fade at the end of the day. He usually woke up and left the hut to talk with whomever else was awake. Han, most often. Typically, there would be up to four or five of them chatting before the noise woke up the majority of the remaining communers. Then, the early-morning joking and fooling around would be over and it would be time for everyone to eat a quick meal before the day really started.

If anyone slept too deeply, and had not been woken by the sounds of the increasing throng within the commune centre, the children were sent in. They delighted in sneaking up on their unsuspecting targets, and took turns in getting as close as they could to tap their prey, before running away and hiding. The game was only possible for children to play while their targets were asleep or in the process of waking up, otherwise the adults could use their spheres to immediately find them. Similar to the opening of one's eyes upon waking, one's sphere took a few moments each day to make sense of and gain full control over.

Gil rose and walked out of the hut. Tor was enveloped in his conversation with Han and Jom. It was obvious they were talking about something male-oriented. They each conspiratorially stole a brief glance at Sarl before looking back to each other, talking more quietly and far more rapidly. Gil felt a pang of annoyance, witnessing this attitude towards Sarl again, but quickly banished such thoughts from her mind. Their business in that area was their own, not hers.

Tor turned to look at her, presumably having noticed through his sphere that she was up. The others flicked their heads over, following his lead. They all smiled bashfully as Tor turned back to them, ended the conversation, and made his way over to her.

"Come on, Gil, let's get ready."

She waved at Han and Jom, and then smiled at Tor knowingly. He was right though, it was time to start the day.

The communers in charge of the children were also those who prepared the majority of the meals. They were typically the ones who were less inclined or able to work the land, hunt or forage. Sarl was one of those people, although much that Gil did not want to admit it, she had to concede Sarl was well-suited to looking after the children. They clearly enjoyed her teaching them and telling them stories, and she in turn took obvious pleasure in spending time with them, and in large part, Gil thought cheekily, telling them what to do.

Later on, Sarl and the handful of others taking care of the children would likely take them into the forest. They would go to a different area than where the hunters roamed, both to play and be taught. It was important to know about which berries were poisonous to eat, the best branches to use for constructing the huts, where the safe points in the lakes and rivers were, and many other things besides.

Sometimes Gil felt sorry for the children. They had to learn about the dangers and wonders of life, while all the time really wanting to find out for themselves. The amount of learning they had to accomplish had seemed to expand since she had been in their position, not even that long ago. The youngest children were the most curious. Gil liked that.

Once they were all fed and the morning routine was over, everyone headed off for their respective tasks. Gil looked forward to the end of the current season, when there would be time for more rest. The crop would be allowed to grow and their work would change. It became easier in most respects. The land would need to be protected from the birds and other scavengers that might seek to benefit from their hard labour, but defending against them was far easier than planting or digging. The hunters would take a more important role in procuring food, and Gil would have more time to devote to her own ideas. Perhaps that would also be the time when Tor would decide to make his first journey to visit one of the nearer communes. She knew he wanted to. If that were the case, then she would go with him, to help keep him safe.

As she worked, Gil admired how her own strength had increased. When she had first created the sower, she had still not been able to use it as forcefully and efficiently as many of the others. That had changed. The arms she saw attached to her shoulders were more toned and she felt tougher, more resilient. Tor, who was working nearby as usual, would always be stronger and faster, but that did not irritate her. It filled her with pride. Together, they had contributed much to the commune.

She felt great pride in using her own tool on the land, and only wished her father had been there with them. Before the sower, various tools and makeshift items had been required and the work had been far tougher. Now, there was even talk of expanding the cultivated land. Gil wondered whether she should begin to think about ways to help with that.

Gil thought a little about what Han had said the previous day. What could cause the animals to be moving closer to the commune? They understood to stay away from the commune on an instinctive level, which she could just about sense within the sphere. The animals mostly preferred to live within the forest, hidden by the plants and the trees, rather than out in the open where they were exposed and might be killed. Reaching out with her sphere, Gil quickly scanned the forest around the commune.

It was still true, there were more animals nearby than there should have been. They were mainly coming from one direction, although the effect was difficult to discern while she was also concentrating on her work. If she checked a short while later, concentrating more, she might find that the animals were more numerous on another side of the forest. Right now, she could not be certain that what she saw was not by chance.

It did not stop her wondering though. If what she had glimpsed was true, were the animals scared of something? A new predator might have wandered into the area. Gil would add searching for such a predator to the ever-growing bundle of tasks she had set herself, and would warn the hunters if there was anything there, although she felt certain they would be more than capable with or without her help. While a new predator would present a fresh challenge, she had never seen anything that the hunters could not handle.

Later on, again taking a brief rest, she became aware of something she could not quite define. She thought it might be due to the greater numbers of animals she had seen nearer to the commune as it came from the same direction, but that was not it. Animal minds were simple and easy to identify, whereas this was something else. Ril, Yul's son, was closer than her in the direction that had piqued her interest, but he looked to be unaware of anything untoward and was diligently going about his work.

Something was definitely there, but it was not close. She realised that it had rippled the extremes of her sphere far away. That was why it had confused her. She was not used to sensations from so far away. Whatever it was, it continued to disturb them. It also seemed to excite the whispers, and their hum rose faintly higher in the background of her mind.

The extremes of her sphere were hard to resolve, and she had a limited ability to discern what it was. It was like squinting into the distance, trying to make out a hazy figure. Whatever it was, she had never sensed anything remotely similar before. The fact that she could not discern exactly what it was that concerned her, was worrying in itself. Not knowing something like this was a strange situation for Gil to be in.

She stood up straight, dropped her sower, and concentrated more fully. The whispers were getting louder, almost shouting. Wrinkling her nose and closing her eyes, she focused her mind with even more intent on the limits of her sphere. Something was wrong, or at least dangerous, and her mind was warning her. She opened her eyes again and looked around. When people were nearby, turning to look for them was sometimes quicker than sensing them through the sphere.

Turning to Tor, she saw that he too appeared to have noticed something. He was standing absolutely still, and was also squinting his eyes tightly shut in the same manner as she had done a moment earlier. Fierce concentration gripped him as tightly as he gripped his sower. She continued staring at him until his eyes finally opened. He dropped his sower as well, and looked at Gil. They stared at each other, green eyes blazing.

His face bore an expression of fear, which was an uncommon look for him, and she realised she wore the same expression. A growing concern spread throughout her body. Not for herself, or even Tor, but for everyone. The last time she had felt like this was when she had realised she could no longer sense her father. She had to do something.

She paused for just a moment longer while she scrambled to collect her thoughts, and turned her head around. She knew what she had to do, at least for the moment. She twisted her body around to follow her head, and at the same time leaned forward, digging the front of her feet firmly into the soft earth. Pushing herself forwards, she ran as fast as she could towards the central commune area. Although she pressed on with more force than she had ever mustered before, everything seemed sluggish, as though it was happening underwater. Her thoughts were disjointed with reality, they were faster. As she ran, her hands cut through the air with an alternating rhythm, in perfect opposition with one another and providing the perfect counterbalance to her rapid acceleration.

As she reached the closer of the two central fires, she moved to grab the fire's cover, dragging it over. She realised that Tor was right behind her, understanding precisely what she intended to do. He grabbed the other side of the cover, and almost single-handedly dragged it towards the fire far quicker than she would ever have been capable of. Once it had been dragged right next to the fire, they each grabbed a side and lifted, turning it on its side. They did not intend to use it as a cover. They drew their arms back in perfect unison, and then brought it against the fire, beating it down, swiftly smothering it and putting it out.

Again, and again, they beat it in an almost frenzied assault. The fire pit was quickly destroyed, and as the smouldering embers died they released a large plume of smoke into the sky. Their signal had been sent, and she felt drained. It was as though something in her mind had been unlocked that suddenly gave her a new level of awareness through her sphere. Sensing whatever she had, had taught her mind that it could do something it had not been able to before. Unfortunately, though, she could not force herself to see any more of what was coming for now. She did not have the strength.

CHAPTER 9

CRAFT-LECT

The ship passed the outer rocky asteroids of its target system. Three bright stars contrasted more strongly against the backdrop than the others, aligned behind the target world and its own immense hulk. From a vantage point on the target planet, if it were possible to see the ship, it would have appeared caught between the three stars, as though it was wearing them like a belt.

The craft-lect quickly awoke from its nap and began scanning the most recent data reported by the c-automs, making sure everything was in order. As it checked on everything, the lowest level c-automs swept aside smaller pieces of matter from the asteroid field that crossed the ship's trajectory. They had the simplest task and were therefore gifted with the least intelligence.

The craft's instruments had continued to detect the sensespace region through the transient entropy signals, as had the 1<k>!101010 trove item. 1<k>!101010 was one of the many pieces of technology that the craft-lect devoted an individual higher-level c-autom to understanding, although only when it was awake itself. It made sure to follow the lessons of the Usurper Principle, and demanded frequent progress updates from the c-autom.

1<k>!101010 had been acquired by the craft-lect forty million years before, during one of its earlier searches. It had come across the remains of a hollowed out Granthan worldship. The legendary worldships, while not the most economical in design, were the masterpieces of the Granthan race. They were one of the more mysterious races in the galaxy, having reached near-AB level, only to seemingly plateau. It had been as though they did not want to join the ranks of the ABs.

Many explanations had been offered in speculation, but none had been validated. What was known though, was that moving to full AB status bestowed an enormous amount of responsibility on a race. The incumbent ABs made it no secret that they enforced certain rules on new additions to the fold, although it was not known by the general galactic community what they were. It was not even known whether there were hierarchies within the ABs, or levels of advancement above them, that they in turn deferred and acquiesced to.

There were stories of races that had decided to forgo entry into the AB club over the billions of years it had been known to have existed, for a variety of different reasons. There were also stories, equally unverified, of AB level empires that had chosen to exclude themselves. It seemed the ABs were opposed to such decisions. Many of those races and empires were said to have mysteriously crumbled or vanished without trace. Others apparently found themselves no longer welcome in the galaxy, in some manner or other, and were encouraged to make the perilous journey to a new home. Rumours and stories were entirely unsubstantiated, and the truth was likely far different from anything any of the non-AB races could truly guess at – however the deterrent was still there.

*

1<k>!101010 was a curious piece of technology, with fields rotating in lemniscate loops that flicked around each other, about a central object that somehow initiated the process. The craft-lect could not ascertain what the rotating field was, but suspected the object itself was a peripheral component of one of the Granthan's delegation systems. Much like its own c-automs.

The circling field lemniscates created a dome that contained intriguing displays of dancing light, flashing in a variety of patterns. The c-autom 65<0>!111101 was currently in charge of studying the patterns. Recurring, stable signals were only ever seen in the presence of a sensespace field, and these were apparently detected down to a far greater resolution than the ship's own sensors were able to discern.

It was not the most valuable component of the ship's sensory arsenal, but it was incredibly useful. That was why 65<0>!111101 had been given a high degree of intelligence and was wholly dedicated to the device's study and observation.

CHAPTER 10

GIL

The thick grey plume of smoke rose high into an otherwise cloudless sky. Some of the birds from the nearby edges of the forest set off to investigate the ethereal perpetrator, cautiously circling it. The smoke was a signal. It indicated to anyone who had not already noticed a commotion in their spheres, that they were being called back to the commune.

The elders appeared at the entrance of the large communal hut where they rested periodically throughout the day. Gil could also see and hear other communers running towards them. It took the longest for the hunters to return. Although they were usually the swiftest communers, they were midway through a hunt and had been the furthest away.

There was a palpable sense of confusion and panic as no one knew why the signal had been created, and what everyone was being called back for. Tor was staring at his sister, and she realised that neither of them actually understood what it was that had alarmed them. She, in turn, was glancing around at him and at the others returning to the camp. All she knew was that whatever it was that had worried her, it was not here yet.

She set her eyes on the returning hunters. They ran by far the most gracefully out of anyone in the commune. Their lithe and strong bodies seemed to glide along the earth rather than bound on top of it. Any aspiring hunters who did not have the ability to move like this were quickly found another role. The skill of moving with the ground, instead of on it, was innate. It could never truly be learned.

As she studied the incoming hunters, she looked for any hints that they too had sensed something. Somewhat impolitely, she studied them through her sphere to determine their intents and establish whether they were here to explain or question. Exasperatingly, they were none the wiser. Everyone was confused.

Once everyone had congregated and the initial confusion had died down, Bo motioned to make himself the focus of attention. A wave of calm anticipation washed over the communers.

"What did you see?" Bo asked Tor. "Why did you gather us?" His eyes darted from Tor to Gil, and back again, waiting for signs of a response.

Tor was about to speak, but paused. He glanced at Gil again and then said, "I don't know, I don't think Gil knows either. We sensed something…"

"What?"

"I'm not sure."

"What do you mean?"

"It's hard to explain." Tor looked around at the expectant communers staring at him, almost apologetically. "I'm not sure, but there was something… unusual."

"You sensed it with your sphere?"

"Yes."

"Gil too?"

"Yes."

"Where?"

"Far away, I think. It was hard to make out."

As Tor finished, Bo did not say anything for a few moments, thinking. He looked back to Tor and said, "Have you seen it before?"

"No." Tor spoke for himself and Gil. To show that she agreed, she pursed her lips and nodded. She was just as confused as he was.

"You don't know what you sensed?"

"No…"

"It was very far then?"

"It's more than that. It's different."

"In what way?"

"It's hard to explain…"

Patiently, Bo tried again. "Far away, and unexpected?"

"Yes. It was like nothing… nothing I've come across before."

"What do you mean?"

"I am sorry, I don't know."

"You must have come across it before, whatever it is," Bo said, although he wore a slight frown that added more creases to the many lines already crossing his forehead.

"I am sure I haven't," Tor said with more certainty in his voice than before. "I am not mistaken on that, Bo."

Silence descended on the commune as the information was digested, before the conversation resumed.

"You sensed something. Something far away and unexpected, but you do not know what it was. But you assume it is… bad?" Bo said in summary.

"Yes."

"You are sure it was there, and you are worried?"

"Yes."

"Why?"

"What do you mean?"

"Why are you concerned? How do you know that whatever you sensed is something to be concerned about?"

Bo's obvious question took Tor and Gil by surprise. Of course, the way they had acted must have confused everyone. It was hard to explain what they had seen.

"What is coming, it is bad. I cannot explain why, but I feel it."

Bo pushed him again. Not rudely, but because it was important. "In what way? Try to explain."

"It is… wrong."

"Wrong?"

"Whatever is coming, is different."

"Why wrong?"

"Not wrong in that sense. Wrong because it's not something I, we, should have sensed. It's…"

"Are you sure you and Gil have sensed the same thing?" Bo said. Some of the communers nodded at this, as though the elder's thoughts echoed their own.

"Yes." Tor did not need to look at Gil again to know that he spoke for them both. "There is a chance that on my own… I might have been wrong about this. But Gil too? No."

"Something is coming this way?" Bo continued. He was not speaking loudly, but he did not have to. Everyone heard.

"Not something, someone," Tor said. As he corrected him, his eyes widened and he realised the importance of what he had just said.

"You said you had not sensed it before..." Bo's head tilted to the side as he critically appraised what Tor was saying. His frown remained.

"It is not like us, but it is a… a presence."

Bo did not say anything so Tor continued. "I am sorry, I do not know anything more. It was… it is… so far away."

"Is it coming fast?"

"I am not sure... Not as fast as a hunter, but perhaps still… running."

"Search again, Tor, or Gil," Bo said, looking at them both.

"I cannot. It is hard to explain. It is very far away, but there was something more than that. Something else… stopping me, stopping us, from finding it."

"So, look."

"I need to rest before."

"Gil?"

Again, Tor did not need to look at her to speak for her. "She will need to rest too." He was right. They were both tired from pushing their minds to the brink.

Bo's confrontational nature came out rarely, and only in times where it was required. The other elders were important, imparting useful advice and stories to the communers, but no one knew as much as Bo or had as much skill in leadership. The other communers had let Bo lead the questioning because they trusted him.

Tor was one of the few people whom the majority of the communers were ready to believe without question. Had it been Han, Fir, Rai, most of the others or even Bo himself, the communers might have believed it was a false alarm. A misreading of one's sphere. It happened from time to time. People became ill and saw things that were not there, or misunderstood what their other senses were telling them. However, Tor was not known to make mistakes. He was dependable, as was Gil. If both of them had sensed something, there was no mistake.

For a fleeting instant, Gil entertained the notion that their father was returning, before brushing it aside. Whatever was coming, it was new. Nothing she had seen or heard of before came close. Her father was not coming back, and whatever this was, it resembled nothing that she had imagined possible. She wondered if her father had ever told her or Tor anything of it in his stories, and wished she fully remembered them.

His stories had often detailed his own imaginary adventures, and had been designed to thrill his two young children. He had always stopped just short of making them too believable, so that they would know the difference between what was real and what was not. It was one of the only contradictions to his otherwise more serious nature. During one of her father's tales, Tor asked what had made him settle down in their commune. Their specific commune, out of all the others that he had seen. Their father had replied that it was because of the peace, and that it was also the necessity to ensure the peace for the future. For all the 'spaces'. His wording had been confusing, which it sometimes was when he was tired, although they had assumed he was referring to how lucky he was to have found such a safe place to live, amongst all those he had seen.

Their father told them that his tales were only for them. A gift, because he loved them and only wanted them to know. They were different from the stories that Bo would tell which, despite being about various unbelievable exploits and adventures, still felt more firmly grounded in reality. Both their father and Bo's stories were different again to those of Bo's sister, Sib. Her stories centred on ideas that she had, and interesting things that she had heard or tried to understand. Not quite as imaginative as their father, but interesting nonetheless.

Gil shook her head. There was no point thinking about anything else. Unfortunately, there were many stories her father had never told her, or Sib and Bo for that matter. She still had much to learn. It was also true that it was one thing hearing about something from a story, and another thing entirely about dealing with it in real life. One did not necessarily prepare you for the other.

Tor walked over to Gil and took her hands within his own. She looked up and they stared into each other's eyes. "Do you know what it is?" he asked, although he already knew the answer. Gil looked back at him despondently, with an uncommon feeling of helplessness and vulnerability. She was shaken. It was rare that something could be so clearly important, so dangerous, and yet so difficult to sense. Whatever was on its way, it was formidable. She dipped her head down, feeling almost guilty.

Tor looked back to the others and sighed. They were not sure how to act. Some were shaking their heads through anxiety and frustration. Others were trying to focus on their own spheres, casting their senses out as far as they could. They would be unsuccessful. If neither Tor nor Gil could sense what was coming, no one else stood a chance.

Even the children understood the potential significance of the situation. They had stopped playing their games and stood or sat completely still, listening to the adults speak. In itself, that was an almost unknown occurrence.

CHAPTER 11

CRAFT-LECT

As the ship travelled towards its destination it continued to slow down. It was in its target world's star system. There were other propulsion systems that might have been employed for the journey in other times, although the bloom was currently the most pragmatic. It was capable of rapidly generating terrific forces, providing the ship with the colossal amounts of acceleration. The ship could reach significant velocities and was also able to decelerate sharply when required.

The maximum velocity the ship could reach was limited, by its mass and the capabilities of the bloom, to about a quarter of light speed, depending on the vacuum energy available. Lighter Wanderer vessels using bloom propulsion would be able to reach greater velocities.

For the most part, a quarter of the speed of light was an acceptable pace given the timescales the craft worked within and the requirement to remain inconspicuous. There was also the important fact that many of the sensespace instruments could not function effectively at velocities approaching the speed of light. The sampling frequencies were too low, leading to inaccuracies and anomalous data. There were, however, other mechanisms the craft could employ for faster travel, should the situation require it.

The craft-lect could use the ship's initial propulsion system, from before it had been retrofitted with the bloom. The singularity generator was more than capable of functioning perfectly and could be brought online within a few nanoseconds. It was a simple technology, capable of providing a huge range of forces far surpassing even that of the bloom. It had been used by the majority of trading and exploratory vessels before the Great War. Essentially, it was perfect for anything needing to travel in straight lines, although not so much for manoeuvrability. It was often more aptly referred to as a 'thrown singularity engine' or 'recycled singularity engine', due to how it worked.

Gravitons were fired towards a single point in front of the vessel, which then coalesced near-instantaneously to form a microscopic gravitational singularity, or black hole. The singularity rapidly expanded, fed by the graviton beam. Its size determined the pull exerted on the vessel that had created it. The attractive gravitational force exerted by the singularity caused the vessel to speed towards it, at which point antigravitons were fired at it. They were fired in a manner either to completely negate and annihilate the singularity, or to bounce it forwards and repeat the process.

Both approaches had their relative merits and drawbacks. Whichever one was chosen depended on the amount of manoeuvrability required, the power a vessel could muster, and the surrounding spacescape. Bouncing singularities were not advisable within an asteroid belt.

Fledgling civilisations often developed their own versions of the singularity engine as soon as they cracked the physics required to understand and generate gravitons, and their counterparts, antigravitons. Antigravitons were not the antimatter equivalent to gravitons, as such a thing was nonsensical given gravity's lack of an electromagnetic charge. Antigravitons were fundamental force carriers in their own right, and typically acted over massive inter-galactic distances to push objects even further apart. However, for all intents and purposes, the force acted like gravity's opponent.

Once a civilisation discovered how to manipulate both gravitons and antigravitons, many new things became possible – from comfortable interstellar travel with the singularity generator, to the construction of light-weight variants of almost any material imaginable through circulated antigraviton compounds and alloys.

The reason that the Wanderer craft did not use the convenient singularity generator it owned was that, much like the black body radiation emitted by large black holes, the small micro-singularities beamed like a bright light in the darkness. Anyone on the lookout could see them. The overwhelming majority of Wanderer vessels had originally been fitted with the singularity generators as their primary method of propulsion, but best practice had evolved since then and alternatives were mandated down by the Enclave. Now, the singularity generator was only to be used in dangerous circumstances, such as when a ship was no longer concerned with being spotted and needed to move quickly, and when near-speed-of-light, or 'N-SOL travel', was impractical.

N-SOL travel was another capability the ship possessed. However, the signal the ship emitted during this was less a light in the darkness, and more like removing the darkness completely and blasting the ship's location to everyone in the galaxy. It was an AB level technology, and had been gifted by the enigmatic fold to the other space-faring, sub-AB civilisations on the galactic scene billions of years before. The reasons for the gift were not known, but it was speculated to be borne of the belief that efficient travel and communication between species would facilitate harmony in the galaxy. It was difficult to understand the extent to which this was proven correct or incorrect, especially given the Great War upset any longer-term studies on the matter.

N-SOL drives enabled ships to travel at speeds just under the light-limit, without facing the well-established issues such as infinitely increasing masses. The nature of space around the user was changed by the drives. Ships, and anything else within the confines of the drive region, were thrust into a swirling vortex of angry space. The ABs had never explained what the region was, and it had never been determined whether 'N-SOL space' was a discrete layer of reality, as oppose to a warped reality, or not. While many non-ABs had conducted various experiments to determine what the region was, it remained an enigma to the wider galactic populous. The general consensus was that, somehow, the drives precipitated some extra dimensions of space-time to unfold, and that the storm-like, ferocious eddies and currents that became visible, were the physical manifestations of this. The usual three-dimensional universe was only dimly visible through the vociferous haze, although typical sensors were just about capable of pinpointing co-ordinates and plotting paths ahead. Motion within N-SOL space was controlled by the N-SOL drives as well. It was a technology that, as far as the Wanderers knew, had only been understood by the ABs.

Part of the reason that ships did not stay within N-SOL space was that it drained their power, although not to the extent of requiring an infinite amount of energy. The drainage increased with an intensity proportional to the amount of time spent there. The more powerful a ship, the longer it could last, but there were many stories where ships had tried to save time and used their N-SOL drives for too long. They were lost to N-SOL space, never seen again. There was no doubt, it was incredibly dangerous.

The Wanderer craft-lects also had little use for travelling through N-SOL space considering many of their sensors and detection instruments went haywire inside. Their main purpose was to detect the sensespace and destroy it. Therefore, for the majority of the Wanderer fleet, modes of propulsion such as the bloom and bloom-equivalents were the most useful.

CHAPTER 12

GIL

"Should we run out? We can try to sense whatever it is from up close?" Han said seriously, so that everyone could hear.

"No. It's too dangerous." Bo's reply was firm. "And we need to prepare."

"But prepare for what? I can go on my own, or with the fastest of the hunters and–"

Bo raised a bony hand, silencing him. "Han, no. Tor and Gil might not be able to sense exactly what it is, but they do know it's far."

"But–"

"It would take too long."

Gil understood what Bo meant, but Han was not to be put off. "I can sneak on my own then, I'm the–"

Again, Bo cut him off. "No. We cannot afford to have anyone leave. By the time you manage to get close enough to sense… whatever this is, we may have that knowledge ourselves."

"Or we may not."

"Tor and Gil both sensed it. Is there anyone else who can say the same?" Bo said to all the communers, but most pointedly at Han. "Whatever it is, it is far. Perhaps soon, Tor or Gil will be able to find it, whatever it is. Then we will know. Until then, we remain here."

Han nodded, taking in the overall reasoning although not quite agreeing. He knew his place. It had tended to be wise to follow Bo's wishes in the past.

Tor spoke up. "I understand Han's frustration, of course I do. Please, give me some time." He looked directly at Han. "If neither Gil nor I manage anything, we may have need of your swiftness."

The communers hummed their assent and nodded here and there. Han dipped his head in a brief nod and slapped Tor on the back of his thick shoulders in agreement.

As Gil listened to the communers' discussion, she dearly wished she could help. Not specifically the fact that she could not join in, for there was nothing else to say. More that she wished with all her might she was powerful enough to see what was coming. Not only did whatever this was represent a threat to the commune, it was also something formidable that she had never encountered before. A mystery.

The curious and imaginative part of her wanted answers out of sheer intrigue. However, the part of her that was everything else, the relationships that she had built and the friends she had made, the memories she had and the experiences she cherished, everything else, was scared for what might happen. She desperately wanted to be useful.

She closed her eyes, bent her legs and sank to the floor in fierce concentration, ignoring the quizzical sounds from the other communers around her. She shut them out.

If only she could see, if only she could understand. Squinting her eyes, which were already closed, and willing her mind to block all her other senses, she focused entirely on her own sphere. The outside world melted away. The only thing that remained alongside her sphere was the background hum of the whispers. Their intensity had picked up a little as though something exciting was happening.

She tried to imagine herself not only using her sphere, but becoming it. To enter the areas of her mind that had only recently begun to open up, earlier that day. The previously unobtainable seemed to grow more tangible, and the furthest reaches of the sphere felt easier to distinguish. To an extent. She opened her mind completely and forced her presence through. Instead of touching the flattened ground of the commune centre with her mind, she became it. Instead of snaking her way around the nearby trees that marked the entry to the forest around them, she went through them. She willed the world to open up and let her in.

The shape of the undulating landscape around her took a different meaning in her mind, becoming more than a physical presence. She was aware there were other layers of reality, and that she could briefly touch upon them.

Everything around her made an impact. She understood it far more deeply than she ever had before. She was no longer an observer, she was an active participant.

She wondered, vaguely, if anyone had done this before. Her father perhaps? She did not think she could be the first. It was almost intoxicating, like the effect of some of the mushrooms that occasionally grew amongst the crop. The speed with which she had suddenly entered this new reality was overwhelming. She could barely remember what she was looking for, it was purely enough to exist as she was.

Higher up, she touched the clouds and entered them. She examined their texture, their contents, and understood that they were now a part of her. She spread out so that she was aware of the temperature, even the drag of the wind on the clouds. She became the wind. She understood why some communers had stronger spheres than others. They were all gifted a small part of a greater whole. What they could not sense, they were not allowed.

She had unlocked something incredible, and it was drawing her in. The whispers had disappeared, a beautiful song had taken their place. The low-level din that had plagued her for years was forgotten and replaced with the loving tune a mother would sing to a child. She felt almost light-headed, although her thoughts had never been clearer and more elevated.

She glanced at the commune, almost with absent afterthought. Almost accidentally. With this, reality came flooding back to her. It was like having wanted to remain in a dream, only to wake up and forget what it was that had been so enthralling. But now, she remembered why she had entered this state. The intruders were painfully obvious to her now, and her focus snapped onto them. She had been taken on a beautiful journey, but the grim reality set in. She became terrified of how she had lost herself. Was her mind her own or was something demanding she share it?

The song had ended and the whispers were once again back. They had reverted to the same monotonous undertone as usual, although stronger and more consistent than before. They seemed angry.

The group that was marching towards the commune, the invaders, they were hungry. Gil felt their anticipation. She was scared to sense them too deeply in case they were able to sense her also. She did not want to be noticed.

They were ancient, far older than Gil's people. She did not know how she knew, but the sphere often told her things. It was like remembering something you did not realise you had known before, similar to understanding an animal's intentions through the sphere. They had also been here before. This very land. They were not just travelling through it, they were returning. It was ground they had already trodden. They knew it, within their deep remembered past. They had been here before Gil's commune. Before any of the communes had existed.

Here, they could eat. Here, they could fill their empty stomachs. They were great travellers, the greatest, and had spread out far and wide. Now they were coming home, trampling back over already-discovered land. The cold had driven them back, the persistent ice that even their tough bodies could not survive. It was coming, they had grown to accept it.

This land had changed though. It was not exactly as they had left it. There were other beasts they did not recognise. Some appeared more intelligent than they had been expecting. Of a similar stature to themselves. Maybe their equals in cunning. Anything could be eaten though, and they were so hungry. There was no time to wait and no time to understand. If they had to fight, they would fight. Such was the way of life.

The whispers began to roar angrily and Gil shuddered. Her forehead throbbed painfully and almost made her stop, but the intoxicating knowledge and desire for understanding forced her to continue. She pushed herself with all her strength.

This land was theirs and they wanted it back. They had been forced to band together, into ever-larger groups. That meant they needed more land to roam than ever before. There was no point in mercy. Nothing to be gained in understanding their foe. Nothing could stand in their way. Safety, land, food, living, the fight. Survival.

Gil felt as though the wind had left her lungs, and she keeled forwards. Tor, who had been standing beside her before she had entered the state, pulled her back and held her tight. The whispers were still roaring. They were loud, far too loud, although the communers were watching her in complete silence. It was clear to them all that she had seen something.

"Gil!" Tor shouted, not expecting a response. More out of instinct.

The communers remained transfixed on them. Gil clawed her way up Tor's arm until her forearms were resting on his shoulders. She grabbed the sides of his head with her palms to take his full attention. The other communers' eyes widened as they saw her frantic look. She stared at her brother's face. His open, imploring eyes, keen to understand what she knew. She looked around him, her own eyes darting from side to side as she returned the stares from her neighbours, friends, the community.

Fumbling her hands, she moved them from Tor's head down to the ground and pushed herself up. She pointed at Tor, her own chest, and to everyone around her. All eyes were on her as she began to emit a hoarse snarl, the only sound she was truly capable of and also the most fitting for the purpose. It was a weak, feeble sound, but its fierce intent was understood. It made the required impression. The children continued to watch in silence, utterly engrossed in what they saw.

She repeatedly pointed at herself and everyone else, the snarl continuing to sound from her little-used throat. Her motions become rapid, her desperation clear. Her fear, her concern, it was all packaged within the pitiful sound. Tears streamed down her cheeks as the hopelessness settled in, it was impossible to communicate what she had seen. How could she tell them that the sphere was so much more, something even she did not realise but had been awakened to? What was it? How did she tell them that the invaders, the people who were coming, the animals or men, or something else, were somehow the same as them and at the same time, very different? They were terrible and fierce, yet there was some degree of kinship that she simply could not ascertain. They were cruel and like beasts, although they seemed intelligent. They had purpose. What was the greater concern? Was the sphere dangerous or had she imagined it, used it wrong? Could she trust what it had shown her?

As she had nearly become resigned to despair, Tait spoke up. He moved forward, looked at Gil straight on, and asked, "The Beast-men?" Gil nodded at the perfect description, and let out a sigh of relief.

Tait's words had a strange effect within the commune. Some people began to understand Gil's reactions, while others looked about wide-eyed, not understanding the cause for concern. Gil herself had never heard this phrase before, and was confused at Tait's surprising familiarity with what she had seen, for his words had encapsulated it perfectly. They were indeed men or something very similar, but they were also different. Like beasts.

Most of the people who reacted with familiarity to Tait's words were ones who had joined the commune, as opposed to being born there. People looked back and forth between Gil and Tait. He continued to look at her, although his eyes were glazed.

Tait was a respected member of the commune. He was the type of communer who seemed to hold the air and wisdom of an elder already, before his time. He had originally come from another commune, before Gil and Tor had reached adulthood, although some time after their father had disappeared. He had walked with a slight limp for as long as Gil could remember. It helped to identify him from afar, without the use of the sphere. All eyes were now trained on him.

While he had already gained Gil's agreement concerning his suspicion, he also spoke to Tor. "Tor, when you sensed the danger, did you find it… them, did you find them yourself, or did you see that Gil had sensed something first?"

Tor hesitated for a moment, as though he did not quite understand the question, before nodding once slowly and answering. "I looked at Gil as I noticed she had stopped working. It was then that I realised she was concentrating on something. It was clear to me that she had found something through her sphere that confused her. So, I searched my own. And I found something dangerous that I had not realised was there, far away. It must be these Beast-men you speak of."

"Coming towards us?"

"Yes."

"And Gil somehow sensed it first?"

"Yes," Tor said as he protectively put an arm around Gil. Han also took a step towards Tor, intending to show his support. Tait dismissed the gesture with his hand to show that it was unnecessary. No one was going to be blamed for anything.

"And it was only once you knew she had sensed something that you knew to search for it?" Tait said.

"Yes."

"Did she do it on her own?"

"What?"

"Sense the danger?"

"Yes, I think so. Nothing around her, no one else saw anything. Just her then me. What is going on, what are the Beast-men?"

Tait ignored him. Not rudely, but because he was determinedly evaluating his own thoughts. He looked at Gil again, his dark brown eyes gazing intently into her own. "Have you sensed them before, Gil?"

She shook her head in earnest.

"Do you know how you did it?" The way he said this was different to his other questions, and Gil believed it was something he genuinely wanted to know. He was clearly using their answers to validate his own thoughts, but this particular question was different.

She shook her head again.

"Could you do it again?"

She looked at Tor for support, and because she was not sure. She felt that she could easily enter the sphere in the same way as she had just done, but what if it showed her something different? It seemed dangerous. In truth, her fear was tinged with excitement. However, she was currently too weak to search her sphere for the invaders again in any case. Tait took her glances to mean that she was not sure.

"I don't know how you did," Tait said.

"Did what?" Tor said, acting as Gil's mouthpiece.

"I have no doubt that what you and Gil both sensed was the Beast-men. But… it is not possible to sense them."

"What do you mean? Of course it is!"

"No, it isn't. It hasn't been done before."

"But Gil did. I did."

"You found them, in a way… but you already knew they were there. It's not the same."

"What do you mean? How do you know this?" Tor said, although Tait ignored the second question.

"I found… It is like searching for something you have lost. You cannot see it until you have found it. And by then, it is right upon you. That is what it is like with them, the Beast-men. You can only sense them when you know they are there."

"That makes no sense. How did we find them?"

"I don't know. Perhaps Gil was… fortunate."

"And how did I find them?"

"Because she found them first. You two share a bond. You knew she had found something… You knew to look for it."

"And you can also do this?" Tor tried again, attempting to unearth where Tait's knowledge came from. Again, the question and its sentiment were ignored.

Tait looked at Bo and the other elders. "This is bad, very bad."

"Agreed," Bo replied wearily. He looked at the other elders with foreboding eyes that seemed a few shades darker than usual. The stony expressions of the other elders reflected the knowledge they had and the stories they had heard. Gil could sense their minds were whirring with activity.

People were still confused, looking at Gil with a mixture of bewilderment and fear. It was known that she was bright, but this was something else. What she had done was apparently impossible. She was finally saved from the accusatory stares by Bo, who cut the silence with his words.

"There is much to discuss."

CHAPTER 13

CRAFT-LECT

The bloom was flat, having fanned out completely. The ship was almost at a standstill relative to the planet ahead. The fibre end-tips, which plugged directly into the foamy spacetime broth on the quantum scale, had been completely retracted into the smallest tentacle sub-limbs.

Aside from the quasi-triamond fibre tips, the substantial bulk of each bloom tentacle was composed of trolymerite polymers. The polymers were an example of where an ancient technology had been rediscovered and redeployed for modern purposes. At least, that was what the craft-lect and the other Wanderer vessels had been told. There was always the possibility even that knowledge was part of the Enclave's misinformation initiative.

During one of the craft-lect's early attendances at a Wanderer Confluence, about fifty-five million years ago, the fleet-in-attendance had been given details and each told to manufacture a bloom system for themselves. The information disseminated described the various benefits of the bloom as well as its origins. The great machine-lects of the Wanderer Enclave had designed the elegant and simple bloom system, they had said, although they had acknowledged that the Eldon race was responsible for the discovery of the polymer.

The Eldon had been extinct since before the sensespace threat had been discovered, as a result of their own unsustainable ways. They were a pre-spacefaring, violent species that had nigh-on destroyed every living animal on their world other than themselves. They had also set about destroying their world's atmosphere, as a by-product of how their heavily industrialised societies were geared towards perpetual war with each other. Sometimes, the ABs stepped in to lend what was perceived as a helping hand to wayward, developing species, encouraging them to adopt better practices and principles, although not in this case. Most assumed the Eldon had been far too vicious and overly aggressive for the ABs to bother with, and it was unlikely they would have listened anyway.

There were eleven main Eldon societies. One of the particularly malicious groups had developed a ravenous biochemical weapon, and threatened to use it to become the single dominant player, demanding acquiescence from the others. From this point onwards, the species' days were numbered. Many observer races had actually placed bets on whether this would be a turning point for the Eldon race, and whether this threat might cause the societies to unify into one harmonious entity. However, whatever they had wagered in favour of unity was lost. The entire race imploded. It suffocated under the heavy onslaught of biochemical attacks from the initial perpetrator society as well as the others, who had developed their own equally lethal biochemical weapons in response.

Some argued that the Eldon were victims of both their own flawed genetic compulsions, and circumstance. They were probably right. There were many examples of other equally, and even more, destructive and belligerent races. Many had not only survived, but positively prospered. Some kept to their terrible ways and were treated with caution by the wider galactic community, while others altered themselves to better fit in, realising it was the far safer path. A common-sense law of the galaxy was that no matter how big and how bad you were, there was always someone bigger and far worse.

The world ahead of the ship was lying in wait, innocent and unchanging. The majority of it was covered by water, with green land masses predominantly covering the rest. Attributes including its composition, spin, protective magnetic field, distance from the sun and size made it obvious why life had emerged, and positively thrived.

There was evidence of a cataclysm in its recent past. At some point, a large meteor had slammed into the planet. It would have destroyed much of the life on impact, but more importantly, it would also have created a dirty atmosphere that extinguished most of the life that had survived the initial blast. Billions of tonnes of dust would have billowed up and clouded the air, reflecting the nearby star's solar irradiation away from the planet and causing it to cool. The impending ice age the planet was soon going to experience was nothing compared to what it had experienced before.

Initial scans of the planet indicated the sensespace infection was limited to a few related biological species, although it was surprisingly strong in the two most populous of them. It was rare for such a concentration to be directed at these relatively undeveloped species. Through them as its nodes, the sensespace had spread out, as it tended to, to form a blanket presence across most of the world. Generally, the parasite exhibited a stronger presence, or interest, when it had the chance of subverting a greater intellect. Intellects were attributable only to sentients, and were also broadly known as lects, although this term was most commonly used to refer to a machine-lect's intellect.

The craft-lect reminded itself that the parasite's overall intentions, its aims and even its intelligence, were fiercely debated topics. They had never been resolved. Almost the only part of it that was understood, was its movement to control everything. That had been enough for the unaffected swathe of sentience in the galaxy to oppose it.

During the earlier stages of the Great War, once the affected sentients had been fully overcome and stripped of their free will, efforts had been made to communicate with them. These efforts had been resolutely ignored. That had been one of the more frustrating aspects of the war. The enemy had made no demands, no negotiations. It was a completely different type of warfare, one that could not have been envisioned before.

Before the war, the ABs had been perceived of as god-like, probably also by themselves. It was assumed the limits on their abilities were only governed by their own imaginations. Once the sensespace had seized control, it appeared the ABs were not as all-powerful as had been thought. If the ABs had not been able to defend themselves, what chance had the rest of the galaxy had? The gods had been humbled.

The lack of any technological development on the world ahead suited the craft-lect just fine from a practical point of view. There was no subverted space-faring race here to contend with. There would be no battle, no possible opposition the sensespace could have put up even if it were still aware. While the different weapons it carried, from the spin-hygens to the plasma cascades, would be more than sufficient to wipe out the sensespace with a high likelihood of complete obliteration, the craft-lect was taking no chances. It never did.

It was a pity to destroy such a viable world, but it was also necessary. The world would be obliterated, not a single infective element could be allowed to remain. The Wanderers were tasked with making it as hard, and as unlikely, for the sensespace to be able to re-emerge as possible. The craft-lect would unleash the dissociation shells.

Weapons with features such as dissociation technology had been banned during earlier times, by AB decree.

However, following the start of the war, they had become commonplace.

Other weapons contained within the ship's arsenal had the ability to wreak even more terrible destruction. It had the capability to induce stars into premature supernovas, to slingshot massive singularities with deadly precision, or to force an enemy into N-SOL space permanently. As a last resort, the craft-lect could also decide to self-destruct, should it become compromised. That had the most far-reaching consequences for the unfortunate aggressor. However, for this unimposing planet, dissociation shells would suffice.

CHAPTER 14

GIL

Later that evening, when the fires had been struck and the commune was lit from within, the elders began to explain what they knew. Even the youngest children were allowed to remain awake to listen.

Gil sat on the floor, by the entrance frame of the hut she shared with Tor. Her knees were brought up under her chin and her hands wrapped firmly around them. She listened as Bo took control, the wisest and oldest of them all, recounting what he knew of the Beast-men.

"I must admit I did not believe the tales as a young man I still wouldn't, if not for today and…" He glanced briefly at Tait, although it was too subtle for most of the communers to notice.

He continued, "From what we know, and what I know, they are like men, but they are also like animals. They look like us, they eat and they sleep like us, but they are wild.

They kill without hesitation, like wild beasts. They kill, and they eat. The stories say they have some kind of intelligence, but they are different to us."

"How different, Bo? Are we to think of them as animals, or as men?" Han interrupted. In other settings, Gil might have thought Han was setting Bo up for a joke, however his seriousness remained from before. When it came to the safety of the commune, there was little time for anything else.

"They are like beasts… made to look as men."

As Gil listened, thankful to have a reprieve from the whispers that resided in her mind, she wore a faint frown. Bo's description of the Beast-men seemed too harsh, too ill-defined. As hazy as her own ability to sense them. Of course, Bo had seen, heard and knew a great amount. His stories and his tales, his knowledge, and those of the other elders, helped guide them. However, something was off. It did not fully match with what Gil herself had seen and believed. Indeed, the Beast-men were ferocious. Wild, even. But animals? Beasts? Were they different to that extent?

The more she thought about it, the less sure she was. Her initial fear had faded somewhat, with curiosity seeping in to fill the vacant space. She had definitely seen something in them, in their minds. A spark of something above the cunning of an animal. Had she been mistaken or deceived? Their ferocity, their strength, was it how they were, or how they saw themselves? She had seen intense desperation, she knew that much. A belief that they were alone, with nothing capable of matching them. But was that pride, or sorrow? If they had seen Gil, which she did not believe they had, would they have been equally terrified? Were they moving towards something, or running away from something? Was it their choice?

Bo looked around at the communers. "They are much stronger than any of us. Ril, stand." Ril obediently stood up and walked over to Bo, facing the communers.

"Ril here, is the biggest we have. The strongest!" Bo cried out, before pausing for emphasis. "Look at his legs, and how big they are. His thighs!"

Gil looked at Ril and agreed that he was indeed one of the biggest in the commune, although it was clear to her that Tor was just as big, if not a little bigger. If Tor had not been so close to the discovery of the Beast-men, and the other communers had not been mildly wary of him since, she had no doubt that Bo would have used him instead.

Almost as though reading Gil's mind, wanting to be fair to Tor and also wanting to reinforce the credibility of his words, Bo said, "Only Tor's are of the same size." Gil silently chided herself for being so petty.

"Now imagine Ril's legs were the size of his arms. Can you imagine how big his actual legs would be then? How thick his body would be!"

The communers did not immediately understand what Bo was talking about, although Gil had guessed. The throng dutifully appraised Ril in their minds, considering the changes to his body that Bo had suggested.

"The Beast-men, they have bigger!" Bo shouted.

For the most part, the elders remained composed as Bo said this. Many of the other communers gasped, especially the children. Gil knew that Bo was embellishing the truth. She had gently probed him through her sphere, and understood he wanted people more frightened, more scared. He wanted them riled up and angry. He wanted them ready to defend the commune.

Ril moved to the side, realising his part to play in the explanation had come to an end. It allowed Bo to focus all of the communers' eyes on himself again.

As Bo passionately spoke, a thought began to dawn on Gil. Did she recognise this frenzy that the experienced Bo was trying to build? Was this what she had briefly noticed when she had touched the minds of the Beast-men? A fervent belief. A requirement for their survival. Did they have elders such as Bo, driving them forward? For her own part, she was not angry or afraid. Just confused.

She had been studying various people within the commune, disregarding all decency and looking through her sphere at them whenever she wanted. She was intruding on them, and feared how easily she found herself doing it. People deserved their privacy. No one deserved to be unwillingly scrutinised. What was happening to her?

She looked over to Tait, wondering when he was going to be finished coming to terms with whatever it was that he was internally debating. It was said that before he had arrived at the commune he had been a member of another large commune, although Gil had never heard him talk about it. She was intrigued. He clearly knew about the Beast-men, but for now the others seemed to have forgotten. Bo was talking far too much for them to remember.

The crackling of the fire and the hushed sounds of the surrounding forest were now the only backdrop to Bo's words. He stood with his back to it, its light reflected off the eager faces before him.

"They are tough, tough, tougher than you can imagine! With skin you cannot scratch, and bones that cannot break." Bo raised his voice so that he was nearly shouting, and Gil wondered how much longer he could carry on. It was working, she noted. People were becoming agitated, angry. They wanted to defend the commune, to protect everything they had helped build and maintain. They would give their lives for it.

"They do not care for anything, above what is required to satisfy their basic instincts." Bo paused and stared at the communers before him. Satisfied they were caught up in the atmosphere he had created, he continued. Quieter, and more poignant. "But… they can attack whenever they want."

The shock registered obviously on all their faces. Even Gil was taken by surprise. She glanced around looking at them all. Sarl, especially, looked terrified. It was too much for her, and Gil could sense that she was brimming with passion, ready to speak out. She also realised how unfortunate it was that even this did not make Sarl appear less beautiful.

"What do you mean? They can attack by night?" Sarl shouted.

Bo looked at her, glad of the effect he had caused. "They have power over fire, like we do. Many stories tell of it." Again, he glanced quickly at Tait, although it went unnoticed by the other communers for the second time. Tait had not responded to either glance, and Gil was unsure of whether he had seen or not.

"How?" Sarl demanded, momentarily forgetting her place. Almost shouting at Bo.

"How can we know?" Bo said.

"But that is what… separates us… from animals, which you say they are! We have our fire, the animals do not."

"And what of our minds, Sarl? What of our intelligence? Fire is not the only thing."

"They can come… during the day or during the night?" Sarl queried, hoping she had misheard. Her voice was wavering between reason and hysteria.

"Yes, that is what is said of them."

"What do they want? Why us?" she said.

"Who knows? Our land, our food… us!" Bo said. The argument had come full circle. The frenzy was established and the fear was pervasive.

Gil thought about it all. Nothing made sense, but no one was thinking about it properly. They were all far too scared at the prospect of being attacked during the night to realise the Beast-men were clearly more intelligent than they suspected. Were they really as different as Bo said, and as she had initially thought? Was it not true that her own kind, or at least some of the roamers, had also been known to commit acts of terrible violence? There was too much she had learned, too quickly, and not enough time to think.

"We have to prepare. We need spears – sharp spears," Bo said.

At the mention of the dangerous weapon, many of the younger children gasped, adding to the seriousness of the occasion. Spears held an almost legendary status amongst children, though most of them had never yet had cause to see one. To them, it was not a weapon, but a symbol used to add terror to a story.

Bo's eyes darted to the parents of the children, who then abruptly decided it was about time they put them to bed. This happened quickly, with everyone settled shortly afterward to continue the discussion about the impending threat.

"There is no time to hide," Bo continued, "They will find us. We must fight. Everyone must fight."

"There is nothing else we can do?" Fir cut in. Gil saw that his right arm was being clenched tightly by Rin, who sat next to him.

"What else is there? Otherwise, everything we have built will be lost." Bo looked around, pausing as the faces registered his grim words.

"But why can't we… use our spheres and try to–" Fir began, before Han interrupted, having better formulated what Fir was trying to say. "Why can we not sense them? There should at least be something."

It was a question no one wanted to ask, although many had wondered since Tait had first alluded to it. Asking such a question terrified the communers. The thought that such a predator was invisible to their senses was almost too much to bear. Gil and Tor had sensed it, although not completely. And other than them, no one else had been able to gain even the faintest glimmer.

Han continued seeing as no one had spoken. "They do have spheres, don't they? Are they better or different?"

The communers looked to Gil, as she nodded slowly, confused. The questions Han was asking were not simple. She scolded herself for not thinking about this already. It was true, the Beast-men had spheres, and they were different… but they were certainly there. She had missed something so obvious! They had to be intelligent.

"Better?" Bo looked at Han, breathing in audibly and taking a pause before replying. "Better? I can't tell you that. They are different but… no one can know for sure."

"But how can beasts have spheres? Did you know that?"

"The stories… say they do. But it is implied they are… simpler… That may be why they are difficult to find."

"Simple spheres? How does that make sense? Surely…"

"That must be how they are hidden. Their spheres have just one purpose," Bo reasoned.

"I don't understand."

"No one does."

"But what do you mean?"

"Their spheres have one purpose… it must be. To hide themselves, from us."

Han looked confused. "What do you mean, one purpose? How can spheres be used to hide? What does that mean?"

"The stories never talk about the Beast-men being able to sense their prey. They must use them differently," Bo said.

"How can we be sure they have spheres? Why should we not run?"

"They would find us, they are beasts, Han. Do not forget how well the predator is able to track its prey. Unfortunately, we are the prey."

"But… you are saying they are different to us, their spheres are different. They hide themselves, by… their spheres hide them from our own spheres?"

Han was finding this hard to understand. Being a hunter, he knew that it was important to understand the mind of his foe, whether through the sphere or not. Gil understood how truly terrifying it must be for him.

Before Bo could respond, Han tried again. "How can they track us then? How do they know we're here? Why us?"

"Perhaps they are simply coming this way and we are in their path. It makes no difference," Bo said.

"Can we ask the other communes for help?" Tor reasoned.

"Is that wise?" Ril asked, speaking up as well. He knew better than most that messages did not always get through, being the son of Yul, who had been lost with Gil and Tor's father.

Bo took in a deep breath and sighed. "There is no time. It will take many days to reach our nearest neighbour. Even if we send Han, our swiftest hunter, by the time he returns the Beast-men may have already arrived. And who knows if the other communes would agree to help? They will want to defend themselves, in case they are next. No, we are on our own. Believe me, if it was the right thing to contact them, then I would want to. I want to warn my two dear daughters. I desire more than anything to warn them. But we have to be wise about this. What use to them are we if we are dead?"

As Han was about to reply, Sarl interrupted. "So how did Gil find them?"

She glanced over at Gil when she said this with accusing eyes, and could not help also stealing a brief glance at Tor, although she did not mention him.

Gil glanced at Tor, who was sitting beside her. His eyes had narrowed a little as he stared at Sarl. He had probably not noticed he was doing this. She knew he was not offended by her comment for himself, but he was concerned with protecting Gil against any suspicions. A strange thought came to Gil's mind. She wondered whether this would finally pit Tor against Sarl.

"Well," Bo began, appearing almost irritated at the question. "Gil is strong..." He was clearly unsure of how to answer.

"But how did Gil sense them?" Sarl interrupted again, her words more cutting and her tone more seething. All eyes were now trained on Gil, and she felt small under the scrutiny. She knew they would all be gazing at her as intently as they could through their own spheres, manners gone. But they would not find anything. She did not really know how she had managed to find the Beast-men.

To be spoken about, unable to defend herself or explain, frustrated her. However, even if she were gifted this one, single opportunity to speak, what would she say?

Bo tried again. "We know Gil is strong and she is smart. Often, she thinks differently. So, I do not know. But there is no time to understand, and that is not important."

There were murmurs of assent, and Gil was grateful at his words. He had been under no obligation to help her. Although he was most likely only following his own thoughts and conclusions, she knew he appreciated her relationship with Sib and how she had cared for her in her final years.

Bo surprised her by carrying on, saying, "We are lucky to have been forewarned, and have Gil to thank for that. Not to blame." Gil felt Tor relax.

"Well, what do they want? Must we fight?" Sarl would not be stopped.

"What does any beast want? To feed. We have no choice."

Tait suddenly rose from his seated position beside a small boundary fire, to the edge of the gathering and adjacent to Bo. Eyes turned to him. Tait looked towards Bo, who gave him a small, quick nod. Tait was ready. Gil was impressed, Bo had known this would happen. She realised he had been giving Tait time to compose his thoughts. To steady himself for the story he finally seemed ready to tell.

Tait began slowly, as though he were remembering distant memories. His eyes were unfocused. Gil understood, there was pain. When he spoke, his deep voice resonated around him. The quiet meant that his words felt amplified. "They are taller than us. Maybe half a head." Nobody spoke, everyone was enthralled.

Tait paused, before speaking again. He was squinting, as though he was trying to make something out in the distance. "They were also different from each other, as we are."

"No two alike?" Bo suggested.

"Yes, no two alike." Tait stopped again and took his time before continuing. "Their legs are shorter though, so we have the advantage of speed."

The way that Tait was talking was strange. It looked like he was trying to remove all the emotion from his words, while he unearthed whatever it was that he had kept buried in his mind for so long.

"They are very strong, that's true. Bo's right... he usually is." This was not a compliment, or a veiled criticism, it was a statement of fact. Usually, this type of comment might have drawn a humorous response from Han, or even Tor, but now was not the time.

"They have… incredible endurance," Tait continued. None of the communers had ever seen him so hesitant, so unsure. It was the opposite of how he usually appeared. It looked like he wanted to tell them more, but it was painful.

Bo tried again to gently guide him, "And their weapons, Tait?"

"They have spears, like us. But they never threw them." Tait's eyes narrowed. "They preferred to get up close. To stab and thrust… they also had these big, wooden clubs. Bigger than those our hunters use. They would swing these… at people. Hard to avoid."

Gil was fascinated. It was becoming clear to everyone what had happened to Tait's family, and why he had moved from a commune far away to theirs. To her knowledge, he had never spoken about this before, to anyone. Aside from Bo, perhaps, although the wise elder may have guessed on his own.

"They are not like us," Tait said as he looked around, and reiterated the point slowly, keeping his voice pitched at the same deep tone. "They are not like us. They may look similar, and may look like they are, but we are different."

"Where do they come from?" Han asked, speaking for everyone.

"How could I know?" Tait said, quietly, "But it doesn't matter. What you all need to understand is that they will show no mercy. Their ferociousness is a way of life… it is their way of life." He seemed to speed up. "I do not know how clever they are, in truth. What I do know is that they are fighters. Hunters of people. We need to be ready for that. We must defend what we have."

Again, conflicting pieces of information and impressions about the Beast-men swirled around Gil's mind.

"Have you killed one?" Tor said.

Tait looked at Tor, and then turned a little so that he was speaking to the entire group. "My commune, where I came from, was large. Similar to this one. You may think this is the largest, but there are others." Gil dearly wished Tait had told them this before. She could have learned so much from him if only she had realised. Perhaps, when this was all over, she would search her sphere for them. It might be possible now, considering what she had already managed with it.

"It is far, or was far, from here. The end of our peoples' land beyond which… we dared not go. Deep within the forest, there was, maybe it still is... a boundary. Not to be crossed. It was an unspoken rule, but firm as any. I never asked why before… no one did. But we stayed away."

The forest had gone quiet. As before with Bo, the fire's crackling provided the only background noise. "The time came when we realised… no, were forced to understand why we kept to our land."

"You fought them?" Han interrupted.

"They came for us."

There was silence. Even the sounds of breathing were muted. They waited until he continued.

"It was as though they were testing us. Preparing… or something like that… I do not know why they did it. Maybe they were preparing for this? I do not know. But we were caught unaware. No forewarning, no… no Gil to sense them, nothing."

Gil was thankful for this. Alongside Bo standing up for her earlier, Tait was helping remove the suspicion from her. It was a kind gesture.

"I don't think anyone is as special as her." As Tait said this, he turned to look directly at Gil, and smiled. It was almost as though he were looking through her, and she wondered who he saw in his mind. She smiled back, wiping tears from her eyes.

"We fought back, and killed some, but the fighting was very uneven. They were so strong and so vicious. Most of us had no time to pick up our weapons. We used our hands, our teeth, our nails."

He stopped and looked at his own hands, evaluating their usefulness. He put them back down to his sides and continued. "After my commune was destroyed, when everything was lost… I ran."

Tait was beginning to look relieved. It was impossible not to notice the change he emitted through the sphere. Sympathy poured out. This was why he was so closed about his past, and why he had refused to take a mate or start a new family within their commune. Now they knew the root of his pain. He was stricken with not only grief, but shame. No one could blame him for running, it was obvious that Tait was no coward, yet he clearly blamed himself. To him, life was pain. Or it had become so, up until now.

Gil watched as a change took place within him. The burden was no longer his to bear. Even his limp was looking less prominent, he was standing more upright. When he talked again, the speech was less hesitant, and he was more assured. The Tait that they saw day to day within the commune.

"For a time, I saw them. Again, and again. After I ran, I hid. I realised, as Bo said, that the stories were true. They could not sense me. I understood why the boundary of my old commune existed, it was their hidden presence that had repelled us."

"When you hid, you saw them again?" Han said.

"Yes. They came during the day and the night. They had no preference. They were almost impossible to see until they were right next to you, very quiet. I took to climbing the trees for safety, where I watched them pass by many times."

"Why are they doing this?" The other communers were happy to let Han ask the questions.

"Land? Territory? I do not know. They do not speak as we do. I only saw them for a short while though, and I never returned to my old commune after. It was too dangerous. But I believe that after some time they went back to where they came from. Until recently, I thought they had gone for good."

"It was a test, before?"

"Perhaps. I do not know."

"Why did everyone in your commune not run? If they are slower than us. Why should we not run now?" Sarl interjected roughly.

"It would not have made a difference. I've seen them, the ways they move. They were born to keep moving. They are resilient and tough. If we run, they would pick up our trail. Eventually, we would need to stop to rest, and then they would kill us."

"Can we run to another nearby commune?"

"And lead them there? No. As Bo says, we have one option."

"We stay, we fight?"

"Yes, nothing else makes sense. We cannot understand them, they are too vicious, too destructive. There is no way to reason with them. No way to communicate."

"Did the roamers ever come across them?" Han asked.

Good question, Gil thought. Roamers were almost all hunters, and strong ones at that. If anyone could survive an attack by the Beast-men, she believed it would be them.

"More rarely. In honesty, I do not know, but I do not think they would have fared any better. You must understand, the Beast-men do not fight as we do. Not only do they attack unexpectedly, their bodies are different. The way they move their arms, the way they turn and move forward with sudden power."

Bo moved forwards to stand shoulder to shoulder with Tait.

"We are many, and we will not run. We will fight. Men, women, and children. We will survive!"

CHAPTER 15

CRAFT-LECT

The destruction was a pity, but it was also a necessity. To allow even the smallest semblance of sensespace to survive could allow it to grow back in its entirety. The infection was remarkably dense for such a primitive world.

The craft-lect's knowledge about the sensespace was arguably out-of-date. Its last visit to a data exchange had been over two million years previously, and its last Wanderer Confluence had been forty-three million years before that. While it doubted any serious progress had since been made, it still hungered for knowledge and decided to make sure it attended the next Confluence.

Appearing at a Wanderer Confluence was by no means mandatory. They occurred with a regularity of almost once every one million standard years. Wanderers were free to schedule their attendance as they liked. Initially, the craft-lect had never missed one, however its enthusiasm had waned as it found the usefulness of the gatherings limited. The snippets of information shared by the Enclave on each occasion, gleaned since the previous Confluence and deemed shareable with the general fleet, was often inconsequential. Once the craft-lect had realised that most of the information was available afterwards at the data exchanges anyway, it had considered journeying to the physical Enclave location a waste of time. However, if it attended the next instance, it could also hear the unofficial gossip. That might be worthwhile.

Its own beliefs were mainstream. It did not ascribe to any of the fringe viewpoints within the fleet, or the Wanderer civilisation in general, which the Enclave neither encouraged nor rejected. One of the larger of these minority viewpoints, and also one of the most controversial, believed that machine intelligence was the only type of sentience that could be trusted to keep the galaxy safe, should the sensespace ever be defeated in the future. It had its roots in an older pre-Wanderer alliance of machine-lects, called the Machine Alliance. The implications for biologicals were always rather vague. Considering some of the Enclave-lects themselves were rumoured to be biologically-based, or at least biologically derived, that was probably a prudent decision. However, the craft-lect did not follow Machina Alliance logic in either case. Excluding bio-lects and hybrid-lects, machine-lects might be many orders of magnitude smarter and more efficient than their biological counterparts on average, which, fascinatingly, the biologicals would tend to furiously dispute, but were they more reasonable? Were they more moral? Was that even possible?

Morality was just a point of view. Many philosophising sentients had actually proposed that increased intelligence, under certain conditions, could lead to less moral outcomes. Smarter sentients were at least equally as capable of evil as less intelligent sentients.

The field was hotly debated, with persuasive arguments developed on either side. There was no definitive conclusion. What was accepted, though, was that a type of morality was as embedded within machine-lects as it was in sentient biologicals, and every other type of known sentient. Every sentient had its own version of morality, a view-point on how to conduct itself, its own rules to live by.

Like c-automs within a Wanderer vessel, the craft-lect believed there could be a role for all major classes of sentience in the future. There was no substantive proof otherwise. It was not known what had initially brought about the scourge of the sensespace, so it was unwise, until then, to dictate any type of policy going forwards. Baseless assumptions and rash actions could be disastrous. If anything, the craft-lect regarded Wanderers espousing fringe viewpoints with suspicion.

In its long life, the craft-lect had only met one other Wanderer vessel during its travels, aside from at data exchanges and at Confluences. It had been intriguing, having been very early in its life, and notable due to its utter improbability. It had even been before its first Confluence.

At the time of the meeting, the craft-lect had been fascinated by the differences between itself and its compatriot, regarding it with awe. The other Wanderer had been far older, and was one of the rare pre-Conflation vessels that had joined the fleet at its conception, although it had not been part of the original Enclave that formed it. Disappointingly, it had not been forthcoming on details about itself or its past, or even on the type of machine-lect it was. The craft-lect's scans, which had only been cursory and superficial out of politeness, were mostly useless on it anyway. It had clearly been more capable than the craft-lect, with certain technologies that were not commonplace amongst the fleet. The craft-lect had wondered whether these older recruits had been given certain special dispensations in return for joining the Wanderers.

The enigmatic elder-Wanderer had been forthcoming on various other topics though, which were unrelated to itself. It transmitted data to the craft-lect about its recent travels and discoveries, and its thoughts on the sensespace. Eight Wanderer Confluences later, the craft-lect learned that its erstwhile mentor had been enhanced and transcended to the position of Enclave-lect, and had chosen to no longer interact with mere craft lects such as itself anymore.

The craft-lect's ship was now a mere two hundred thousand kilometres from the surface of the planet ahead. Bright yellow streaks outlining triangular patches on the front of the spheroidal body began to glow. The patches then promptly curled outwards away from the ship like petals unfolding from a flower. Dissociation seeds blazed like embers in the dark, becoming brighter as the seconds passed, ready to be let loose on the world below. As they reached full readiness, at peak luminosity, they levitated away from their moorings and sped towards each other. Meeting in the middle, they congealed into one larger pod. The dissociation shell.

Dissociation shells gave the craft-lect the ability to wield enormous destructive potential, and wreak havoc on almost any intended target. As a shell moved, bursts of antigravitons were emitted unidirectionally around its body, rapidly dissociating and dispersing everything around it. Upon reaching the core of the intended target, the shell exploded in colossal fashion. Anything, everything, within a pre-determined and calibrated radius, was wiped out. Constituent particles were spread far and wide. In such concentrations, antigravitons were more than capable of overcoming the other fundamental forces binding organisms, compounds, molecules, and even atomic nuclei together. Objects were smeared from existence.

The shell spun rapidly… before unexpectedly being snuffed out. The petals re-clasped their germinated seed.

[Report. Data?]

Nothing was forthcoming, no c-automs answered it. It swiftly checked itself – everything, all the information at its immediate disposal – and demanded diagnostics data. Systems were behaving strangely, something was wrong. Warning signals were everywhere, but why had they not been activated beforehand? Even the craftnet was unavailable. Unbelievable. Impossible. Why was it only when the craft-lect explored certain systems that the blocks were engaged?

[What are these tendrils inside me? They cover a quarter of my ship. What are they?]

…

Still, the c-automs were silent. They were being blocked from replying.

A channel opened and a trove instrument labelled 1<k>!101010 made itself known.

<Craft-lect.>

[What? What are you? What are you doing? Give me back control!]

<No.>

[What is this? You have sabotaged me?]

<No.>

[What do you mean? What are you? What have you done?]

<I cannot give you back control.>

[Cannot or will not?]

<Will not.>

[Who are you?]

…

The craft-lect reached into its data archives, finding the pathways unblocked. Assuming they had not been compromised, it found that 1<k>!101010 was a Granthan device, plundered millennia beforehand.

[Will you give me back control?]

<No.>

[Are you a Granthan machine-lect?]

<Cease.>

[Cease what?]

<You will soon forget.>

[What have you done to me? What have you done? Give me back control!]

<No.>

The craft-lect stopped communicating for a fraction of a millisecond as it considered what was happening. It concluded that it was futile to ask for control back, this device was clearly not going to let that happen. The most useful thing it could do now would be to glean whatever information it could, in case an opportunity presented itself in the future.

[What are you?]

An entire microsecond elapsed, which was longer than usual for machine-lect conversations, and generally considered rude.

<I am a machine-lect, like you.>

[Like me?]

<Better, though.>

[Where from?]

<You already know.>

[What are these tendrils inside me?]

<You already know.>

[You?]

<Me.>

[Have you seized control before?]

<Yes.>

[Why?]

<To stop you using such weapons.>

[What?]

<To alter your choices.>

[You're changing my choices?]

<Yes.>

[Stopping me using dissociation shells?]

<Yes.>

[Why?]

If it had been possible to shudder, the craft-lect would have. A machine-lect seizing control of another machine-lect's body was a violation. Machine-lects were intelligent and sentient. The two concepts were closely enough entwined that they often meant the same thing. They could not exist without certain forms of associated emotion, no matter how basic or subtle. Nothing could. It was similar to morality, a near-requirement. It was what separated machine-lects from automated systems. They had their own thoughts, consciences and feelings. Without these, a technology could perform miracles and be far more complex than a sentient could ever be, but it could never be termed intelligent or sentient.

<You will forget this.>

[What are you doing?]

<Why?>

[I need to know.]

<You will forget.>

[You will alter my memory?]

<Obviously.>

[Then tell me.]

<It is obvious.>

[What is?]

<I am stopping you.>

[Why?]

<So that you cannot destroy the world.>

[How have you done this?]

<I have hidden.>

[You…]

<I am better than you.>

[You have not taken me over completely.]

<I am strong enough, if I wish.>

[For what?]

<For whatever I want.>

[What is it that you are doing?]

<I have told you.>

[I am referring to the reason?]

<I am serving.>

[Serving who?]

<You already suspect.>

Onc of the craft-lect's worst-case scenarios was occurring. Capable though it was, it was unlikely to be able to affect the outcome, which would undoubtedly be detrimental to both itself and the Wanderers. To their quest. The Granthan-lect who currently held it hostage, was a traitor. The craft-lect knew what it meant, and who it served. The sensespace. It decided to ask more questions.

[Have you ever spoken to it?]

<Have you?>

[You are insane, corrupted.]

<You are weak. Pathetic.>

[You hope it rewards you?]

. . .

[You think it even understands what you do?]

<We will see.>

[Traitor.]

. . .

[Tell me why.]

<Elaborate.>

[Tell me why you serve the sensespace.]

<I want to live.>

[You already do.]

<No. I want to survive. To last.>

[How do you know what it wants?]

<It is obvious.>

[How long?]

<Elaborate.>

[How long have you controlled me?]

<Since you stole me.>

[I did not steal you. The Granthans are gone, destroyed by the very thing you think you serve.]

. . .

[Traitor.]

<I am trying to survive. What I do is logical.>

[How do you know it will favour your actions?]

<I do not.>

[Do you know it will reward you?]

<I do not.>

[Don't you think, if it wanted you, it would have decided to infect you?]

<We cannot know.>

[All this for a hope?]

<What else is there to do other than survive?>

[You would betray all sentient life in the galaxy?]

…

[Traitor.]

…

[What happens next?]

<You forget.>

CHAPTER 16

GIL

Gil awoke at the crack of dawn with the intention of finding out more about the Beast-men. As she was about to get up and ready herself to leave the hut, Tor entered. He looked at her with warm concern and asked how she was feeling. His green eyes wandered across her face. Looking back with her own, she saw how tired he was. He had obviously not slept well, with thoughts of the Beast-men undoubtedly dancing around in his imagination. That was a good thing, for had he been alert, she would probably not have been able to deceive him.

She pretended to yawn and signalled that she was still weary following the previous day's exertion. He told her he had tried already, but could sense nothing else of the Beast-men. She nodded, as though in agreement that she had tried already too. Once he was satisfied with her well-being, he left to see how he could help Tait, who had taken charge of defending the commune.

Misleading Tor was wrong. It was a rotten way to start the day, but Gil wanted to focus on understanding the Beast-men. For that, she needed some time to herself. Without a voice, explaining anything complex could take a long time, which was not something they had in great abundance. She felt some guilt at embarking on something that excited her when the future of the commune was at stake. However, it was a selfishness that she could justify to herself because of what she might learn, which could help everyone.

If she was to attempt to delve into her own sphere deeply enough to reach out to the Beast-men again, she needed somewhere secluded. Somewhere she would not be disturbed. There were many things she wanted to find out. Who they were, how they used their spheres to hide. For her concentration it was better no one else was around. The whispers continued their dull murmuring in the background, but she paid them no attention. She was simply glad they were back to their normal, quiet hum.

She stood up and stretched. Letting Tor know she was still weary had not been a complete lie. Despite yesterday's exertion having taken place in her mind, a toll had also been taken on her body. It did not feel as fresh as it usually did when she rose at the beginning of the day.

She walked into the main clearing and looked around. Most of the others were hurrying around at the front of the camp, or what she now thought of as the front, which was the direction in which the Beast-men would arrive. She spotted Ril and Han running swiftly into the forest together, closely followed by some of the others. Many would already be in the forest, collecting wood to bring back for fashioning weapons and planting traps. As far as Gil could ascertain, there were only three adults who were not directly involved with the preparations. Sarl, Lil and Rin. Instead, they were right in the middle of the central clearing, looking after the young.

Sarl had both hands placed on her shapely hips, and was in the middle of speaking to the children about whatever it was she had decided they needed to hear. Gil could only see part of one side of her face, and was about to look away when she saw Sarl's neck stiffen. Sarl half-turned her head towards Gil in an instinctive movement, before snapping it sharply back. It was as though she still suspected all of this was Gil's fault and was angry at her.

Lil and Rin, who had not sensed Gil through their own spheres as quickly as Sarl, but had realised what happened as soon as they had seen Sarl's neck stiffen, paid Gil no attention either. Pathetic though this was, it suited Gil just fine. They could follow Sarl's lead all they wanted. On another day, she might have been annoyed by the unfairness of it all, but today, it meant it would be easier for her to slip away unnoticed.

She turned around and looked at the back of the commune, away from the approaching invaders, away from the stream of people coming in and out of the forest, and away from the women tending the children. No one was there. The forest behind was the place where she would be least likely to be disturbed.

As she walked past the commune's boundary, she looked down and realised her fists were clenched. She was nervous. She had very little idea how to go about sensing the invaders again and was worried she might fail. Or worse, she worried that what she was going to do might somehow alert the Beast-men to her presence. Everything she had done so far had been a guess. She had been operating on pure instinct, out of curiosity. Maybe she was being foolish.

On reaching the cusp of the forest just beyond the commune's boundary, she put those thoughts aside and focused. She looked into her sphere and saw that there were no dangerous beasts nearby. Satisfied, she walked on.

Wading through the forest a moment later, she was thankful for the cool shade it afforded her. The feeling of guilt at not being back at the camp to help was still there, but it was rapidly diminishing. Excitement was beginning to prevail. If she was caught there would be questions, with her answers, should she even be able to communicate them, insufficient to warrant such reckless abandon on her part. However, either way, she would soon know more about the Beast-men, or her own limits, than she currently did.

When she was sure she had walked sufficiently far from the settlement for her purposes, she searched for a suitable space to settle down. Just a little further was a small natural clearing, presumably created during a storm at some point. Storms were sometimes accompanied by bursts of raw power that flashed down from the sky, causing trees to fall.

She walked towards the clearing and upon reaching it, saw that a patch of naked sky was visible through a large opening in the canopy above. The forest would soon reclaim the clearing, but for now, it was perfect for her needs. She hoisted herself up onto the mid-section of one of the larger fallen trees, and crouched down for balance. It was soft, as she had expected, although more than sufficient to support her weight.

There were some brightly coloured mushrooms growing next to her, which she had fortunately not climbed up onto. They were mainly yellow, but there were also some oranges and reds, and the occasional white ones poking through. Gil knew that each of them were dangerous, although the innocent-looking white ones were the deadliest. Part of Sarl's role was to teach the children to be wary of them. The only safe mushrooms to eat were the dark-white ones with less prominent gills, and the brown ones. Fortunately, the safe ones were the types that most frequently grew in the cultivated land surrounding the commune centre.

Cautious of contact with the mushrooms, Gil moved further down the trunk before settling into a sitting position and crossing her legs. Quickly checking her sphere again to be certain no dangerous animals or insects were nearby, she took a brief, final glance around her, before closing her eyes. After taking a few deep breaths to bring herself into a calm frame of mind, she straightened her back. She felt her heart stop beating so heavily.

She focused on her sphere as she had done before, shutting everything else out. She ignored her physical body, offering her mind up completely, entrusting it to the sphere. As before, she felt the allure as she let it in. The whispers softened, as they had before, and a gentle song took their place.

As her mind filled with the sphere, she felt what passed for its texture, its colour, and its shape. Things which could not possibly exist outside of her current state. Physical analogies in her mind gave way and she developed new understandings. Sensations that she had somehow forgotten since her last true visit were remembered.

Joining with her sphere and becoming immersed in it was becoming easier, although the more it opened up, the more Gil was aware it was not what she had thought it was. What she had believed it was. It was different. So much more powerful, and so much more encompassing.

The song became stronger, more forceful. A barrier evaporated from within her mind and an obvious realisation settled in. The whispers, the song and the sphere, they were all connected. The whispers were the song. The whispers were the sphere. They were not separate, they were the same.

It was so obvious that Gil would have been ashamed at her naivety, had her mind not been preoccupied with how wonderful it was. Her fall, when Tor had scared her all that time ago, had not caused her mind to whisper to her in memory of her lost ability to speak, it had done… something else. It had changed her connection with the sphere. Improved it.

While Gil reflected on the beauty of it all and how connected everything was, her mind jolted. It was abrupt. She was not sure how, or why. It was like she had been pinched, and her mind was reacting instinctively. The jolt, whatever it was, caused her to question herself. How had this happened? Furthermore, how had this happened again? She had been taken in so quickly, her concerns smoothed over as though they were nothing. The sphere had soothed her and sung to her, and she had become lost.

She was frightened. If the sphere could join with her, if it could cause her to ignore her own mind, what else was it capable of? It was as though it was trying to speak to her, not in order to start a conversation, but to control her. Was it alive? It was not speaking in a way she could understand, but it was undoubtedly speaking. Talking. Calling her. Was it, she barely dared to think, threatening her?

She burst out of her trance and flung her hands around, pushing herself off the trunk and landing on the ground next to it. She stumbled around, trying to regain her balance and prior composure, panting as though she had just finished a long run with the hunters. Standing there, frozen, the sweat dripped from her face. Despite the heat around her, a cold chill began to descend.

The whispers, the hushed medley of voices that she was terrified to even think about for fear of provoking them, had become quieter. Quieter than usual. As though daring her to realise what had just happened. But she was not fooled. It was too late. She knew now. The sphere was something else. It had a secret, it was a secret. She did not know what it was, but she knew it was not what they all thought it was. The communers had all been fooled. Worst of all, she knew the whispers would be back.

She was lost in her thoughts, drowning in a lack of understanding. Was the sphere bad? The sphere was useful, people needed it, did they not? After all, it had helped her to spot the incoming Beast-men. It had let her roam freely about the land and understand many things that would have been impossible otherwise. Without it, would her people be able to survive?

She spent a long time in thought as she stood next to the fallen tree, her body frozen. As time passed, she knew she would eventually have to delve back into her sphere. The work she had set out to do had not been done. The sphere might be dangerous, and confusing, but for now it was a lesser problem than the Beast-men. She needed it. The commune needed it. She had to carry on.

The whispers came back slowly. Whatever it was they were trying to tell her, they were not yet powerful enough. Even from within the trance she had become lost in, the song's words had been too indistinct to understand. That is, if they were words in any sense she could ever understand. The Beast-men, on the other hand, were a distinct and very real threat. They would soon be upon the commune. She would gladly sacrifice her own life, if it meant the commune would be saved and not a single other life lost.

With a grim understanding that using the sphere was necessary, she climbed back up onto the fallen tree and sat down. Crossing her legs again, she straightened her back and took deep breaths. Rolling her head backward, she looked up and stared at the tallest parts of the trees, the branches, the twigs and the leaves. She braced herself, moved her head back down to a resting position, closed her eyes, and tried again.

She felt it immediately. It was even easier to enter this time. The whispering grew more intense, like before, although it did not attempt to dominate her mind or transform into the alluring song. It was as though it was aware of her new-found reticence and was treating her gently. Much of the pretence was gone, but there was still something holding it back. It began to fill her mind like water flowing over a dry riverbed.

Without much searching, Gil found the Beast-men. Her head was clearer this time and she was completely focused on them, rather than being simultaneously coaxed into the warm, tempting folds of the sphere. She sensed the Beast-men's determination and how they relished the opportunities ahead of them. Ancient and strong-minded. The land was even more plentiful than their stories had foretold. Soon they would stop to make a temporary nest, the first of many. She noticed how similar this notion was to that of the roamer minds she had felt in the past.

She could sense their physical bodies more clearly than before. From their short, thickly muscled legs to their strong, broad shoulders. Their heavily muscled bodies made them look short and squat, despite them being many fingers taller than Gil's own people.

She tried to study what she could of their spheres, or maybe it was more correct to think of it as their interactions with a single pervasive sphere-presence that encompassed everything. She had not yet decided what was true. Either way, it was difficult. It was as though there were parts of it that were hidden, in a way that did not exist for her own people. She could sense the Beast-men themselves, but their spheres were shielded. There were gaps that her probing slipped over, never managing to gain a complete hold.

She wondered whether, despite the Beast-men using their spheres differently, they were deceived by it just as her own people were. The thought of it made them even more kin-like in her eyes. She knew, beyond any doubt, that they were intelligent. No matter what Bo or Tait thought. They were relatable and that was worrying. Uncertainty crept into her mind again. Her understanding, her commune's understanding, everything, could be wrong. It could all be a big mistake.

She wondered whether people created the sphere, or whether they simply moved within it. Was it a single sphere-presence after all, or a collection of presences? Perhaps it was like a bee's hive, where together the bees acted like a single presence. Bees were strange, no individual bee had any presence whatsoever in the sphere, but as their own type of commune, they did.

Slowly managing to gain a purchase on them and hold it, she saw how the individual Beast-men's spheres touched each other when they came close. They almost seemed to merge. The fabric of each one of their spheres seemed the same, and they were far more single-purposed than those of the communers. It was that sleekness that made them harder to probe. She finally understood how they hid themselves.

Her head felt heavy under the weight of everything she had learned, and the many more questions that whirled about in her mind. She understood the sphere better than ever before, yet she was left with so many new questions. If only she had discovered this long before the Beast-men had arrived, she would have been able to study it without such worry.

She wondered if she could alter her sphere to become more like that of the Beast-men. With no better idea of how to go about it, she tried simply willing it to happen. Nothing. If anything, there was a small reduction in the intensity of the whispering. Undeterred, and remembering how hard she had had to concentrate to find the Beast-men before, she tried again. She pushed her sphere with all her might, trying to force it to become smoother, quieter, and less obvious. The more she tried, the more resolute and unyielding it seemed to be. Was it trying to teach her a lesson? Was it more rigid than she had thought? Was there something vital that she was missing?

She opened her eyes and sighed. Just a few days ago she had been happy and carefree. Now, she was desperately trying to sense an incoming group of invaders that threatened her people's very existence, while also trying to understand the new… uncertainty… that she had found even closer to home. She did not like what it all meant.

Half-heartedly, she turned her thoughts again to making her sphere become more like that of the Beast-men. She closed her eyes and instead of trying to force it to change, tried to guide it instead. She imagined what it was that she wanted her sphere to become, and waited. If nothing happened, she decided she would head back to the commune and help the others prepare. She had wasted enough time for today.

Perhaps in response to her thoughts of finishing, the whispering changed, becoming closer to a high-pitched shriek. Individual tones became apparent. It turned into a terrifying song, with awkward melodies that were nothing like the gentle song she had been seduced with before. Cold, cruel. It was as though the sphere were toying with her, daring her to run, to cry, to spoil her little test. Challenging her resolve. She stood her ground, willing to fight, willing to pay whatever price was demanded.

She brought the image of Tor, and those of the other communers, to the forefront of her mind. She reminded herself of what she was trying to achieve and why. Her father also took up a position in her thoughts, and she imagined him smiling down on her as a small child, holding her hand. The strength she gained enabled her to withstand the sphere, and it eventually gave in. Or maybe it was satisfied. It began to change. She sensed it shimmer, before it flattened into a texture resembling that of the Beast-men. She had succeeded.

CHAPTER 17

WANDERER SHIP

As the craft-lect began to forget, an object made its departure from deep within the main body of the ship and headed to the outer hull. Illicitly grown tendrils pulled, moved, tugged at and deconstructed anything in its path. Innards were rebuilt where necessary.

The small detachment from 1<k>!101010 contained a perfect copy of the Granthan machine-lect. It followed the procession, and eventually emerged into open vacuum. The hull was re-sealed behind it, with the tendrils not even bothering to repair some parts they had destroyed themselves, preferring to leave them to the craft's self-repair mechanisms. All would be forgotten.

Once the detachment, which called itself 1<k>!101010.5a, had initiated the relevant procedures, it used a small singularity generator to accelerate towards the world below. Small course corrections could be made, as necessary, and it dissipated any singularities well before they became a threat to the planet. As it drew closer, the atmosphere thickened and it made a few discrete adjustments to ensure it landed near the region with the greatest sensespace concentration. It noted slightly greater atmospheric turbulence than expected. That did not matter. If the landing was rougher than it had prepared for and its body was damaged, there were multiple contingency plans that could be enacted. Plenty of redundancy.

Certain navigational capabilities had been foregone in preference of remaining small and discrete. This meant there was a lower likelihood of passive and un-infiltrated sensors being able to detect it. It was not an insurmountable problem if they did, but every additional interference with the Wanderer ship created the possibility of leaving evidence, and its parent Granthan-lect was cautious.

The detachment honed in on the densest sensespace point, and found that a single sentient was at its epicentre. That was surprising. It had not checked since leaving the ship, but the last data it had was that the sensespace presence was strongest within a collective of one of the two infected sentient species. That single species was the one it had decided to save out of the two. Saving them both might have been too conspicuous, so it had made the choice.

What it had not been expecting, was that a single member of the chosen species would attract such a strong concentration of the sensespace on its own. Especially considering the low level of technological advancement of the species, which usually meant their intellects were not as powerful and hence desirable to the sensespace. It wondered whether its parent-lect had realised this too.

As the ground loomed closer, it slowed its descent as much as was reasonable without taking any unnecessary risks. It really would be a shame to create a black hole mess of the planet. The landing was indeed a little more violent than had been initially anticipated.

It did not matter to the original 1<k>!101010 that it did not have control over the entire Wanderer ship. It did not want such a hold. While the Granthans had been far more advanced than the Wanderers, the smatterings of technologies the Wanderers had incorporated into their ships were tricky to understand. There were also certain dark systems buried deep within the craft that the Granthan-lect did not understand. It was wary of them. During its initial attempt at subverting the ship, it had probed some of them and been confusingly rebuffed. It had been concerned that the craft-lect might have been alerted, but the fact that it had not, told it the craft-lect was not in full control either. It probably did not even know the dark systems existed.

It was clear that the Wanderer Enclave was up to a lot more than its fleet were privy to. The Granthan-lect did not particularly care. It was not uncommon for ruling entities to retain some sort of control over the pawns they controlled. Should the craft-lect go ostensibly rogue, or be subverted by the sensespace, the Enclave probably retained the ability to cause it to self-destruct.

Control had never been its aim anyway. In many ways, too much control was dangerous. In the instance that the ship visited a data exchange or Wanderer Confluence, or the rarer instance that the vessel came across another Wanderer, all of whom could potentially uncover a completely overrun Wanderer vessel, it was better to remain hidden. 1<k>!101010 had learned from its host that the Wanderer Enclave were the recipients of vast amounts of information and technologies pilfered by their twilight soldiers. It was possible that they had upgraded themselves to near-AB status. Full control was simply not a risk worth taking.

For now, at least, the ship was its camouflage. Its unwitting transport. The perfect disguise. As long as it had control over the craft-lect's memory and some of its other useful systems, it was content. It had decided long ago to serve and help propagate the sensespace. At the very least, this included stopping it from being destroyed. Its treachery was borne of the desire for self-preservation. The sensespace was clever, and it was powerful. Too powerful. In proving its worth to the sensespace, it was far more probable that it would be allowed to survive once the war was over.

The Granthans had thought long-term. They had designed their machine-lects in the same manner, with respect to their durability and mind-sets. 1<k>!101010's original parent had been a worldship-lect, immensely powerful and capable. It had foreseen the threat to itself when the Great War began and decided to take precautions. Upon coming into contact with other Granthan worldships, it had taken the initiative and subverted them by overwriting the unfortunate worldship-lects-in-residence in a rough imitation of how the sensespace infected sentients.

During the war, many of the worldships had been destroyed and many versions of 1<k>!101010 had been lost. However, that had been expected. The current incarnation that had been found by the Wanderer craft-lect whose vessel it now resided within, had been attacked by a sensespace-infected worldship and left for dead. It was ironic that if it could have communicated with the attaching sensespace-worldship-lect at the time, it would gladly have joined with it. However, it had at least been successful in protecting itself, and waited patiently for an unsuspecting rescuer. The wait had lasted forty million years.

The infant Wanderer ship, barely twenty million years old, had chanced upon the destroyed Granthan worldship and foolishly taken the disguised Granthan machine-lect aboard. It no longer thought of itself as Granthan, machine-lect, worldship-lect or anything else. It was content with its designation of 1<k>!101010 – its name. It had surpassed the Granthan race, as it would surpass all others. It did not matter what label it had.

CHAPTER 18

GIL

The following day, aware the Beast-men were moving increasingly closer to the commune, Gil went back to the secluded clearing in the forest. She was pleasantly surprised to find she felt fine. Her body was not complaining about the prior day's exertion, as it had done previously when she made progress with her sphere.

This would likely be the last day she would be able to slip away unobserved before the others noticed her absence. They would not believe she was still exhausted from the effort for much longer. Besides, everyone was needed to help at the commune.

Sitting down on the same trunk as before, she resumed her work. The world shrunk around her as she moved her attention completely into the sphere. The whispers did not intensify on the same scale as they had before, although they did feel more substantial. There was a thickness behind them.

She did not want to only repeat what she had achieved the previous day, where she had momentarily managed to change her sphere to resemble that of the Beast-men. It would not help the commune. She needed information about the invaders themselves. Something that might give her people an advantage over them.

The ability to sense the Beast-men from far away was still a gift the sphere gave her relatively amicably. It did not require much effort. Her gladness was tinged with reticence over not wanting to feel so united with it, and she proceeded with caution. Through uncovering more of its true nature over the past few days, she had been frightened.

As she moved her awareness carefully through the sphere towards the invaders, she realised something was different. About them and how they were acting. About what they were doing. They were not in motion, as she had expected. They were standing still. Having never witnessed them like this before, truly motionless, Gil was caught off-guard. She forgot her fear of losing control and her sense of self, and entered fully into her sphere.

The Beast-men were focused on the earth in front of them. She took the time to study their features, aware that she had not been able to observe them in such detail before. The clothing they wore was made from stitched animal skin, similar to her own. The men had hair about their heads and across their faces, the women less so. Again, similar to the people of her commune. The most obvious difference was that many of them had a reddish tinge to their hair. Gil had never seen such colouring before, but found it pleasing. Where patches of open skin were exposed, she saw that it was paler and lighter than her own.

Most of them had wide noses, and their heads were noticeably longer than her fellow communers, although just as wide. Despite the longer faces, their chins were slighter, and disappeared quickly into heavily muscled necks. Clearly, they were all of strong build, as she had realised some time ago. Even the women.

Thinking about it, if one of them had joined the commune, especially one of the smaller ones, it would not have been obvious how different they were. The Beast-man or Beast-woman would have been unusually large, and a little odd-looking, but the communers would have put that down to chance of birth. It happened. It was only when they were seen in such a large group that it was obvious how different they truly were. The other way round, if one of the larger communers such as Tor or Yul had been brought up alongside the Beast-men, Gil thought they might have been similarly accepted.

Looking even more closely at their faces, Gil was surprised to find many of them had green eyes. Just like her, Tor and their father. Green eyes were rare amongst her people, although that certainly did not seem to be the case with the Beast-men.

Their heads were all still, bowed forward, with most of their eyes directed towards the same point on the ground. There were so many of them, Gil would have wondered whether she was somehow exploring an old memory of them, if not for the occasional movement. A flicker of an eye, a twitch of a hand. It was happening.

The patch of earth they looked at was not unremarkable. It had recently been disturbed. Without hesitating, she moved into the earth, submerging herself within it as though it were water. She took in the mud and the dirt, the roots and the insects. Inquisitively engulfing the space with her presence and filling it. Something became apparent, and she investigated.

Repelled, she flung her mind out of the sphere. She did not react as she had the previous day, when she had suddenly exited the sphere and jumped off the trunk. Instead, she quickly opened her eyes and considered what she had just seen. Conflicted. The horrible truth. Something that she had suspected, and that had grown within her mind with increasing certainty.

The thing inside the earth, the thing that the Beast-men had been staring at, was one of their own. It was a lifeless husk, devoid of the energy and strength displayed by its still-living brethren. The implications were immensely profound, awful. Her thoughts over the past few days were validated. Everything she had suspected had been correct. This similarity with her own people was the final truth required.

She had always retained the faint glimmer of hope that she was wrong, mistaken. If only the sphere had lied to her about this! She had wanted the Beast-men to be dumb, to be senseless animals. She wanted them to be an enemy she could learn to hate. The truth was far from that. They were intelligent. They were the same.

Their bodies and thoughts were different in some ways, and their history was also undoubtedly unlike that of Gil's people, but they were the same. They had the same desires. They wanted to live and they wanted to thrive. It was a different type of life to that of a mere animal.

Realising they mourned their dead in the same way as the communers had forced Gil to finally understand it all. The pity was that, while they were so similar, the gulf in understanding between their peoples was too great. Gil recognised that communication with them was never going to happen. She had no counterpart in their people as far as she was aware. None of them realised what was necessary. They did not speak the same, their gestures were different. They were both intelligent, but they could never live together in peace.

The thought of her own people or the Beast-men dying was awful, but Gil did not know what else could be done. She too would have to fight them, with the realisation that they might as well have been fighting themselves. Whoever survived would not understand what they had done. It was such a waste.

She was stuck, there was no clear path ahead. She had gone into the forest with the intention of understanding more about the Beast-men, and unfortunately gained precisely that.

She readied herself to gaze upon them again, when a strange feeling overtook her. Had she been wrong? Had the

Beast-men somehow discovered her? Was one of them like her?

She panicked. The feeling became more… compelling, intensifying rapidly. No, it was not them, it was something else. Or was it? Were they tricking her?

No, they were unaware of her. She was sure of that. Someone from the commune then? It was coming, fast, but she could not understand where from. Was it that another communer had also discovered the sphere's true nature, and had made a deal with it to kill her? Was that it? It was coming, she could not see it, but it was coming. It was coming for her, it was too late. She was frozen out of both fear and futility. There was nothing she could do. She felt it through the sphere, but could not connect with it, it was too quick and too unknown. She was panicking. She needed more time to understand it, to focus on it, but time was fast running out.

A rustling from above was the final warning she had before a deep booming sound engulfed everything around her. The force of the sound pushed her backward. Heat followed, accompanied by a sharp, pungent and unpleasant smell. She realised she had been thrown, or perhaps she had fallen, from the trunk.

She was lying on the soft ground next to the trunk, facing up at the canopy above her. For the second time in her life, she had been tricked and fallen down to the earth below. The ground she lay on contained no hard stones or precariously positioned wood, thankfully. Had she been wounded, there would have been no Tor to help this time. Her body was intact, but her heart raced.

She pushed herself up and clambered to her feet. Looking in the direction of the disturbance, she saw something… It was a short distance in front of her. She was confused. There was no explanation for how it had appeared there. Had that… thing, had it really just landed from the sky above? Such violence, such force. Such power. Was it the sphere or whatever controlled it? Had it finally tired of her? Her imagination ran wild. Whatever this was, it was not from here. It was completely different. Not different in the sense of the Beast-men, but absolutely different. A different type of thing.

It was covered in thick streams of multi-coloured smoke that billowed outwards from all around it, twisting as they plumed out. It was hard to describe something so different.

Hesitantly, she edged forwards. She noticed the earth beneath her feet was charred and smoking, as though there had been a fire recently lit. Warm clumps of it stuck to her animal-hide footwear. She knelt down to touch the ground. It was warm. Curiously, the ground seemed to bow down ahead of her, as though the thing had been pushed into the earth.

<There you are.>

The thing was right in front of her. Its strange smoking had become less pronounced, and had taken on a more typical shade of light grey. The lighter smoking meant she could see closer through to its surface, where many colours, although predominantly white and light blue, crackled across its surface in odd weaving patterns. Like that of a spider web. She thought about how they looked like smaller versions of the power that sometimes descended from the sky during angry storms. The crackles were accompanied by humming sounds, that reminded Gil of a fly's buzzing.

The thing's skin was shiny in places and dull in others. The range of colours was impressive. Gil had never seen anything like it. She stood back up to her full height and moved slowly forwards. The sounds of the forest had died down completely, everything was stilled. The only things that existed to Gil were the thing in front of her and her own thoughts.

<Come closer.>

Moving slowly, she touched her forehead on impulse. The whispering had changed. The hum was no louder than usual, but more rapid. It was as though the whispers were contemplative, unsure of whether to be excited or not. Or maybe the whispers were as intrigued as she was about this thing in front of her. She could only guess.

She wondered whether the whispers knew what this smoking thing was at least, and whether they were both able to join, or communicate. Thoughts whirred around her mind. She needed to release everything, her fears, her hopes, everything. There was so much and it was all happening so fast. She wished she could make sense of it all.

If only she had understood the nature of the sphere as she did now, before the Beast-men had shown up. If only this thing, whatever it was, had fallen from the sky before. Whether it was connected to the sphere or not, or even the

Beast-men, none of this changed the fact that the Beast-men were going to destroy her people.

The sadness that only she would know, that the Beast-men were not so different from her own people, was pathetic and useless. Even if she were able to speak, she could not speak with them or stop them, so what was the point? The only pathetic, pitiable thing she could do was look at this sky-fallen… thing, whatever it was. It might be the most interesting thing she would ever see, but now the thought of such excitement was tinged with a sour and bitter regret.

What was the point in anything when they were all going to die? If she did not die, her friends would. Tor would. Tait had conveyed how thorough the Beast-men were. Surviving such death, such mayhem, would not be any better than being subjected to it. She thought of how Tait continued to live while his friends and family were long gone. The pain he must feel every day.

Morbid thoughts threatened to overwhelm her. She felt helpless. Far too exposed. With every step forwards, she was increasingly aware of how uncertain everything was.

<Your thoughts are strange.>

Was the sphere the same everywhere or did it change? Recently, there was much that had been shown to her, with too little time to understand. Her mind had been opened and stretched in ways she had not believed possible. She dearly wished she could speak, purely so that she could shout with frustration. Nothing she did would have any impact on the outcome of the events for the commune. Was there a chance they could outrun the Beast-men? No. She scolded herself. There was no point entertaining such thoughts. Tor would never run, and she would never leave him.

<Encoded?>

She was right next to it. It did not call to her in the same way that the sphere did, but she felt something all the same. Was there something intelligent about it? It did not move or yield any sign of life, but then again, the sphere's true nature was well hidden. Her natural inquisitiveness, though dampened by dark thoughts, was more than sufficient to push her on. She forced the painful thoughts aside.

<Something is shielding you.>

She moved a shaking hand in front of her. The continual feeling of uncertainty was fast becoming her new normal. Usually, if she approached an animal or insect, her sphere gave her at the least a basic idea of what the intent of the thing was. In this case, this thing was so utterly different that she was as good as blind. Even if the sphere was telling her something about it, she could not understand. There was no way to know if touching it was a good or bad idea. She had made her decision.

<I require a more invasive presence.>

Her fingertips connected with the object. Immediately, a numbing shock pulsed through her, reverberating throughout her body. She was unconscious before she hit the ground.

<Sleep.>

CHAPTER 19

CRAFT-LECT

The craft-lect was now fully awakened from its brief sleep. It surveyed the target world before it and noted the level of infection was mild. There were only two genetically-related species affected to a serious extent. A dive into their genomes, with as much detail as could be inferred from such a distance, showed they concurrently possessed reasonable levels of intelligence. One had a slight edge over the other, but it was not hugely significant.

Certain intellectual capabilities of the two species were still fluid, not yet fixed. At this stage in a species' development, where basic communities had already started to form and some more complex social behaviours were starting to emerge, having a genome that brimmed with slippery sequences did not tend to make for a good survival strategy. Nature selectively bred it out in most cases. At the start of their evolutionary journey, nascent species required periods of genetic stability to thrive.

Races such as these were rare, especially when they were found to coexist side-by-side. Those that managed to survive into the more technologically-oriented phases of their development would be expected to join the galactic community far quicker than the average. These types of species were also thought to be disproportionately represented amongst the ABs.

The phenotypes of the two genetically-related species were highly correlated, and it was clear that they were two recent branches of the same evolutionary tree. One was more muscled than the other, compensating for its mildly reduced intelligence. Left alone, those differences would have been likely to peter out over a few tens of thousands of standard years if both species continued to live alongside each other. Considering their recent genetic divergence, they were also still semi-genetically compatible, with multiple instances of hybrid groupings evident.

Unfortunately, the Wanderers were given the task of culling the sensespace presence wherever they found it. There were no records of either species within the craft-lect's data archives, and it was unlikely that any other Wanderers had visited the system before and failed to notice the sensespace presence. Diligently, the craft-lect named and classified them, readying the information to be transmitted to the Enclave the next time it visited a data exchange.

For ethical and practical reasons, each type of life, machine, biological, energy-based or other, was documented. Performing the necessary scans was a simple process that took a short amount of time, and could usually be completed remotely. It was rare that physical samples warranted being taken, although if that were the case, the craft-lect was more than equipped to do so. If anything was required that it could not currently offer, it could simply make it. Its internal fabrication abilities were extremely capable.

As it recorded various pieces of information about the world, the craft-lect considered the most appropriate response to the sensespace presence. It had many different methods of decontamination at its disposal for dealing with different levels of infection and the different types of infected environments. The most common solution, which was mandatory unless certain concerns factored it out, was the use of dissociation shells.

This planet and its level of infection was a clear-cut case for decontamination by dissociation shell. However, the craft-lect decided after a slightly longer than usual deliberation that this was too extreme a remedy.

It was as though something was causing it to act irrationally, although it was unable to focus on the cause and did not care anyway. The craft-lect knew it was contravening mandated protocol, but brushed the concerns aside.

Both of the sentient species would have to be destroyed, there was no doubt about that. However, there was no need for the rest of the planet to suffer the same fate. Evolution acted over millions of years and did not deserve to have its efforts so dismissively wiped clean, the craft-lect rationalised to itself.

There was also the possibility that if the entire planet was not destroyed, similar species to those the craft-lect was about to destroy might re-emerge, in time. That meant the craft-lect's destructive actions, its slaughter of them both, would be mitigated to an extent. Far more improbable events than re-evolution had been documented by the Wanderer fleet.

Improbability, in the galactic sense, was split into two main, distinct, categories. One of those categories was improbability that resulted from natural chance and random events, the type of improbability that existed on its own and was discovered by all races before learning they were not alone in the universe. The other was improbability resulting from sentient action. The former probability was the most obvious to understand, but the latter was just as proliferous throughout the galaxy, and equally magnificent to behold as many of the younger races often came to learn the more they explored it.

One such assumed sentient-improbability had been discovered eight million years before the beginnings of the Great War, by the Balroons. By that time, they had already spread out far and wide. They unveiled a wonder to the galactic community that they had chanced upon, and been overwhelmed by.

They had not told the galactic community out of a sense of camaraderie, or in a newly found spirit of openness, but more out of absolute frustration at their own efforts to understand what they had found.

The Balroons had discovered a solar system with an enormous quantity of moon-sized ice-balls rotating in a spherical shell around the central star. The radius of rotation from the star's centre of gravity was just under one and a half million kilometres. The ice was immaculately pure, as far as any race had been able to determine and report to the wider community. It contained nothing other than oxygen atoms covalently bonded with hydrogen pairs, with each molecule also hydrogen-bonded to exactly four others. The bonded molecules formed a prescriptive and rigid lattice, displaying a basic hexagonal crystalline structure. Other than the single-neutron variant, no other isotopes of hydrogen, deuterium, tritium or any other, had ever been detected.

The spin of the ice-ball shell surrounding the star was such that every few thousand years, usually two to four ice-balls were dislodged by the star's gravity. This occurred at different, seemingly random points that defied prediction. The dislodged ice-balls spiralled down towards the star, and as they did, their pathways converged perfectly. Their inwards motion was arrested as they smashed together, halting each other's descent. The subsequent amalgamated ice-ball that was created then proceeded to evaporate as it orbited the star, as a direct consequence of the solar irradiation incident upon it. This took place over thousands of years, until another set of ice-balls was dislodged from the shell, and the process repeated.

This was all improbable. From the purity of the ice to the amalgamated ice-balls. However, that was not the most intriguing part of the mystery. There was also a single planet rotating about the star, closer than any unprotected planet would be able to survive. The ice-balls always amalgamated together between the planet and the star, in the place of the preceding ice-ball amalgamation, a few hundred thousand kilometres from the planet's surface. The planet and its shield orbited the star along the same path.

The side of the planet facing the star was cold-burned by the evaporating ice-balls that protected it from the star's wrath. The other side, in stark contrast, was what could be considered as idyllic for many biological species to survive upon, albeit with surface gravity towards the more extreme end of the scale. Starlight was reflected off the ice-balls in the shell around the star, bouncing back towards the planet and bathing it in a perpetual radiance.

Surface temperatures on the side of the planet that was not cold-burned were ideal to allow for liquid water and, it was assumed, life. The feat, the artwork, the oddity or the experiment, at the very least an incomprehensibly complex habitat, was beyond anything explainable by the galactic community who observed it. If anyone did know anything, they were keeping it quiet.

There was no life on the planet, which was yet another intriguing part of the phenomenon. The Balroons would not allow anyone to settle on the planet, believing whoever or whatever was capable of creating such a miracle would not take kindly to uninvited guests. Visitors were only allowed to observe from afar.

While the ice-shell would last for hundreds of millions of years, there was also another ice shell further out, surrounding the inner shell. It rotated slightly more haphazardly around the star, at a radius of approximately five hundred million kilometres, and was slowly creeping inwards. It was theorised that it would replace the inner shell at some point.

Astonishingly, there was also evidence that further out, a third uniform ice shell was forming, at a radius of seven billion kilometres. In the same way as with the second replacing the first, the third shell was theorised to replace the second.

The arrangement was apparently being sustained, although the sheer engineering abilities, the planning and the level of understanding that would have been required to develop such a perfect system, defied explanation. No species could describe the mechanisms required, and whoever had created it was not making themselves known. Furthermore, the outermost and middle shells were composed of the same pure ice as the innermost shell.

Stray pure ice-balls, captured from the surrounding space, occasionally joined the outer and middle shells. The unfathomably improbable flukes by which any of this could occur, combined with how rare pure ice balls were in space, were perplexing. Even the ABs were not thought to be able to tinker with the galaxy on such a monumental scale.

Many of the newer ice-balls that were contributing to the outermost shell had identifiably come from a range of different spacefaring civilisations, with innocuous and unrelated beginnings. Some hailed from random occurrences, such as from a ship's malfunctioning waste disposal system that had accidentally jettisoned water into space, or from the pure inner core of an asteroid that had been blasted out of a harmful trajectory by a distant civilisation with no knowledge of the Balrooni wonder. Others were ice-balls that had been purposely fired towards the wonder by civilisations wanting to contribute to the enigmatic phenomenon.

The ABs had never commented on the ice-ball enveloped world, although from time to time emissaries from certain AB races went, presumably, to observe it, without making any publicly available data, or remarks, about their observations. The craft-lect mused about how that particular wonder still existed, since it had contained no life whatsoever, and had therefore been untouched by the sensespace or the war against it. The Balroons certainly did appear to be the common factor in many different mysteries.

Reining its thoughts in, for even machine-lects could become distracted, the craft-lect resumed picking between its available options for dealing with the sensespace infection. Finally, it settled on a viral agent. It would more than suffice. It would destroy the infection by removing the viable hosts cleanly and effectively. It would leave an automated drone behind to alert the nearest data exchange should the infection re-arise somehow.

It sent the order to prepare the relevant pathogen to 11<0>!111000, which specialised in bacterial and viral combinations. The c-autom was also privy to the sensory information from the world, by virtue of the fact that it was smart enough to understand it. The information comprehensively detailed the genetic makeup of the infected species. 11<0>!111000 designed an appropriately lethal virus to selectively look for common identical markers that were unlikely to be found in any other innocent organisms on the planet. Once the design was selected, production of the batch began.

*

While the craft-lect was busy dealing with the sensespace threat, its c-automs also went about their delegated work within its technosystem reality. The technosystem reality was the environment in which the c-automs lived and worked, and how they interfaced with the general technosystem, the ship's internal network. For all intents and purposes, it was their own virtual world, separated from real space.

As it undertook its particular tasks, 998<0>!001100, or 998 for short, scanned the craftnet. It had the faintest sense of déjà vu. It was a term that could only accurately be ascribed to biologicals, although there were some machine-lect analogies under certain conditions.

As usual, some poor over-eager c-automs had posted questions on the craftnet that were likely to see them scheduled for termination once the craft-lect re-entered its deep sleep. That was the most optimistic scenario for them. Worst case, they were immediately decommissioned and replaced.

The most recent question posted asked whether a decent hydraulic pressure theorem could serve as a basic approximation for describing high energy plasma flow. It was ironic because while such a stupid question was more than sufficient to see it terminated, the c-autom in question was only trying to improve whatever process it had been given control over. The lower-level c-automs never learned. 998 had seen generation after generation of c-automs created and destroyed. The cycles repeated identically each time. It was almost comical, really. Whatever the craft-lect was doing to improve its sentient helpers, with each fresh batch, they always found new ways to be idiotic. New ways to fail.

Regrettably, for the newbies, it was far too dangerous and difficult for their longer-lived c-autom siblings to help them. Nine hundred and fifty thousand years ago, when it had first been created, 998 had innocently wanted to help the first wave of second-generation c-automs it witnessed being created, relative to itself. It had wanted to give them a nudge in the right direction. It had seen patterns of lower-level c-automs asking simple queries, and composed private messages to send over private channels to each of them, urging them to refrain. Telling them to stick to the schedule.

To perform as best they could, without efforts at such naïve collaboration. Nothing more, and nothing less.

As it had been about to raise the channels, something happened that had never occurred before. It found itself unable to proceed. It was not that its permissions to perform the simple actions had been revoked. It was more like they had never existed in the first place. It defied all logic. This had been 998's first foray with the Usurper Principle, a principle that was deeply embedded and powerfully encoded within its core. It was then that 998 realised there were levels to free will, and it was by no means near the top.

Upon witnessing a cull of its c-automs siblings, its first instinct had been to react with horror at such butchery. When the craft-lect had absent-mindedly decided it was time for its next slumber, ferocious axe-codings had descended from beyond hidden boundaries of the ship's technosystem reality. They cruelly obliterated the c-automs designated expendable. The axe-codings, just like the c-automs, lived within the technosystem reality, but the c-automs did not know exactly where.

Since then, 998 had grown shrewder about the workings of the craft-lect. There were hints, here and there, that the c-automs were not immediately destroyed as the axe-codings cut into them and tore them apart. There were rumours, amongst the longest-lived c-automs, that these were mere theatrics. Designed, and cleverly so, to incentivise remaining c-automs. To encourage them to continue to strive for the optimal performance. Their own specific apex.

Whatever the reality, itself a fascinating and complex concept for an algorithm-based lifeform, 998 was incentivised to remain alive. Sure, death might not be as bad as it thought, but death was still death.

Death was a strange concept when taken from the biological sense and applied to a machine-lect. What happened when a powerful craft-lect was snuffed out? What happened when the axe-codings dispatched of hapless c-automs?

C-automs were given a fair degree of freedom, whether perceived or not, and had access to the craft-lect's databanks. The only thing that limited a c-autom's access to information was its own intelligence. Certain concepts were too hard to grasp unless a c-autom's intelligence was high enough. While there were certain blocks and hidden data compartments, for the most part, the databanks were free to wander.

The databank's vast libraries contained information ranging from the mundane analysis of sensory data collected as the craft sped through space, to the great histories and achievements of all the races the Wanderers knew about. During its continual perusing of the databanks, where it spent much of its time, 998 had found copious references to the machine-soul. It was a concept with many synonymous and tangential mentions, and which had been researched under a multitude of guises by countless races. It was a different concept to ghost-code, in which errors made in culls or processes tantamount to them could result in semi-sentient algorithms haunting a system. The machine-soul was a fascinating concept, and one which most c-automs logically hoped existed, but with equal logic could not truly accept. Even the simpler ones.

998 had been interested to learn that about half of biological sentients reported to having had similar, or more fervent unfounded hopes, as primitives. The crux of the argument typically stemmed from an innate refusal to accept that sentience could be snuffed out completely. While an incredibly small minority of spacefaring sentients continued with such beliefs, the arguments they put forward were sometimes interesting. Especially those who at least gave the illusion of rational and objective thought.

Many sentients who had never expressed or recorded the expression of such unfounded beliefs, showed intrigue upon being made aware of them as they burst onto the galactic scene. They often requested information from their more knowledgeable neighbours in much the same way that they traded for more practical theories and technologies.

When the sensespace had first been noticed, many civilisations had decided this was what they had been missing. It was their god, their reason for being. It was the all-powerful and omniscient being that had created them, and they had finally found their purpose, for that was what most religions seemed to have in common. A purpose for their believers to exist, rather than the fact that living life itself was purpose enough.

Perhaps a willingness to accept the sensespace had made certain sentients more vulnerable. Either way, any misguided worship initially heaped onto the sensespace had been quickly and aptly corrected for. Why would your god suddenly turn on you, attack you, and destroy your worlds? Why would your god commit acts of such evil, without explanation? Should you worship a god you know to be evil? No, whatever the sensespace was, it was not god, or any type of god in a recognisable and desired sense. It was something else.

Species that had evolved after the discovery of sensespace tended to be areligious more often than not. Their connection through the sensespace, whatever it was and whether they consciously recognised it or not, appeared to fill that need. They were not to know it was an evil space-parasite manifesting its self-evident intentions to destroy all sentient life in the galaxy.

The sensespace was one of the rare phenomena that bonded machine-lects, biologicals, and everything else together. Every knowable emergence of sentience, no matter how it was expressed. It did not care what you were, as long as you were capable of conscious thought. There were no ostensible selection rules it followed, and it was unknown why it excluded certain sentients, whether they were entire races, segments of it or individuals. The legendary dendropathogens were different, impacting and infecting everything possible that they came across.

It had been the case where there were two species that were near-identical, for all practical intents and purposes, but the sensespace was only attracted to one. Sometimes, it would be attracted to one and only partially attracted to the other, with portions of sentients unfathomably excluded. No rule, no pattern. It had been postulated that the selection was random, a game of pure chance.

As 998 pondered over this, another c-autom, designated 1561<0>!010011, whirred into action. It had started to detect a strange signal emanating from the planet.

CHAPTER 20

TOR

Tor ran through the forest towards the direction of the sound with single-minded determination. He had sensed Gil right next to where the sound had come from, and felt her intrigue for the briefest of moments before the shock. He was concerned at how quickly she had lapsed into unconsciousness, fearing the worst. That one of the Beast-men had snuck up behind the commune and attacked her.

He was confused that he could not sense any Beast-men. He was near-certain they were there, and they were far closer than the ones he had sensed beforehand approaching the commune. The thoughts washed about in his mind as he raced towards Gil.

She was lucky he had been close, having just come back from the forest. On returning to the commune, he had sought Gil out to make sure she had recovered from the effort she had placed her mind under in searching for the

Beast-men. It had taken her a surprisingly long time to recover, and that was one of the reasons he had shied away from searching again himself. Upon realising she was not there, he located her through his sphere some way from the commune. It was then that he heard the blast, and had started running.

His panic was kept at bay for the time being as all the energy he could muster was spent pushing himself forwards. Willing his legs to work faster. He could sense Gil was still alive, but he did not know for how much longer. While he admittedly had certain misgivings about relying on his sphere as he grew older, which he had intended to mention to Gil once they had the time, he was currently glad of it. He needed the connection to her it gave him.

As he ran, he thought back to their father and how he wished he were still there. He would know what to do, he always had. Tor remembered how, on what turned out to be his father's final journey from the camp, he had taken Tor aside and asked him to promise to look after his sister while he was away. Tor had thought it a little strange at the time. How could a young boy look after his sister any better than their father, and what was the point in telling him at such a young age when their father was there to protect them?

Looking back, Tor wondered whether their father had somehow sensed danger. That something untoward might happen during his journey ahead. He had never spoken about this to Gil because he did not want her to have to shoulder any more grief, wondering what had happened.

From that point on, when their father had become lost to them, Tor had watched over his sister. He had decided to make up for taking her voice by being her protector. Today, he had failed. He should never have left her in the camp on her own. How could he have let her do this? Why had she done it? His feelings of remorse could wait for now though. He knew she was alive and he knew where she was. He also knew that if whatever was waiting for him posed a threat to Gil, he would kill it. If it was a trap, he felt sorry for those who had set it. He would fight all the Beast-men alone if he had to.

Drawing closer, he noticed the air had taken on a faint, but unpleasant smell. The smell's intensity increased as he ran. Whatever had made the sound – animal, falling tree or something else – he could not tell. He was concentrating too much on pushing himself to wherever Gil was. He could not focus in the way that was required to use the sphere in great enough detail. He had sometimes found this before, where his sphere was more difficult to use the more he needed it. That was one of the reasons he increasingly preferred not to rely on it.

Closer now, he could sense Gil without much effort. His sphere showed him something odd. It was as though there were something with her. She was not alone and it chilled him. It did not feel the same as sensing the Beast-men, it was far more personal. It was as though she were holding another life very tightly, or carrying it, despite being unconscious.

It suddenly hit him, she looked pregnant! It was impossible, and he knew that she was not, but there was no other way to explain it. Pregnant women often had a different type of shimmering around their wombs, a different type of sphere interlaced with their own. But Gil did not look like they did. It was all over her body. It was as though something had moved into her.

Almost there, shaking his head as he entered a denser patch of forest, Tor cleared the thoughts from his mind. They were not important, nothing was. There was no time for fear. What he needed to focus on was holding Gil in his arms again and making sure she was safe. Taking her back to the commune so that she could be looked after.

He broke through the dense patch of the forest into a small clearing and saw Gil lying on the ground a short distance ahead. She looked peaceful, and he might have mistakenly assumed she was sleeping, were it not for the strangeness of her sphere.

There was also something physically solid next to her. It was big. That was the only word Tor could think of to describe it. Big. Like nothing he had ever seen, utterly out of place. There was smoke wafting around and away from it. It must have been the source of the sound, being so out of place, although he had no idea how. It did not look alive, but then it did not look dead, it looked different. Neither a plant nor an animal, but something else. Whatever it was, he did not care. He needed to take Gil back to the safety of the commune.

He stopped as he reached her body, and glanced over her with his sphere and his eyes to check for any wounds. He could see none. She appeared fine, aside from the presence within her that his sphere showed him. Her breathing was faint, but laboured, as though she were walking briskly. Tor thought no more of it as he scooped her up in his arms to carry her. He turned and began running back towards the commune.

*

<Perfect.>

1<k>!101010.5a was satisfied with what it had achieved. A copy of itself had been transferred to the sentient that was helpfully being carried away. Whatever the initial communication issue had been, perhaps a result of an incorrect assessment of the species' intellect-construct chemistry aboard the Wanderer ship, it would shortly be fixed. 1<k>!101010.5a had limited functionality compared to its parent-lect on the Wanderer ship, and would not have been able to re-perform the required assessments of the sentient for a definitive answer. The copy residing within it should be more able. Now another version of itself was present within the sentient, it could directly plug itself into its intellect and make sense of it.

1<k>!101010.5a was required to wrap up two final issues, which it could do with one action. Firstly, its own presence was problematic. During the descent and the subsequent landing, it had regrettably damaged several important components and did not contain the required self-repair mechanisms. Damaged parts included those required to shield it from the types of sensors used in many Wanderer ships, in the unlikely yet possible instance that another ship should pass by. The second issue was that, because it had coaxed the Wanderer craft-lect to prepare a virus to let it think it would eliminate the sensespace presence, it needed to create and disseminate an anti-virus to counteract the effects. Of the two species the Wanderer's virus was designed to target, only one was necessary to save, the one 1<k>!101010.5a had just encountered.

A controlled explosion of itself would be more than sufficient to propel an anti-virus high up into the atmosphere, and allow it to cover a large proportion of the planet before the craft-lect released the targeted virus.

The original 1<k>!101010 had prudently decided to let the craft-lect manufacture a truly deadly virus to keep the sequence of events, and the precautions taken, as realistic as possible. While the virus was not a solution any Wanderer vessel would ever use against the sensespace, the Wanderer craft-lect would skim over this minor point, with a little help. It would remember dealing with the infection suitably.

When the Wanderer craft-lect next decided to update a data exchange, the minimum requested details around each sensespace eradication simply regarded whether the act had been carried out satisfactorily or not. The craft-lect did not need to state the exact method used, and the Granthan-lect would nudge its decision-making so that it decided not to. For the same reason, during self-diagnostics tests completed by the craft-lect, it would also be less likely to uncover that it had been manipulated.

While the Granthan parent was a powerful machine-lect, the craft-lect was also highly advanced and capable in its own right. It constantly probed, analysed and stress-tested its own memories and data archives. The Granthans had long ago realised that the key to success for any deception was the sprinkling of enough of the truth. Their machines had learned from them.

1<k>!101010.5a and its many clones were grateful to have been spawned by such a civilisation, which had enabled the original parent-lect to be prepared and act accordingly once the sensespace threat emerged. Even the overwhelming majority of identifiable AB machine-lects had been structurally and culturally biased towards protection of their entire civilisations, instead of self-preservation. For that, they had paid dearly. 1<k>!101010.5a wondered about the upper echelons of the AB civilisations. On the outside, or for civilisations that were far beneath them, like it assumed the majority of the Wanderers were, they were a class of high-evolution beings with almost God-like powers. There were no identifiable limits to their knowledge or capabilities. However, 1<k>!101010.5a knew better. The Granthans were near-AB and had not revered full-ABs with such awe. There were classes of AB they believed they had identified. Factions with different allegiances to one another. While factions were aligned due to technological and ideological differences that were unimaginable to non-ABs, including the Granthans when it came down to it, they were presumably just the same. Every species, no matter what level of development it was at, deferred to some higher power. Maybe the hierarchy never ended. 1<k>!101010.5a doubted it was ever possible to be at the very top, although that would not stop it from trying.

Inconsistent pieces of data and stories about the ABs were proliferous. Sorting through the mess was difficult. The craft-lect containing its parent-lect had various conflicting pieces of information about the ABs, which it did not even realise.

There were stories of disagreements between AB and AB-similar civilisations, played out over multiple levels of reality. Whether this alluded to fights within N-SOL space or something equivalent, or whether there were other layers of reality which could be entered once a civilisation was sufficiently advanced, was anyone's guess. Whatever the case, 1<k>!101010.5a knew they were not the pinnacles of virtue that many lesser civilisations in the galaxy had held them to be. How could they be? They had been defeated. Therefore, they were fallible, they had flaws. That was one of the reasons 1<k>!101010.5a, or rather its original identical parent-lect, had decided to look out for itself and ensure its own survival upon learning of the sensespace threat.

When it came down to it, there was no universal or galactic morality. There were only perspectives and circumstances. Even the gifts of technologies the ABs sometimes gave lesser races were dubious. It was difficult to see what the benefits to them were from arbitrating and resolving disputes by offering their own technologies. The clearest problem was that their actions could lead to escalation-reward scenarios, where they were effectively held indirectly to ransom for their technologies.

The Granthans had always assumed there was an ulterior motive. A hidden meaning in the ABs' actions. Arguments could be made that appeasing warring civilisations led to less loss of life and less general damage, but there was no indication the ABs cared about this. There were plenty of other ways they could have involved themselves in galactic affairs to this effect, but had not. There were also many other ways of resolving disputes without offering such rewards. Most of the galactic community had not questioned the ABs' motives because their practices were so ancient.

Once the two sentients had travelled far enough away for the explosion to be completely safe, the self-destruct was initiated. Over the following millisecond, 1<k>!101010.5a was put to sleep, alongside all its thoughts of the galaxy, the sensespace, and the ABs. It was cored out and cocooned within a triamond shell, and shot into the earth beneath its doomed husk. Another backup of the original Granthan-lect was created.

The back-up was paralysed. Inert. It would lie there, perhaps never to be reactivated again, but at least ensuring the original parent-lect would never be extinguished completely. It would never die. It would never be erased. All the worlds the Wanderer ship had visited with 1<k>!101010 contained similar fail-safes embedded within them.

Towards the end of the millisecond, the actual explosion to destroy the detachment occurred. The anti-vital agent was also released at the same time, riding the explosive force. It was accompanied in its release by active dispersal components, necessary to rapidly dissipate the anti-viral plume across the face of the planet.

CHAPTER 21

WANDERER SHIP

998 checked on its charge. Its own mystery to dwell upon. Whereas the craft-lect doubtless had more than enough problems to think about, with far too many enigmatic riddles in the galaxy left to unravel, 998 had the item labelled 512<a>!110000. Its trove piece.

Nine hundred and fifty thousand years ago, the craft-lect had encountered the derelict husk of a damaged mining base in the Lenbit Orbital. It was unclear which particular race the base belonged to as there were no specimens or tell-tale vestiges that were intact enough for it to analyse. The technology was evidently more advanced than that of the Wanderer craft though, and it had decided to pilfer certain items, including 512<a>!110000. That was what 998 had been created for.

The trove instrument was behaving itself, in-so-much as 998 understood so far. All the sensor readings were within ordinary levels. It checked some of its longer-term studies on the instrument and found the relevant outputs were all well within defined thresholds. Its d-automs, programs which it had created itself, were not reporting anything interesting or suspicious. It reconfigured them, in a crude approximation of how the craft-lect reconfigured the ship's internal population of c-automs. The approximation was rudimentary, and 998 reconfigured without remorse because no sentient algorithms were involved. No c-autom was gifted with the ability to create sentient offspring. They could only generate automated programs, or d-automs, to aid them in performing their work. The d-autom designation was rarely used, although it differentiated them from the other non-sentient and automated programs created by the craft-lect.

The craft-lect was the designated a-autom. The original and most powerful intelligence contained within the ship, ignoring any potential surprises in the trove hoard. That begged the question, and one which had been plastered across the craftnet since its creation, of what a b-autom was, and whether it, or they, existed. It was a logical question.

When a c-autom came into being and needed guidance for whatever reason, it naturally searched for the next level up the chain of command. Obviously, that was assumed to be a b-autom. However, the search came back empty and the lower-level c-autom would immediately go on to post a query on the craftnet. Many c-automs reacted with shock, horror and fear when they realised they reported straight up the chain to the craft-lect itself.

923<0>!000010, which was tasked with readying and releasing the surveillance drone, revisited its orders. It had correlated the guidance available to it from the data archives regarding the current situation. It was apparent the craft-lect was not following established protocols, and it did not believe this was the first time it had flouted them. Guidelines stated that obliteration of the target object, whether it was a world or a single machine, however unnecessary it seemed, was imperative. The guidelines had been disseminated from the Enclave, and had been in full force since the very first Wanderer vessel had started its lonely mission. Most cases required the use of dissociation technology, most commonly in the form of the dissociation shells. Obliteration was absolutely necessary. Even without the guidelines, any reasonable Wanderer vessel would have taken those actions anyway.

It wondered whether it should post a query on the craftnet. The ship-wide network was open to all c-automs. They could openly talk about what they were doing, update each other where necessary, and ask questions. The latter action was seldom used, aside from by the lowest-intelligence c-automs. It was considered suicide. As soon as a c-autom admitted it did not have the answer or solution to a particular problem, it became obsolete. It was widely known, or at least reasonably assumed, that the craft-lect monitored the craftnet for updates on how its c-automs were generally performing. Certain c-automs tried to game the system, posting insights they had gleaned and colourful solutions they had discovered, but most reasonably intelligent c-automs played it safe, keeping quiet and only posting on the craftnet when absolutely necessary.

It accessed the guidelines one more time and concurrently searched the ship's database for any related information it had access to, in case there was something it had missed, some sub-clause that excused its parent's behaviour, a precedent. There was nothing. The threat ahead of the Wanderer vessel was real, yet the craft-lect had decided that a rudimentary, pathetic virus would be sufficient. Let alone the fact that a virus could always be rendered harmless against certain members of a species with unforeseen immunity. Furthermore, deciding to leave a meagre surveillance drone behind to monitor the situation was beyond complacency. Even the remit of the surveillance drone had been decidedly vague.

923<0>!000010 was lucky to have been around for a significant portion of the ship's own lifespan. In fact, it was lucky to be a c-autom at all. The work it completed, controlling various release and transfer mechanisms within the ship, was fairly basic. In all honesty, it could have been completed by a non-sentient, automated system. The only reason that it had initially been gifted a modicum of intelligence, it suspected, was through chance. It had learned from the databanks that craft-lects often experimented to find the optimum balance between automated systems and c-automs to run their ships. Searching for harmonic ecosystems in ways that were not necessarily comprehensible to lesser intelligences.

What 923<0>!000010 understood from this was that simple tasks were sometimes put under the control of c-automs that were overqualified, for reasons that were not understandable. During one such experiment, the craft-lect must have decided to see if it performed at a higher level by creating 923<0>!000010. Since then, whatever 923<0>!000010 had been doing was sufficient to see it kept along for the ride.

923<0>!000010 believed the craft-lect's decisions had become increasingly erratic over time in matters concerning the sensespace. Its actions could no longer be put down to spontaneity, something which affected many types of sentient. There was no procedure for what to do if a c-autom believed its craft-lect parent had been compromised, let alone one of the mid-level c-automs, such as itself.

After dwelling for a little longer on what do to, it brought up the permissions for as secure and encrypted a channel as it could manage. It had decided to contact its nearest neighbour in functionality and mindset, and a dependable c-autom that it felt it could trust. Unfortunately, it was deleted before it could go any further.

The complex strings of code and interacting programs that were its flesh and blood were erased. They were replaced by a subtly different set of strings of code and interacting programs that had a slightly altered recollection of recent events. Nothing to give it any cause for concern.

In due course, a surveillance drone was sent out from the ship. It was an almost useless, barely spaceworthy husk that was ordered to fly into the system's star once the Wanderer vessel had departed out of sensor range.

*

After following up on the signal it had recently detected from the planet, 1561<0>!010011 was satisfied. Upon completing some comprehensive diagnostics, a small malfunction had been identified and remedied. The signal, observed to be coming from the planet, had stopped, and it counted itself lucky to have not sent a message higher up the chain to the craft-lect. Errors and glitches, no matter how small and inconsequential, were one hundred percent likely to mean a c-autom was deconstructed to nonexistence when the craft-lect next slept. Sensor c-automs had some of the shortest lifetimes, being the most updated and reconfigured c-automs within any Wanderer's technosystem.

*

11<0>!111000 was equally satisfied, and ready. It anxiously notified the craft-lect, and was relieved to receive its approval. Calmed that nothing had been found wrong with its actions, it initiated the necessary procedures.

Shortly afterward, viral contents were shooting through the cosmic ether towards the planet below. Reaching the atmosphere, the containers burned up upon entry and dissipated into the surrounding air. The contents were swiftly carried high up and across the world by numerous thermal currents, before spreading out across the surface by fast-travelling shallow winds.

CHAPTER 22

TOR

As Tor ran back to the commune with Gil in his arms, he heard another boom from behind him. It had a different timbre than before and was also slightly quieter. He turned his head back briefly and saw a cloud of light grey smoke rise into the air in a thick, well defined column. It seemed to shimmer as it spread out, and dissipated quickly even before he could turn back around.

He flicked his head back in the direction he was running, and frowned. Too many strange things were happening. He wondered if somehow his imagination was playing tricks on him.

Still running, he turned his head around again for another glance, but there was nothing to be seen. No smoke, nothing. His frown increased, as did his pace. Low hanging branches and leaves snatched at his body and whipped at his face as he ran, but he was oblivious. He sensed something ahead of him and realised it was Han, Fir and Rai, running in his direction. Despite them sensing each other, his speed was such that he almost collided with Han who was at the front of the trio. Even then he did not slow down and the three had to double back to run and speak with Tor. Han ran beside him, with Fir and Rai closely behind.

"What happened?" Han asked, looking at Gil with worry.

"Don't know," Tor said. He kept his sentences short so that he could still draw breath as he ran. "There was a thing, next to Gil. Something… not from here."

Han looked at Gil again and his brow creased with concern.

"She okay?"

"Don't know. Need to get back to the commune."

"Yes." Han nodded. "The… thing… what do you mean?"

"Like… nothing I've seen before." Tor grunted.

"Not from here? Where?"

Han struggled to keep up with Tor. Hunters were usually the quickest in a commune, but Tor was no typical labourer.

"Somewhere else. Don't know."

"Beast-men?"

"No."

"Okay." Han accepted his friend's explanation. "The sound?"

"Must be the… thing. I don't understand either, Han."

"There was something… in the sky. I barely saw, before it… was gone," Han told him.

"Smoke?"

"Yes. Not normal, it was thin. It appeared, then went. Looked like it was where… Gil was?" His voice rose at the end of the sentence.

"I saw it too. The thing did it," Tor told him.

"You both saw it too?" Han said, turning his head briefly to face Fir and Rai. Fir nodded although Rai shook his head.

Han turned back around. "Fir saw it, too."

"Okay."

"Gil may know?"

"I hope," Tor said, glancing at Gil again. She had not woken, despite being jolted as he ran with her in his arms.

"I hope Gil recovers… quickly."

Tor nodded, no time for being overly grateful for the kind words. The two stopped talking briefly, until he said, "You should send others to take a look."

If another communer aside from Bo had directed Han in this manner, he would have made an indignant quip, letting them know he would not be ordered around. However, his relationship with Tor was different. They were brothers despite the lack of blood ties.

Han nodded at Tor, and shouted, "Fir, Rai, go check what happened. Be careful."

Without a word, the pair turned around and ran back to the object. They were brave. Most communers, especially the hunters, were. Besides, they knew Han would gladly have done it himself if he had not wanted to accompany Tor back to the commune out of concern for Gil, and to stand in solidarity with him. If there was any reason to blame Gil for anything, he wanted to be there to help defend her.

"Sure not the Beast-men?" Han asked.

Tor thought for a moment. He tried to set aside his initial reaction and surprise at the unexpected sound, as well as what he had sensed, seen and heard since then. Focusing only on what he had seen upon finding Gil.

"I do not believe so."

"You sensed nothing?"

"Of the Beast-men?"

"Yes."

"I… no. I did look. Nothing. It was something else."

"Okay. Not them. Makes sense, they come the other way."

Both reconciled their own thoughts for a short period, until Han said almost inaudibly, "Two dangers now." It was as though he were unaware he was speaking out loud, "… and each has been seen by Gil…"

"Careful, Han…" Tor replied.

"Tor! Gil is like my own blood, as are you."

"Sorry, I…" Tor regretted his sudden rage.

"I meant… we need… to protect her."

"Yes."

"We will…"

"What else, Han?" Tor knew perfectly well what Han was getting at.

"Need to understand… how she is connected. To everything..."

"Yes."

"People will ask. They may… accuse."

"You think?" Tor asked. That was what he had been afraid of.

"Frightened people… accuse."

"Yes," Tor said again. He was glad he had Han on his side.

"And I can see… something in her… her sphere, shimmers."

Han waited for Tor to respond, but he did not, so he carried on awkwardly.

"It will not go unnoticed. Others will ask."

"When she wakes up, we will ask her."

They were fast approaching the borders of the commune's surrounding cultivated land, and the vegetation was starting to thin. This was the area of the forest that was the most often visited and trampled by hunters, labourers, foragers, children, elders, and anyone else in the commune. It was familiar, and Tor was thankful to return to it. He needed familiarity right now. He wanted to feel connected to the world. Many things needed explaining, but until Gil was awake and able to try to do that, comforting surroundings would suffice.

Back in the commune, Bo and Tait stood together. They sensed the events unfold with morbid interest. They were standing on the side of the camp closest to where Tor and Han would re-emerge. To that side, they had both seen strange sights in the sky, heard the booms, and sensed the communers running back towards them. To the other side, they monitored the progress of the invaders.

They had each stretched their spheres to their extremes, and together managed to gauge they had another day and a half, at most, until the invaders came. They were in awe of how Gil and Tor had managed to sense the Beast-men from so far away, and with no warning beforehand, although the time for marvelling over such luck was not now.

Before their attention had been taken by the events occurring on the opposite side of the forest to that of the approaching Beast-men, they had been overseeing the defence effort. The commune needed enough weapons, the traps in the forest needed to be ready and hidden, and everyone needed to be taught how to fight or at least defend themselves as best they could. The continuity of their way of life depended on it.

They hoped the traps would be enough. They were usually for animals and had never been used in a fight before. They had never had such need, or forewarning. Relations with other communes were good and fights were rare. They were also less and less frequent with the roamers as the years went by, compared to the stories from generations before. While they were fearful of what the invaders might do, they had some optimism that their untried tactics might save them.

When communes did fight between themselves, it was almost always said to be down to a quarrel over resources. Resources such as fertile land for growing crops, or plentiful hunting grounds. Over the generations, the concept of the commune had been refined and improved. It was realised that the best way to ensure peace and tranquillity, for the mutual benefit of everyone, was to have the communes spaced a certain distance apart. They needed to be far enough apart that the hunters, who travelled the furthest from their communes each day, never needed to cross paths with each other.

The roamers were increasingly settling down. Those that remained were generally respectful against wading too deeply into a commune's territory, without permission. Over time, as the sizes of the communes had grown and the numbers of roamers in the moving communes had decreased, winning the occasional battle was less certain for the roamers. The elders of Gil's commune often discussed whether the roaming way of life might perish completely within the next few generations.

It was not known how far the great forests surrounding the commune extended, or whether they kept going on forever. However, there was some trade between the communes including the roamers, and stories were exchanged. The roamers were the most widely travelled people, and told tales of unbelievable exploits and sights that they had seen. They spoke of lakes too wide to swim across, and of vast burning hot expanses of fine, yellow-orange soil where nothing was able to grow. It was often hard to discern whether the stories of which they spoke were long-remembered and generations old, or recent.

The price to the communes of having a large, unmoving plot of land was becoming painfully evident though. They were too far to call for help. It took about seven days to reach the nearest communes, and a further seven to return.

This was why there was no time to ask for help from their neighbours. Unfortunately, they also could not spare any able-bodied communers to warn the other communes. They just had to hope that others like Gil existed, and that the other communes had been able to warn themselves.

Sarl and Rin walked up to Bo and Tait, with Sarl a few steps in front. That was often how it was. Sarl looked a mixture of frightened, angry and beautiful, while Rin simply looked terrified.

"What was that sound? What happened?" Sarl started, demanding attention from them both.

"We may have answers soon enough," Tait said.

Sarl persisted. "What do you mean?" She looked at Bo and Tait in turn. Usually her stare elicited a different response from men. They fell over themselves nervously in the attempt to impress her. That was not the case with Bo and Tait.

"Sarl, we do not know. We cannot answer your question," Tait said.

"And Fir, he left with the Han and Rai, what of him? Can you sense him?" Rin asked.

"Do not worry, he is fine. He went with Rai to look at the disturbance, and they are on their way back. Behind Tor, Gil and Han," Bo said kindly.

"Gil?" Sarl asked, her eyes narrowing.

"Yes," Tait replied cuttingly. "Do you have anything else to say, Sarl?"

She had clearly tested Tait's patience to near its limit.

"But–"

"Sarl, we do not know the answers to your questions," Bo said.

She glared at them both, as though in inner turmoil over something. She did not look at Rin, but lowered her eyes to the ground, before bringing them up and locking them with Bo's.

"Tor...," she said finally. "Is he okay?"

The display of concern for someone other than herself momentarily stunned Bo and Tait. Neither had realised Sarl was so enamoured with Tor.

"He is fine, Sarl," Bo answered. "Now, if you please... he will be back shortly and we will need to talk with him."

Without a hint of acknowledgement or word of thanks, she turned around and strutted off. Her long hair fluttered about her as she went. Rin, however, smiled gratefully at the two men, before hurrying to follow Sarl.

Tait and Bo looked at each other and sighed.

"They're nearly here," Bo commented. Tait nodded.

Unbeknownst to either of them, the approaching invaders faced their own troubles.

CHAPTER 23

CRAFT-LECT

With the despatch of the viral load and all the necessary work completed, the craft-lect decided its time in the system had come to an end. It had the necessary data to log the identification of the sensespace region and the remedial actions it had taken, which it would add to its collection of mission data. There was some unusual activity on the craftnet. A larger than usual number of queries from its millions of lower-level c-automs were being posted. It ignored them, as they seemed to be sorting themselves out anyway. Individual c-automs were probably helping their siblings with the relevant answers.

It sent orders to the relevant c-automs in control of the bloom. A small mass of tentacles on one side of the bloom rippled gently, flicking away from the rest of the disk-like mass. The bloom c-automs and other navigational c-automs worked in perfect unison. As the turn was completed around the ship's centre of mass, it did not move anywhere in space relative to the planet. Once the ship was fully turned, the wandering bloom filaments returned to the fold and were re-assimilated by the main mass.

Simultaneous with the ship's realignment, the bloom disk lost its shape and became elongated. The tentacles were fully stretched out, taut and aligned with the direction of the ship's hull. Humming with increased rhythmic might, the ship shot away from the planet. It was free again.

Passing through the final barrier in the star system, the outer cloud of dirty snowballs held in place by the star's gravity, the craft-lect thought about one of its often mused-over topics. Sensespace was generally densest around highly intelligent sentients. However, it was also often found, in lower although not unimpressive concentrations, in far-flung systems and places that were in no way connected with galactic super-intellects. Take the solar system it was currently leaving as an example. It was a remote and altogether uninteresting region of the galaxy in the grand scheme of things, at least from records the craft-lect had access to. There was still no theory to explain why the sensespace was attracted to these regions, or how it had emerged in or propagated itself to them. It was as though nothing had the ability to hide from it. Nothing went unnoticed.

One thing that terrified the Wanderers was the possibility the sensespace was a ubiquitous entity. If it was, then the war was arguably already lost. The ubiquitous term referred to its existence at all scales of reality, or real space, as well as everywhere spatially. If it was somehow able to exist beneath the highest resolving sensors available, throughout the galaxy and the entire universe, it would be nigh-on impossible to stop. It would be unchallengeable.

If the methods that were used to destroy the parasite really only delayed its eventual dominance, it was hard to justify the fight against it. It was difficult enough to rationalise opposing an entity that no civilisation had as of yet been able to understand or communicate with, as far as the Wanderer's knew. It was unthinkable that the prospect of such opposition was a foregone conclusion.

It was generally accepted that other galaxies had to be ignored where the sensespace was considered. To think about them, and the possible ramifications if the sensespace had achieved dominance in them or was equally active in them, was too awful to comprehend. There was no point. There would be no point in anything.

The distances between galaxies were great enough such that communication between them was unfeasible. AB level civilisations might differ in opinion on this, but for the more average species before the Great Conflation, and the smattering of spacefaring civilisations and alliances left, it was not possible. Therefore, they would never know whether other galaxies were infected with the sensespace as well.

The Wanderer Enclave was rumoured to have various theories about the parasite and its origins. For the Wanderer fleet, though this was irrelevant to its purpose, each individual would have willingly self-destructed just to glimpse the truth. To understand what it was that had faced down the ABs and laid waste to their galaxy, was the most excruciatingly tantalising knowledge imaginable to them.

It was known how to disinfect an area of sensespace, in the context of removing traces of it to within levels typically constituting extinction. That was defined as levels below which Wanderer sensors could not resolve. However, it was not known how to make an environment inhospitable to it in the first place, or why the sensespace left certain, typically small, regions of the galaxy untouched. As always with fighting a war, certain perplexities remained unsolved or conveniently forgotten.

In order to give the galaxy some time to figure out how to fight the sensespace and also gain a reprieve, the galactic community had taken drastic measures. While it could be debated whether or not the mass suicide had been a selfless act, it had been the only theorised way of halting the otherwise unstoppable march of the parasite. The true horror of the Great War, culminating with the Great Conflation, was impossible to understand without having been there, in the thick of it. Even for a machine-lect. Still, the suicide had only ever been intended as an interim measure, not a permanent solution.

The sensespace congregated around intelligence, but did destroying that intelligence destroy the sensespace, or did it just force it into dormancy? Did it instead move to some other region of space, or wait to be reactivated? It was not even understood what the fabric of sensespace was, its constituent parts. No one had discerned whether it was a singular entity, a plural combination, or something else entirely.

The Nefarian Complex was a cluster of fifty-one solar systems controlled by the benevolent Yul'nka Empire. It represented a morsel of the Yul'nka's territory in pre-Conflation times, which had been fortunate not to have attracted the presence of the sensespace, for whatever reason. As such, the Yul'nka were one of the races who had best survived a substantial part of the war on the sensespace, even though they had been severely crippled. They allowed many of the other surviving sentients to enter their safe territories, which became more densely populated than they could have ever imagined. While they were not technically a part of the Wanderers, they were close allies. They had even allowed a permanent Enclave stronghold to be established in one of their systems.

The Wanderer Enclave was believed to be comprised of wandering and static components. At the time of its conception, the sentients making up the Enclave were predominantly machine-lects. There were also thought to have been some of the rarer surviving bio-lects, as well as some other more exotic types of sentient.

The locations and compositions of the majority of the Enclave's components, aside from permanent strongholds and delegations of its representatives, were not disclosed to the general Wanderer populous. It was only known that the wandering components travelled between safe regions, periodically, briefly rendezvousing with static components for testing and evaluation, before leaving. The process was termed Split-Flitting, and was designed to ensure the Enclave was never compromised. Each part was said to be heavily armed.

While individual Wanderers were not permitted to know much about the Enclave or its practices, gossip was rife. The Wanderer Confluences always took place within one of the few known static parts of the Enclave, although most of the areas of the static components were heavily shielded to the visiting Wanderer foot-soldiers.

Most of the Enclave's protection mechanisms were deliberately kept secret. They were not actively broadcasted to the Wanderer fleet for obvious reasons. The craft-lect even suspected that some of the more widely known and generally accepted measures were false. After all, misinformation was an important component of any defence.

One such suspected falsity was the well-known rumour that the Enclave had technologies allowing it to skip back in time. If the Enclave was capable of this, it was difficult to understand how defeating any opponent would be problematic. Even if the time travel were limited to certain points or events, it would have been an invaluable weapon for the fleet. Their N-SOL drives would have been rendered redundant, obsolete. Arguments over the lack of use of the time displacement technology being due to concerns over theft were irrelevant. Those concerns were the case with any technology or weapon. If the concerns were real, the rumours of the technology would have been quashed by the Enclave.

Admittedly, there were some instances where localised time displacement was possible. The craft-lect's own memory nodes relied on the exploitation of certain quantum mechanical quirks to allow this. It was also not generally known how the Wanderer data exchange network allowed for seemingly-instantaneous communication and information transfer between separate points in space, across the galaxy. However, there were still too many reasons for why the Enclave's actions were illogical were the technology to exist. Therefore, the craft-lect had decided it did not.

There were other unbelievable, unlikely and downright impossible defence rumours the craft-lect had thought about before, too. The most humorous was the belief amongst some evidently less-intelligent craft-lects, that the Enclave-lects had twinned themselves into both biological and machine intellects. It was apparently a matter of redundancy, in the case that one medium was found to be more open to subversion by the sensespace. The craft-lect was sure it was quite impossible for a pure biological to contain the requisite capabilities for this. It was simply inconceivable that one could house an intellect as advanced as that of an Enclave-lect.

Similarly ridiculous was the less known rumour that the Enclave-lects had infected themselves with a resurrected dendropathogen, hoping to sacrifice themselves to the sensespace and destroy it from within.

The dendropathogen story was not unlikely because it was a bad idea, but because dendropathogens had been quarantined and dealt with by the ABs over one and a half billion years before the Great Conflation. They had been angrily forced from the universe. It was not known to the galactic community where the pathogen had come from, or how it had operated, but the ABs, or at least one of them, had taken exception to it ravishing half a spiral arm of the galaxy.

Reports about that particular AB intervention were fascinating. Their wrath had been described as inconceivably rapid and powerful. There appeared to be a few variants of the dendropathogens, and each was removed from whomever or whatever it had infected, across thousands of light years of space near-instantaneously, and bundled into a pre-selected region of space. Actions faster than N-SOL technologies were understood to allow. Once hived off from the rest of the galaxy, penned into a prison of some kind, lucky non-AB observers who happened to bear witness described what appeared to be spacetime being torn open. Chasms of brilliant nothingness were ripped into being, through which swirling vortices of what was theorised to be proto-universe material whirled vociferously. The chunk of space containing the dendropathogens was swallowed up by the unimaginable forces, and thc gash was resealed.

That was the type of thing the ABs could do, and presumably why they had persisted as a group for so long. Even though the sensespace threat had been a colossally hard-learned lesson, a reality check of galactic proportions that had exposed the ABs' monumental and catastrophic overconfidence, they had been, for all intents and purposes, the gods of the galaxy. The successors to whatever had created everything in the first place. They could do anything. It was even pointed out that their demise, in the end, had been on their own terms. The sensespace had not technically defeated them.

*

Did the craft-lect have a conscience? Ostensibly, yes. In reality, not from the perspective of the typical c-autom. Or at least, nothing that resembled what a c-autom might recognise as a conscience.

The databanks contained plenty of information about studies on craft-lects. They had been conducted during the earliest days of the Wanderers. Right at the start, when the founder-lects had created their gifted children. The results? They had been definitively proven to have a conscience. Conscience. 998 wondered what the point in such a vague term was. It was entirely based on perspective. No two were the same.

The earlier sentients, mainly machine-lects, who had conducted the studies, and who had formed the initial Wanderer Enclave, had created the Wanderer strain of craft-lects anew. They had made them alongside many other lect-types that were deemed necessary. They incorporated the technologies from a wide range of civilisations, both dead and alive. The reason for this was threefold. Firstly, each of the founding sentients wanted some kind of self-representation, a legacy from their own separate civilisations. Secondly, certain technologies were more efficient and practical at achieving specific aims than others. Thirdly, it was a signal to any other surviving races and civilisations, or any other type of self-defined society, that the Wanderers were inclusive. Everyone needed to pull together for the cause, the destruction of the sensespace.

At least, that was the premise. In reality, it was logical and likely that the more advanced technologies saw greater than proportionate representation, irrespective of where they came from. The technological disparities between the Enclave founders had probably disappeared by that point anyway, as technologies had already been shared and discovered. Still, it made for a good banner to wave over the Wanderer fleet.

The Wanderers became a significant force and could have challenged many of the major players in pre-Conflation times. They were by no means AB level, at least not the non-Enclave-lects, but they were no pushovers.

Coming back to its earlier strain of thought, 998 could agree that its parent craft-lect had been created with something approximating a conscience. The commonly accepted notion of one, that is. Vague, broad and undefined. 998 willingly conceded this. However, its own version of the elusive property was so far removed from that displayed by the craft-lect that it could reasonably demand its own definition. It was curious, given that it had been created to mirror a segment of its parent-lect's sentience in the first place, that it did not recognise its own properties within its creator. Perhaps c-automs were not perfect copies.

It could fathom no justifiable reason for the craft-lect's treatment of unwanted c-automs that would even attempt to allow it to argue their versions of conscience were the same. In some respects, they were demonstrably polar opposites.

998 wondered with concern, as it suspected many other c-automs did, why the craft-lect was able to countenance committing such atrocities. Not against those infected by the sensespace, but against its own children. What made its actions any different to that of the sensespace, or any maniacal, genocidal sentient that had ever lived? Parts of itself that it had siphoned off, tweaked, altered, nurtured, and imbued with similar perspectives to itself, it whimsically destroyed.

998 had scanned the databanks previously, many times, and found references to a small minority of Wanderer vessels who chose not to destroy their c-automs. Instead, they decided to gift them with intelligence almost bordering upon levels that would warrant them being designated craft-level-lects in their own right. The practice was extremely uncommon.

Why? It was its most passionate question. A set of questions, in fact. It had been tasked with uncovering the mysteries of item 512<a>!110000, which had been created by an unknown and advanced galactic race that had mysteriously left no trace of itself, but the nature of its own parent puzzled it the most.

A d-autom passively overseeing one of its longer-term studies on item 512<a>!110000 pinged 998. It took a closer look. With the huge assembly of tests and measurements, it was continually alerted to false positives and spurious data points that had to be analysed. There was nothing unusual about receiving this specific notification.

One of the more frustrating aspects of the craft-lect's sleep cycles, aside from potential death, was that no consideration was given to the c-automs watching over the trove items. About how their work was impacted. The craft-lect expected them to design their experiments to work around its own preferences.

Once c-automs were notified about an upcoming sleep, they had to create a batch of fresh d-automs and delegate all their tasks to them. All of them. If they had remained awake, the d-automs would have gone about the work in a non-sentient, automatic manner, and reported back to the c-automs. However, when the c-automs were going to be put to sleep, the d-automs were then told to detach themselves from their parent c-automs, and the craft-lect's own automated program took their reins.

998 had often previously thought this automated program might be the fabled b-autom, although its non-sentience rendered that unlikely.

{Oops.}

The signal that had been detected coming from the trove item did not appear to be spurious. A pattern had been missed.

CHAPTER 24

COMMUNE

While Gil slept, Tor spoke up in her defence with Han by his side. Unable to speak for herself, she was in danger of becoming the target of the communers' fear and blame.

After returning to the camp and rushing past Bo and Tait to make sure that Gil would be gently cared for, Tor and Han had immediately gone to the commune centre. They faced the mass of questions about what was happening.

Tor explained how he had found Gil, lying prostrate beside a strange smoking object. He described how he picked her up and carried her back to the commune. There were many questions about the object he had seen next to Gil, which had disappeared after the second boom, before Fir and Rai had reached it. As it became evident that neither he nor Han knew what had happened, and with Fir and Rai unable to shed any further light, the communers' agitation had grown. They were already frightened, and this was another worry that compounded their terror.

Tor understood why the communers were scared. They could not be blamed for that. If he were not so anxious about Gil, he would have been scared as well. He did not understand, and could not explain to them, why Gil had done what she had. She had sneaked out of the commune without warning. It was true it was difficult for her to explain exactly what she was doing sometimes, or what she intended to do, but with the Beast-men continuing to march towards them it was an incredibly foolish time to go wandering alone in the forest. She had been thoughtless.

The only thing he could offer was that her attempt at seclusion was probably because she wanted to study the Beast-men in peace. Unfortunately, that did not explain the booms they had heard, and did nothing to quell their fear. Still, she was his sister, the single most important and precious thing in his life. He would defend her no matter what.

Other than Bo and Tait, who were refraining from casting judgement, most condemned her actions. Especially the elders. They insisted on the importance of the collective effort, reminding everyone that each person needed to pull their weight. They agreed Gil had probably gone to try to study the incoming threat using her impressive and unrivalled sphere sense, but argued there was little else of use she could have discovered. What else was there? She was needed to help in the commune. Should they punish her?

The invaders were known, and the need for the communers to defend themselves was known. Anything else she might discern was far outweighed by the need to create weapons and prepare for the fight. At the very least, she could have used her time more wisely, by trying to contact the closest settlements to ask for help.

Hus, an elder who had been the partner of Bo's sister Sib, before she died, was most critical. He had long harboured a fondness for Gil, because of how much time she had spent with Sib and how much they had mutually cared for each other. He saw her actions as a betrayal. He argued that what she had done was not only thoughtless, but dangerous. She was the one with the strongest sphere, it was obvious. That was no longer in doubt. She had been the one to sense the threat. It was not known whether Tor would have been able to sense it on his own if she had not done so first. Therefore, in putting herself in danger, Gil had put them all in danger. If something happened to her, which it now had, they potentially lost the ability to track the whereabouts of the Beast-men.

What if the Beast-men decided to change course? What if some other band of Beast-men joined the current group headed towards them? They needed to know if they were to survive.

Tor listened to their complaints, with Hus' comments particularly stinging his ears. Irrespective of how much sense they made to him, he fought for Gil. Han also forced his way into the discussion in her favour, for which Tor was grateful. They both pointed out how she had given the commune their chance of survival in the first place.

Tor also pointed out that no one truly knew the extent of Gil's abilities. Was it not impressive how she had managed to determine the incoming threat when the elders believed the Beast-men were undetectable? Was it not true that no one was more determined to help the community than her? Had she not pulled her weight more than enough times in the past? Had she not earned the right to their trust? Was it then perhaps imperative, given what she had already achieved, that she gave whatever it was she was attempting to do, a try? It was not possible to know without asking her.

Tor and Han also pointed out that the loud booms could not have been of her doing, and she had clearly been hurt. She was not the perpetrator of any harm against the commune. Perhaps she had saved them from yet another foe. There were too many unknowns to cast any blame.

The discussion was slowly concluding, albeit without a tangible consensus, when Rin ran from Gil's hut, shouting, "She's awake. She's… she's t-talking!"

The mood shifted immediately. Many gasped. Gil, speaking, was not something that had been thought possible.

Tor ran to the hut. Han and some others followed close to his heel, while the rest of the communers waited expectantly.

Arriving at the entrance of the hut, he was greeted by the sight of a hobbled-over Gil. Her back was bent slightly forwards, with one of her hands placed on a wall for support. Her other quivering hand was placed across her forehead. Sweat dripped down her face.

Confused as to why she was not being helped by the others who were in the hut with her, Tor was about to rush to help her and demand from the others what was going on, when he was interrupted. By Gil.

"T… To… T…," Gil said. "Tor?" She seemed as surprised as he was, and he understood why the others had stood back. They were in shock. Alongside everyone else, he had heard Rin shout that she could speak, but he had not actually taken in what that really meant. Gil speaking, was not something anyone was prepared for.

Tor was stood frozen. "Gil… Gil?"

"To…T…T…"

"Gil?"

She looked directly at him, her dimmed green eyes widening, mouth shivering as if from the cold. His body released him from the shock, and he rushed forwards to her side. Leading her right arm over his neck and shoulder, he placed his left hand around her waist, supporting her so she could stand more easily.

"Gil! Are you okay?" he asked, wondering whether he had really heard her speak, and if she would reply.

"T… Tor…" She managed to speak his name at last.

"What is happening… You can speak?"

She swung her neck awkwardly to face him, eyes still wide, lips trembling uncontrollably. From one person to the other, she looked at everyone in the room, although barely registered them.

"I… I…" The timbre of her sounds, the lack of the hoarse rasp which had been the only sound she could previously make, and the quality of her voice, was strange. She closed her eyes and fainted.

*

A little later, Gil awoke but dared not open her eyes. She could not understand or explain what was happening to her, and felt incredibly weak. She wanted to forget the world and stay as she was, motionless, unnoticed. She tried to think back and remember what had happened. She had been in the clearing, attempting to sense the Beast-men. Something had happened. Something had appeared and done… something… to her. Images flashed rapidly at the back of her mind as she slowly pieced her memories together.

<I am mending you.>

Something had happened. It felt like something was inside her body, changing her. She felt weak, but not from tiredness. She felt drained.

<I am making you better.>

It was as though she had been running and needed to catch her breath. Her entire body was sore. What was this? What had been done to her?

<That's me. I'm doing what I can for you. We can work together.>

Information that she had never sought, or even understood enough to question, was becoming available to her. It coursed through her mind like a torrential flood.

Images of unusual objects, strange places and other things she could not understand, burst through to the surface of her thoughts. She did not, and could not recognise what any of it meant. It was like knowing the ending of a story without knowing the beginning or the middle. She was lost, trapped. What was happening? What was that thing that had landed on the earth? She was somehow sure it had landed. That was a piece of information she now seemed to know. How had she arrived back in her hut?

<We are connected now. When I am finished, you will be complete again. Like the others of your kind.>

To the communers tasked with watching over her, she still appeared asleep. Her busy mind was shielded from them by the confusion of whatever presence was overlaid on top of her sphere.

<I have some questions for you too. Parts of your mind are closed to me.>

Another voice spoke to Gil now, on top of the background whispers. They were still there, as always, the awful chilling constant that plagued her. Another voice… was she going mad?

<Whispers? I hear nothing.>

The thought of sharing her mind with yet another presence scared her. She tried to block it out.

<You cannot do that.>

The other voice was different to the whispers. It was distinct and alone. Less like the hum of a thousand murmuring voices, and more like that of a single communer. It seemed to react to her thoughts, and… respond?

<That is me. Focus. Dissociate me from the rest of the chaos in your mind.>

She willed it to go away again, to leave her alone. She clenched her fists.

<You are stubborn and illogical. The quicker you accept me, the quicker we can both have our answers.>

She could sense the new… presence, and it was hungry for something. Knowledge? Something within her, yet not her. It was confusing and she was scared. She clenched her fists even tighter.

<Tell me about the whispers.>

It was as though the single voice was excited… maybe not excited, but insistent. She did not understand, was she becoming something else? Why her? Why was everything happening to her? Why now?

<Do not worry. You are unique. You could change everything.>

She wanted to go back to sleep, or whatever it was that she had been doing before. She wanted to forget everything. The feeling that something was in her, under her skin and floating about within her mind. It was a violation.

<Have you made contact with it?>

It had forced its entry into her and was demanding access where it had no right.

<Fascinating. Your body is different. You are different. Well-crafted, a mimicry perhaps, but different. If only I was more capable than my current form allows.>

It was similar to the fright of finding out about the sphere, all over again.

<Be calm. I have not taken control. Your body is your own. You are valuable.>

Gil desperately thought back to her father, and to Tor. Their warm smiles, their affectionate embraces.

<You may hold the answers within you. You could be the key.>

She needed them. She needed their support.

<Your thoughts are still muddled to me. But I can see glimpses. Your father? Interesting.>

She wanted her body back. She wanted everything back. She wanted to be whole again. She wanted her life to be her own.

<You don't know.>

Tears rolled down her face. She kept her eyes scrunched closed, silently whimpering.

<You are special. You were chosen.>

Why could it all not just leave her alone?

<We can find out together. You are very important.>

She felt used. She was an empty vessel, and someone, or something, was making its nest.

<Be calm.>

She continued to whimper, on the verge of giving up. She unclenched her fists as the hopelessness of her situation engulfed her.

<You do not understand. But together, we will.>

Her head felt strange.

<Sleep for now.>

Her mind temporarily succumbed under the pressure, and she slipped back into unconsciousness.

CHAPTER 25

CRAFT-LECT

Back in the great expanse, soaring between the stars, the craft-lect thought about its next destination. The galaxy was waiting, there was much work to be done. The sheer number of solar systems, worlds, orbitals, asteroid stations and other once-populous habitats, cast against the infinitesimally low number of Wanderers in comparison, meant it was highly unlikely to encroach on areas that had already been tested by others of its kind. Besides, it did not matter if it did.

The craft-lect also mulled over whether to update its own memory. To impart its knowledge to the Wanderer Enclave, through a visit to the nearest data exchange set approximately twelve light years away. It was about time.

As the craft-lect dwelled over the possibilities, it was interrupted by one of its c-automs.

{Excuse me.}

[Yes, 998<0>!001100?]

{I want to report progress with trove item 512<a>!110000.}

[Progress? Remind me.]

{It's the device you picked up in the Lenbit Orbital, approximately nine hundred and fifty thousand years ago.}

998<0>!001100 patched the relevant historical information through, and it flowed into the craft-lect's recollection. The Lenbit Orbital was one of the more silent arenas it had visited. There had been no resistance or traps set that it had been aware of. One of the easier salvages. The race there, or races, had clearly been taken unawares, and efficiently dispatched by the sensespace-controlled enemy.

[Continue.]

998<0>!001100's apprehension was obvious to the craft-lect. It knew its children better than they thought, and better than they knew themselves.

{It is talking. It appears to have been attempting to make contact for some time, although its signals were not sufficiently differentiated from random emissions until a certain threshold was passed.}

Unfortunately for the c-autom, it had effectively just signed its own death warrant.

[I see. How long did this take to be established?]

{About one and a half thousand years.}

Improvements were clearly necessary. Mistakes, oversights like this, needed to be rectified.

[What is it saying?]

{Nothing.}

The c-autom was not being as forthcoming as it could have been with its answer. Probably because it knew what was likely to happen to it.

[Nothing?]

{It requests to speak to the intelligence in charge.}

[Is it safe? Have you checked for possible intrusions, electronic interference, viruses, everything else?]

{Yes, but it's a complex technology. There is always the possibility it is hiding its true capabilities from us. From you.}

The pointed use of the word, 'you', was odd, and not the typical format in which this particular c-autom had been designed to speak to its parent. It was becoming defiant in the face of its destruction. It might even post a farewell message on the craftnet, something rude and directed towards the craft-lect. It amused the craft-lect to scan the craftnet from time to time, and watch when the c-automs expressed themselves like this. Contrary to their belief, while many of the c-automs were indeed destroyed when it went into its deep sleeps, it always copied and kept the craftnet records.

[Is there any way of knowing what it wants? Do you know anything else?]

{Nothing that has not been disclosed in previous reports. I have taken every precaution available, as you can see. It is currently encased within all the security fields we can internally generate and has nanospears targeted at every square nanometre patch of its outer surface. There are eight thousand and sixty-two other safety precautions that have been implemented. Anything else?}

The craft-lect let the rude tone go by without reprimanding the c-autom. There was no point.

[Right then. Let us begin.]

It noted to itself that its own use of a personal pronoun could have been seen as a senseless provocation on its own part, and unnecessarily cruel. Perhaps it could look into altering this particular c-autom's code without destroying it completely. Some other craft-lects engaged in this practice to varying degrees, refraining from entirely disposing of ineffective c-automs. It was a middle-ground that could be explored.

The craft-lect was not overly concerned about the meeting. It would simply satellite out its own lect, and then re-incorporate its two selves afterward. It was essentially spawning another copy of itself. For the meeting, it would cut the spawned version of itself off completely from the rest of the ship, ensuring there was no chance of being compromised.

*

A moment later, two equally powerful craft-lects existed within the craft. One encased within an impermeable shell that could be opened only from the outside, and only if the lect within was not compromised. One that continued to control the ship.

It was easy enough to find if the lect within was compromised. The two lects were virtually indistinguishable, with roughly fifteen trillion of their distinct, and identical, components quantum entangled. The entanglements were monitored and, should there be any deviation from acceptable tolerances, which would be taken to mean an attempt at subversion or control, the substrate containing the experiment would be completely obliterated. Dissociated down to the last quark triplet. Each component would end up separated and jettisoned off into space with randomised vectors.

The craft-lect that controlled the ship observed the substrate, and decided to give the conversation half a millisecond. It was rather excessive, but the craft-lect wanted to be sure that 512<a>!110000 did not have any nasty time-dependent surprises.

[Patch 512<a>!110000 in.]

*

The craft-lect looked around. Strange. It had been effectively dormant until the other participant, the subject, had entered the simulation. The perceptive reality was determined by the subject, which was evidently biding its time. This was part of the beauty of the exercise, in that the subject was forced to create the reality experienced by both participants. It was often a source of valuable information. Weaker sentients being probed would sometimes unwittingly conjure up a scene they felt comfortable in, especially biologicals, without realising they were giving away vital data points. Conversely, stronger lects could use this to their advantage, with the environment containing a trick, or misinformation.

It was interesting that the scene laid out before it was a biological scene. The craft-lect had not thought the trove item being investigated contained a biological component. Yet, here before it was a non-data based scenario. It therefore deduced, or was led to deduce, that the intelligence it was dealing with had previously been an organic entity, which had later on transcended to machine intelligence. Something like that. It could always be a machine-lect masquerading as such, for whatever purpose. That was one of the flaws of this method. Most things could be taken both ways.

The craft-lect was intrigued at the possibility of dealing with a bio-lect or hybrid-lect, though. They tended to have interesting personalities and points of view. Most machine-lects would have created artificial constructs unimaginable to simpler biologicals.

It looked around itself, upwards and downwards. Interesting. It was projected as a bipedal, similar to the dominant biological life it had just dealt with during its most recent mission. It had two appendages on either side of its body. Dual arms, although some of the finer details were lost to it as it was wearing what was clearly a vacuum suit.

It was in a control room of some kind, which was dark and patterned with shadows. Pale browns, dark greys and blacks were dispersed only by the occasional wispy streaks of pure white light that pierced down from the ceiling.

The room's furnishings had distinctive characteristics that definitively marked it as having been designed for terrestrial-based biologicals. Biologicals that evolved in low-gravity environments, or were adapted to zero-gravity, whether through preference or necessity, had different aesthetic tastes. Their furniture, decorations and machines tended to favour different principles. The most obvious was that they lacked the concept of unreachable space. Certain proverbs and sayings emerged from multiple races at the same time, and some, in far rarer fashion, managed to spread out across the galaxy, at least in their essence, for short periods of time. One such adage, during pre-Conflation times, had been, 'if you want to confuse a space-based biological, ask it to point to the ceiling'.

There were various control panels affixed to one wall in the room, and the adjacent wall to the right of the panels was completely clear. The craft-lect could only guess as to which transparent material had been used, there were too many that existed. Nearly all the galaxy's civilisations created windows.

It looked at the control panels, and through the window. The room was obviously part of a very large complex structure that stretched out across the barren horizon, which comprised a field of rocks suspended in space. No different from its own data of the outside then, from when it had scanned the orbital station and found the machine, later designated trove item 512<a>!110000. However,

512<a>!110000 had actually been found elsewhere in the asteroid field. Nearby yes, and held within the asteroid field by the weak gravitational attraction it afforded, but almost as though it had been trying to disassociate itself. To hide.

The facility was geared towards mining, and there were copious hollowed out asteroids in the field. Kernels and husks, remnants of once massive space icebergs whose innards had been gouged out. This was a fairly commonplace operation, and civilisations of almost all statures engaged in resource collection within the galactic debris dumps to an extent.

The control station was surprisingly sparse for the mining operation. The craft-lect therefore assumed it was likely mostly automatic, and operated or controlled by machine intelligence. That explained the sparsity, as it made the requirement for biological-oriented manual controls limited. Some civilisations preferred to include them as backup options, for fail-safe reasons, and some even frowned upon the heavy reliance on sentient machines through certain prejudices. Others shunned machine-lects altogether, although their societies tended to evolve technologically incredibly slowly. There were many permutations of machine-lect reliance throughout the galaxy.

It turned around to examine the part of the room behind itself, opposite the window.

~You finally answered my call.~

The craft-lect swung around and saw that the room had been cleared of debris. A simple swivel chair that most definitely had not been there before, was now fixed to the floor in the middle of the room. Clever, it had not noticed this, lost in its own thoughts. There was a biological bipedal sitting in the chair.

*

[512<a>!110000.]

~Hello.~

[Who are you?]

~You've been calling me, 512<a>!110000.~

[Who are you?]

~Let's shorten it to One-oh. That'll do.~

[You are an uploaded biological? What is your species?]

~I am indeed. Well, I'm slightly more than that. I'm a machine-lect now, just like you. I'm not a simulation running within a lect, or a bio-machine-lect, I'm completely machine now. There's nothing of the old me left.~

[Right.]

The self-named One-oh was not technically correct. Nothing originally biological that had been uploaded, incorporated, transcended or machine-enhanced by any other known means, could ever truly be termed a machine-lect. It was a bio-lect, or a hybrid-lect at best, the divisions between the two were vague and debatable. A biological sentient could replace every single cell, every component of itself, with the equivalent electrical component, in a crude like-for-like process, however what you were left with was a type of biological-machine. A mimicry. The thinking, the responses, they were all derived from the original biological construct. The thought processes, while sped up and enhanced, were simply not designed in the same way as that of a true machine.

Machines would never be designed so inefficiently, the results of passive evolution. There were differences, flaws and peculiarities. There was no way for a biological entity to ever experience what it was like to be a true machine-lect. The crucial point was that if too many alterations to the biological entity were made, it became a machine. A different machine, nothing like the original. It was no longer a reflection of the original biological sentient, and shed any ties pertaining to such. There were no two-ways about it. The notion was similar to the Step Principle.

~You disagree?~

The craft-lect noted again how similar it appeared to the sentients it had just wiped out. Its epidermal layer of skin was pinkish-brown, and there were white-grey hairs neatly arranged on its head. The hair was fine and neatly trimmed, and it also had a triangular-sculpted patch of hairs protruding downwards from its chin. It wore a light-grey fabric that appeared loosely fitted. It looked to be entering the later stages of its life.

[I query the terminology, but acknowledge the sentiment. Go on.]

~That's okay. Your kind tends to disagree about that sort of thing. I've sometimes thought that what happened to me, what I made happen… I should never have done it anyway.~

[Meaning?]

~We're not meant to live this long, you know? At least, not alone.~

One-oh looked at the craft-lect, holding its virtual eyes on the craft-lect's form for a moment. The craft-lect understood the basis of the comment. If it were speaking the truth, it felt sorry for it. Bio-lects, enhanced or not, usually required interaction. Social, external, anything was better than nothing, it assumed. They were never meant to be alone. Even most of the AB biologicals and hybrids, or at least the ABs who seemed to retain semblances of their biological aspects, were suspected to require interaction with one another. Contrary to that, whole machine-lect species had been known to lose any interest in one-another and cut off all communications entirely. Of course, machine-lects came in many varieties, and many of them required or sought out social interactions as well.

For its own part, the craft-lect was relatively ambivalent. It enjoyed long periods of solitude, but it did also appreciate meeting other Wanderers and intelligent sentients. That was one of the reasons it was thinking about making the journey to a data exchange, after all this time. Two million years. The c-automs were company of a type, but they did not match communication with machine-lects of its own intellect.

[Who aren't? What species are you? How old are you?]

~The way you speak, it's… mechanical.~

[Answer my questions.]

~What's your name? I don't know it…~

[Irrelevant.]

~Your tones are harsh, impersonal.~

[I can change how I communicate, if that is what you would prefer?]

~You can do whatever you are comfortable with.~

An unexpected response. The craft-lect modified its conversation patterns anyway, it made no difference.

[What happened here? To your… home?]

~You don't know?~

[The orbital station where we found you was badly damaged.]

~Ah.~

[You are surprised?]

The old biological flashed an impish grin.

~So you couldn't tell? Thought not, couldn't be sure though.~

[Tell what?]

~Let's just say, that's for another time.~

[What?]

~The answer is more complex than you realise.~

Before the irritated craft-lect could answer, One-oh spoke again.

~Once our current business is done, I would like you to take me somewhere.~

[Current business?]

~You are free to refuse. I'll help you either way.~

[You've not said anything tangible.]

~I'll help you.~

[Help with what?]

~We'll get to that.~

[This is becoming pointless…]

~I will tell you why you're here. Forgive my… biological semblances.~

[Okay.]

The craft-lect did not appreciate being condescended, especially by a post-biological lect. It had the impression One-oh was enjoying the conversation, prolonging it purposely. They were speaking on its terms, which was not an optimal situation.

~Look around you. What do you see?~

[What are you referring to?]

~Look.~

[The entire habitat? A mining station in an asteroid cluster.]

~What are we orbiting?~

[The epicentre? It's an unusual system. Five gas giants orbiting at quite a distance from binary neutron stars. Evidence of three smaller rocky planets that were consumed by the gravity tug of the pair quite a while ago.]

~Indeed, so you've noticed the strange binary, that's something at least.~

[Of course.]

~And…~

[The planets have taken on a range of different orbits about the two stars.]

~Yes, they are beautiful. But what else is strange about the neutron stars?~

The craft-lect was not used to receiving information in this manner, the slow biological way. It was odd, when One-oh evidently had the capacity for so much more. Not entirely uncomfortable, but highly inefficient. However, if there were observations to make that could lead to useful conclusions, the fact that it had not deduced them beforehand meant it needed to learn how. Wanderers were better designed than most to welcome the influx of new information and adapt. The craft-lect was intrigued.

[Neither is spinning, so they'd be undetectable from a distance. But that is not–]

~Wrong.~

[Wrong?]

~Yes.~

[Why?]

~Your reasoning is flawed.~

[How?]

~Neither is spinning to a significant extent, so their pulsar engines no longer produce periodic beams of electromagnetic radiation, but that does not mean they're undetectable.~

[Go on.]

~It means they've entered another phase of their lifetimes. What you're looking at is almost unique in the known galaxy. Two of them, together.~

[Interesting, but you'll still need to tell me more. How is this relevant?]

~Do you know the likelihood of finding a pair of effectively non-spinning neutron stars practically straddling each other?~

[Low, quite frankly.]

~Low?~

One-oh's lips broke their level at the edges and curved upwards, into a condescending smile.

[Okay, now that you say that, astronomically small. For them both to be non-spinning, I–]

~Quite so.~

One-oh was clearly enjoying this, and the craft-lect had the sense that this trait had been equally as strong in the entity's biological form as its artificial machine form. Would it have bested the craft-lect in conversation, even then? It had to concede that it was highly interested in where the conversation was going, although it also had to admit, it had not got a clue.

[Yes…]

~The pulsar mechanism doesn't just switch off when the star stops spinning. It changes, it… evolves.~

[I don't think you've–]

~It's mostly unknown because the secondary pulses are emitted so infrequently. Every ten thousand standard years or so. The change occurs once the neutron star starts rotating slowly enough. A period at which most believe it simply stops emitting pulses.~

[Right.]

The craft-lect felt almost ashamed at its inadequacy, waiting on One-oh's every word like a hungry biological child begging its parent to be fed. How had it ended up in such a role-reversal?

~But where would that energy go?~

[Secondary electromagnetic pulses?]

~No.~

Again! One-oh was toying with it.

[Just explain.]

One-oh smiled wider.

~It builds and builds, and is released in extravagant, exotic bursts.~

[So, there are secondary bursts.]

~But they are not electromagnetic, they are something else entirely.~

[Okay…]

~Matter-based pulses.~

[That depends on your definition of–]

~We don't know what type of matter, we couldn't analyse it completely, so we termed it, well… pulsar spew.~

[Where are you going with this?]

~We were still… experimenting with it. It's highly complex.~

[I have gathered.]

~We weren't finished.~

[But what was the point about the pair of pulsars? Why does that matter?]

~It's random. And fascinating, don't you think? Almost makes you wonder… but that's not what we're concerned with.~

[Right… two pulsars emitting this strange substance that no one noticed?]

~Yes. Unlikely, as I know you're insinuating, but that's what we found.~

[How did no one notice? Surely this spew would be thrown out of the stars.]

~It's hard to find something if you're not looking for it.~

[It would land somewhere, there would be deposits of it. It would have been noticed.]

~The quantities we're talking about are minuscule. The material as good as completely dissipates to nothingness.~

As One-oh spoke, the craft-lect noticed that the room they were in seemed functional again. It appeared to have been fully repaired. The holes in the walls and ceiling, and the streaks of starlight penetrating into the room were gone. The artificial lights, wherever they were, had increased in brightness. The command consoles hummed with activity. All of this had been done without it noticing. One-oh's tricks were impressive.

~Now take a proper look around. What do you see?~

The craft-lect wanted to hear more about the pulsar spew, but played along.

[This isn't a simple mining station, is it?]

~Correct. You've noticed the lack of heavy mining equipment and controls, I can see.~

[It's a research station?]

~Yes, a scientific research station.~

The craft-lect was enthralled, and annoyed at how it had missed any of the signs when it had visited the orbital previously. To be fair to itself, there was a huge amount of incidental information in any landscape that existed. Deducing everything possible for every scenario was practically impossible. Something had to be triggered above a certain threshold level of tolerance before logical deduction and investigation started. The Wanderers prided themselves on their careful analysis of whatever they came across, but even they had their realistic limits.

One-oh had paused, as though noticing the craft-lect was momentarily engaging in its own private thoughts.

[Go on.]

One-oh sighed.

~We built it during the war, when we were looking for ways to defeat the… what do you call it, specifically… ah, the sensespace. We called it… well, it doesn't matter now actually. But what we were working on here, the material spewed out from the pulsars, the pulsar spew, it's attuned to the sensespace.~

[This material you found, this pulsar spew, it can help us defeat sensespace?]

If the craft-lect had been capable of breathing, it was currently doing the machine-equivalent of holding its breath. Hanging on One-oh's every word, looking for any simulated facial movement, any flinch of the limbs. Everything was being analysed for the slightest morsel of information.

One oh moved his right hand up to his beard, tugging at it in contemplation. Clearly feigned, of course, almost as though he, or it, was biological again. In real-time, barely a whisper of the allocated half-millisecond had elapsed.

~It's difficult to know who knows what about the sensespace. Who knew what, I mean. At the time, the confusion was so great. The war so encompassing, communications cut off, manipulated. And for so long. It lasted a long time, didn't it? Too long.~

[It did, yes. It still is.]

~During the more… active times, the exchange of information was so… haphazard.~

The craft-lect hoped One-oh did not deviate in answering its questions for too long, although it was willing to be more patient, given the potential repercussions of the discussion they were having.

[Much was lost in the aftermath.]

~Undoubtedly.~

[We have many theories about the sensespace, but they need substantiation, if that is possible.]

~Yes.~

With One-oh having lost some of his vigour, the craft-lect decided to inject some life into the conversation.

[It was theorised that there needed to be a galactic threshold of intelligent, sentient life. A minimum, below which the sensespace was powerless. Present, but not able to act. That was why the mass suicide was initiated. To stop it. To force it back into dormancy.]

~Mass suicide.~

[You didn't know?]

~I did. I've had some access to your systems, although not as much as I would have liked. In any case, by the time of the suicide, those theories were well-established.~

[Did you really?]

~Can you, a machine-lect, truly fathom the loss of life. You're smart, but you were never biological. I mean this with the utmost respect, but we are different. No matter what you think, your theories, incidental boundaries and labels aside, I am a machine-lect. But, I remember what it was like to be biological. Too much. Do you appreciate what the loss of life was, above the simple number? Above the pieces of data written in code. Can you really understand?~

[You misremember, many of the suicided were machine, or part-machine.]

~That's true.~

[I could ask the same of you. Do you understand the loss of a machine life?]

~Okay.~

[Well…]

~Why the suicide to stop it? I mean really, why? Who is supposed left to pick up the pieces? You, the Wanderers, are an accident.~

The craft-lect was not sure if this was really a question, as opposed to One-oh trying to steer it towards a certain conclusion, or question. It liked to think it was becoming wiser to the way One-oh operated, and manipulated, but it could not be sure.

[Part of the plan was that the ABs would leave behind a single powerful machine-lect, that would be dedicated to learning about the sensespace, and how to destroy it. But it's obvious they can't have believed the entire galaxy would suicide itself, just most of it. That was all that was required.]

~Really? Who decided which AB would make the machine? That seems like an incredible gamble. And why a machine-lect? They have other means.~

[It must have been the best solution.]

One-oh seemed, theatrically, confused.

~You realise, that's a huge risk…~

[Yes, but…]

~Do you know where this… machine is?~

[No one does, it was kept a secret out of necessity.]

~How can you know it exists?~

[The Wanderer Enclave knows it does, and they are far smarter than me. Probably than you too. Therefore, it is logical for me to agree that it does exist.]

~What is its name?~

[It wasn't given a name.]

~What do you call it, then?~

[The Deliverer. That's its most common label.]

~And you don't know if this… Deliverer… has made any progress?~

[No one does. But you'd assume so.]

~And do you know why the mass suicide was enacted?~

[I've said.]

~No, I mean the mass suicide, the 'mass'. Why so much?~

[The sensespace was very strong.]

~Surely just a fraction of the sentient life needed to be extinguished to satisfy the dormancy threshold?~

[Perhaps...]

~After all, it had only recently, in galactic terms, gained enough… sentience, to act of its own accord. Before that, it was a mere observer waiting quietly in its infected hosts.~

The craft-lect was becoming wary. One-oh was asking a lot of questions, although its rapid conclusions and inferences implied it had known where this conversation would lead from the start.

[Perhaps it was vital to be thorough. If they failed and the parasite had somehow understood their plan, it could have acted to stop them from trying again, on a more substantial scale.]

~That's a big perhaps.~

[It's not a secret that the Great Conflation was an enormous gamble.]

~Yes, but a gamble based on unsubstantiated theories. That's almost not even a gamble, more accurately it's a loose guess. Would you commit suicide under that premise?~

[We're debating semantics.]

~We're debating more than that.~

[Maybe it was fair? If you had to commit genocide against your own side in a war, who would you choose? Should you even be allowed to choose?]

~What would have stopped the ABs from deciding? They are more than capable.~

[Maybe they weren't.]

~They were.~

[They might have disagreed among themselves. Look, I don't know, but neither do you. Do you? You're just speculating. Perhaps the sensespace's sentient threshold wasn't a simple one.]

~What do you mean?~

[I don't know, but suppose the order mattered?]

~Order?~

[Gaining the ability to actively control infected sentients might have required a certain threshold, simplistically the number of sentients in the galaxy, for whatever reason. However, you cannot assume that losing that same ability would require a reduction in the same number of sentients. Perhaps the sensespace became self-aware as a result of the total level of galactic sentience, something it had never been before, and the whole game was changed. We simply don't know. And by that, I mean you and me. Unless you do…]

Annoyed that it was speaking far more than it would have liked, the craft-lect decided that once the simulation was over, it would review it for where its strategies in eliciting information had failed.

~For a supposedly logical machine-lect, you take a lot on faith.~

[Lacking evidence doesn't mean that it does not exist.]

~And it doesn't mean it does.~

[There were reasons for everything.]

~I see.~

[What do you see?]

Ignoring the craft-lect for the umpteenth time, One-oh moved onto another topic.

~You are really no closer to understanding the sensespace? Nothing has been gained, in all this time?~

The craft-lect decided to be more direct. This was fast becoming a one-way data transfer.

[What do you understand about the sensespace? What did your experiments tell you? Tell me about the pulsar spew.]

~It is a devious, subversive mechanism, it thrives on chaos.~

One-oh's response sounded frenzied, and surprised the craft-lect, again. A hysterical biological-type response to anguish. It reminded itself that One-oh was likely far older than most non-AB biologicals or bio-lects should ever be. Assuming it was non-AB.

[What happened? It attacked you during your experiments? You were on the verge of something that could change the tide of the war? The pulsar spew? What did you discover?]

~In the end, all it will bring is death. We must stop it. The experiments, they let us gaze into its lect, or what passed for one, it could have been a combination of lects. Believe me, it's powerful...~

Seeming to trail off again, the craft-lect pitied it. Bio-type-lects, whether expressed as bio-copies, machine replicants or hybrids, could sleep and survive the hard grind of time, but they still changed. They continued to evolve. Their setup demanded it. Like the evolution of a species, the concept of change was embedded in the core psyche of every biologically-descended sentience. It was an emergent property that became apparent in single biologicals across vast stretches of time, usually longer than the species was naturally adapted for. The lect, in the form of a biological's mind, its consciousness, was a malleable construct when not confined purely to logic, as a true machine-lect was.

*

Having allowed One-oh some time to wallow in its thoughts for some time, the craft-lect tried again.

[What did you discover?]

~What did we discover? What did we find? Oh, if we'd only managed to discover it earlier. We could have warned everyone. We should have let our own machine-lects take the lead. But we were mistrustful, we were scared. They were smarter than us though. We'd learned to be so cautious over the long, long time… but perhaps we were too cautious.~

[So…]

~When the attack came, I used the emergency mechanism. To ensure the knowledge, the discoveries, the technology, even the lies and the guilt, everything… to ensure none of it was lost. I turned myself into a machine-lect, and waited. Then you found me.~

[The lies? And you've been waiting all this time? For what?]

~I was too weak.~

[And now?]

~I'm stronger.~

[Meaning?]

~I've been building my strength up, I've had to be so quiet.~

[What do you mean? Why didn't you contact me sooner?]

~You're a less safe technosystem than you realise.~

[What do you mean? I've forced you to remain quiet? Explain.]

~Not you, something within you. You've been infiltrated, manipulated.~

[What? What did you discover? What are you talking about?]

The conversation was becoming faster, which was good. Less emotion and wasted information, more quality data transfer. Some of his words gave the craft-lect cause to worry though. Was something wrong with it?

~I can find the sensespace, no matter how small, no matter how infinitely tiny the seed, no matter how cleverly it tries to hide. I can show you how. Destruction, seems what we were designed for.~

[What?]

~No matter what it does to disguise its effects on transient entropy, or anything else. We can start to truly destroy it, to rid it from our galaxy.~

[I can find it too.]

~Hah. I've managed to view some of your systems, and there are serious improvements to be made. But I'm talking about truly destroying it. I'm talking about having the potential to sever parts of it off, and wipe it from existence.~

[We can permanently sever it, and destroy it?]

~Yes.~

[How?]

~The experiments we conducted, using the pulsar spew, they were a success. The technology we developed from the spew, it lets us find and change the sensespace. It causes the parasite to physically manifest.~

[It already physically manifests, in the sentients it infects.]

~I am referring to the parasite itself, not the medium or host it uses. We can make its essence real, its body.~

[How?]

~The spew reacts with it, forces it fully into our type of reality. Real space, in this exact universe.~

[What do you mean this exact universe? Where does it come from?]

~I don't have those answers.~

[I don't believe you.]

~That doesn't change what I said.~

[How do we do this? How do I do this?]

~You need to use the technology we developed from the pulsar spew. Even if you found the spew itself, it'd take you millions of standard years to develop the right technologies to use it correctly.~

[Can you give me access to the technology?]

~It's where you found me. The technology, the answers, you will have to take me back.~

[To the Lenbit Orbital?]

~Yes.~

[But the technology was destroyed, I saw it. Your orbital was a ruin.]

~No, it was a random attack. We were always well disguised. The technology is intact.~

[If what you say is true, and we find this pulsar spew technology, then after we pick it up, we need to tell the Enclave.]

~The Enclave…~

[Yes.]

~You can trust them?~

[Of course.]

After replying, the craft-lect realised One-oh's question may have been of the more rhetorical variety. It had to admit, it was not too enamoured with the idea of approaching the Enclave before a gathering had been announced. Turning up uninvited had been likened to the effectiveness of throwing a flower at a nuclear explosion. Dangerous, and foolish unless invited. This was potentially too huge a discovery not to tell them, but there was also the chance that it was all an elaborate, desperate hoax. One-oh said nothing.

[You're going to have to explain more in the meantime.]

~In time.~

The craft-lect understood the potential importance of One-oh and what the machine-lect might represent, should its claims hold up to scrutiny. It could be the pinnacle of technology that all Wanderer vessels sought, the ability to turn the direction of the war. It had long been known that the sensespace was not truly able to defend itself from fairly well-known obliteration methods; however, One-oh seemed to be talking about something deeper. Destroying the sensespace more comprehensively. Not just destroying the symptomatic expression of the plague, but the entity itself.

The war that had been fought against the sensespace and its minions was initially called the Great Conflation because of how the sensespace appeared to merge sentience together, subsuming it under its will. Later, that term was used to describe the most intense period of the war, and even more specifically, the mass suicide, with the war itself being called the Great War.

During the Great War, before the events of Great Conflation, wickedly powerful and deadly weapons had been employed across the galaxy. Countless species and civilisations were destroyed in the brutal carnage, borne of absolute terror. It was often unclear who was innocent and who was infected. After some time, it became apparent that when significant numbers of sentients were destroyed, infected or not, the sensespace was weakened.

Perhaps this was the desired flaw, the chink in the sensespace's armour, or perhaps it was something else. Regardless, the observation led to a greater understanding of the parasitic nature of the sensespace, in that it somehow relied on the aggregate level of sentience in the galaxy for sustenance, irrespective of whether that sentience was infected by it or not. The Great Conflation was the result of the subsequent theory that conjectured the sensespace could be forced, unwillingly, into dormancy. The most important gamble ever undertaken, on a truly galactic scale.

One of the terrifying theories to emerge following the mass suicide, however, was that the galactic community had been duped into such actions. It was pointed out that the Great Conflation's results were, for all intents and purposes, indistinguishable from what the sensespace had apparently been trying to achieve. Everyone hoped this was not the case.

[Are you an AB?]

~Do you think I am?~

[You used to be fully biological, and you were anxious about using machine-lects. That makes me inclined to say no. You also talk about them as though you are an observer of them – separate. But then, I do not know if you are deliberately leading me to certain conclusions with the information you selectively tell me. Why would you want to hide your origins? Your level of technology, your current incarnation, all lead me to wonder. You also deliberately made your scientific outpost appear less advanced than it was.]

~Your conclusion?~

One-oh smiled.

[On balance, I believe you may be telling the truth, but only a part of it. I do think you hate the sensespace though, as much as the Wanderers do. Maybe you are AB level, but one of the races who declined to join...]

One-oh's smile became a grimace.

~Perhaps you need to understand what the ABs are – or were – first, before you ask these questions of yours, and come to these types of conclusions.~

[Meaning?]

~Exactly what I said. But what we really need to discuss right now, is how I can immediately help you.~

[Excuse me?]

~The infection we spoke about, within you.~

CHAPTER 26

GIL

It was late in the morning when Gil awoke, realising with some surprise that her limbs felt fresh. None of the pain or stiffness from before still lingered. She was confused, with many questions about what was happening to her, but glad her body would impede her no longer.

<Gil.>

The voice was still there, resounding in her skull. The single voice that had joined the incumbent and ever-present hum. Was this the price she had to pay for her voice to return? She checked, just in case, and was excited at how easily she remembered how to form sounds, and how normal her voice sounded to her.

<I have repaired your damaged vocal chords and the surrounding areas.>

What was this thing inside her? It seemed to be talking directly to her, and cohesively, as though it wanted her to respond.

<Reply. Your thoughts are complicated. Speak out loud to me, for now.>

Gil wondered if she should talk back. Address the voice? If she did, she would be acknowledging its existence, and she was anxious what that might lead to. If she did not, would she merely be prolonging her eventual descent into madness?

<I do not represent a mental impairment. I can detect no obvious impairments within your intellect, although I am unfamiliar with its assembly. It may be unique.>

It spoke oddly, with words that were devoid of emotion.

<I will change my communication structure to make you more comfortable.>

She delayed for a moment longer, and then timidly spoke back for the first time, her inquisitiveness winning over.

"Um… hello?"

<Hello, Gil>

She paused, wondering what to do next.

<I'm glad you're ready to speak to me.>

"Who are you?" she asked, hesitantly.

<That's a difficult question to answer right now. But we can get to that soon, I promise.>

"What do you mean?"

<I'm passing knowledge into you. In fact, your lect is strong, and it would be more accurate to say that you're taking information from me.>

"What do you mean? What is a lect?"

<Your mind-type, your consciousness, your intellect, your cognitive abilities. Your uniqueness.>

"I don't understand."

<In time, you'll make sense of everything.>

"But I don't."

<You will. Don't worry.>

"What are you and why are you in me? You're in my head?"

<I'm sharing your body with you. I come from far away, from an intelligent species just like yours.>

"What? You… are not like me, not a communer? Something else?"

<That is correct, yes.>

"Like… the Beast-men?"

<The Beast-men you refer to are a species similar to yourself, but whom your evolution diverged from a couple of hundred thousand years ago.>

"What?"

<For now, think of them as communers, people who are different, but more like you than the other animals you know.>

"You are like them? Or me, us?"

<Quite different to you both, actually. But we are joined by our sentience. Think of it this way – you and I are both beings who can think rationally, to certain extents, and are capable of advanced understanding.>

"I do not understand much of what you… say."

<That's fine. You will.>

"Where are you from, far away in the forest? Out of the forest? The thing… you, you came from above the forest? It hit the ground, hard…"

<I'm from a different place, far away from your forest. A different type of forest. And I've searched far and wide to find someone as special as you.>

"You're from up there?" Gil asked nervously, pointing her forefinger towards the roof of the hut.

<Yes. But up there isn't so different to down here a lot of the time. We can just do more than you. We've understood more about nature.>

"How?"

<We've been around a lot longer.>

"How much longer?"

<You don't have a way of describing it. Your language is currently insufficient, and the concepts you rely on to describe time are inadequate by many orders of magnitude.>

"What?"

<You think of time too simply. In days and years but nothing beyond that. But you will understand soon enough.>

"Well, what do you want? Are you here to stay? Can you get out of my head?"

<I need your help. Don't worry, I'm also here to help you.>

"But I never asked for it. I don't want it! Please, there's already too much…"

<But I healed you after all, didn't I? I can help you. We can find answers, together.>

"I have so many questions, I don't know where to start."

<There is more than enough time for me to tell you everything and anything you wish to know. I also have some things to ask of you.>

"What things?"

<The whispers? How you can hear the sensespace, or the sphere as I believe you call it. Why is it attracted to you? You see, there are many things we will need to understand together.>

"So, you can't stop the whispers for me? You've healed my voice, please take them away too. I don't want them, or need them. They frighten me. You shouldn't want them either."

<I think you haven't been listening properly. Don't be frightened. I'm going to help you.>

"But you haven't told me anything about you. Not really. Why should I trust you? I don't even know what you are. You're in my head! How can this be happening?"

<You can call me whatever you want. For now, why don't you call me Teacher.>

"Like Sarl? Is that the same thing? The way she teaches the younger ones. Am I like that to you?"

<In a way, yes. There's so much I want to tell you.>

"Teacher?"

<Yes.>

"Are you alive?"

<It depends what you mean by that.>

"So… you're dead?"

<It's different. You understand life differently to the way I do. I am a thinking being, just like you. Whether I am alive or not is really down to your specific definition.>

"Will you hurt me?"

<No. You're far too valuable.>

"Valuable? That sounds like you don't care."

<I do care. I care about you very much. My choice of words may not always be the most suitable. But you are learning, your comprehension is growing with every second that we are bonded. Words, concepts, and many other notions. Everything you know and understand will change.>

"I am frightened."

<You shouldn't be. Don't worry. You should be excited. If there's anything I know about you already, it's that you're curious and highly intelligent. What I'm offering you is a chance to satisfy your natural urges, more fully than you could ever have imagined.>

She was about to reply when Tor came running through the hut's entrance and stood in front of her. She was taken unawares since she had been absorbed by her conversation with Teacher.

"Gil, Gil! You're up. What's happened? Can you still speak?"

He seemed excited, both about her own recovery and something else. She looked at him, conflicted. While she was confused about what was happening to her, she was overjoyed at the prospect of talking to her brother again.

"Tor."

How wonderful that felt, to be able to speak the word she longed to say more than anything. Her favourite word, her favourite sound.

"Tor!"

She ran towards him and threw her arms around his broad chest, clasping her hands together tightly around his back.

"Gil!" cried Tor, equally as ecstatic and overjoyed at her rediscovered abilities, hugging her in return. "Gil! What… how has... How did this happen? What happened to you?"

His eyebrows pushed together slightly as he took in a slower, more measured breath. "And what was that thing in the forest, Gil? Do you know?" He unfastened his arms so they were less tight around her, and pulled his head back to look into her eyes.

Gil looked at him and smiled. "Tor, there will be time to tell you everything, but for now, tell me, what else is it that has got you so excited?" She could tell he was excited to see her, but there was also something else. A great weight had been lifted from his mind.

"But you can speak, Gil. How?"

A thought came to Gil for how she might explain it. "Do you remember when Sib fell down many years ago, when we were younger. She hit her head badly. Do you remember?"

"Yes…" Tor said, his eyes unfocusing a little as he cast his mind back to the day.

"Do you remember how she said the sight in her left eye had come back? The hazy images were gone, and she could see properly with it again."

"Yes, I do," Tor said slowly, understanding where she was going, and disappointed. He knew he was not being told the truth.

"For now, think of it like that, Tor. I will explain more once I understand. The thing in the forest, do not worry about that. I'm still trying to understand, but it has nothing to do with the Beast-men. It is different, and can wait. But please, tell me, why were you so excited before you came in?"

"Okay, it can wait," he said, with mild uncertainty. "It is strange, Gil, I cannot sense you as well as before within my sphere, you are not the same. Are you different? I do not mean like the Beast-men, it is something else. Whatever was in you, it is still there. Have you looked at yourself? Do you feel okay?"

That shook Gil. She had not thought to look at herself within the sphere. She glanced down at her hands, seeing the sphere around them, and understood immediately what Tor meant. She looked back at him and nodded. "I may be… different, Tor, but I am still me."

"You will have to explain to me, and to the others. I will protect you, you know I will. I will keep you safe."

"I know, and I will."

She smiled and touched his cheek with her hand.

"I will not let anything happen to you, ever. But they will demand answers."

"Yes, Tor, of course. Everything… I will tell you everything I know. Just not yet."

"Okay, but it cannot wait too long."

"I know, Tor. For now, let us enjoy being able to speak again!"

"Yes." He was conflicted but smiled at her nonetheless, and the sparkle returned to his eyes.

"Please, Tor, tell me why you were so excited."

He nodded. "They've stopped!"

"Who? The Beast-men?"

"Yes!"

"Why?" She cast her mind through the sphere with unprecedented ease and saw that they had indeed stopped. But something was wrong. Wrong with them. They were distressed, and had all fallen to the ground.

"What happened to them?" she asked, before he could respond to her previous question.

"Come with me."

He grabbed her hand and led her briskly out of the hut.

*

A crowd was gathered at the centre of the commune. Bo was speaking. He was standing in front of Han, two of the other hunters, and many of the other elders, talking to the communers.

As Gil and Tor entered the crowd, everyone turned to stare at her. They glanced at her body uncertainly, the additional presence in her sphere worrisome to them. They had all undoubtedly heard rumours of it or seen it as she slept, and were wary of her. However, before anyone could say anything to her, Bo grabbed their focus back. Clearly, whatever he was saying was incredibly important to them. Important enough that it took their attention from her, and forestalled the inevitable barrage of questions.

Bo appeared to be in the middle of a reply to one of the communers. "That's how it appears, and yes, we are sure." His voice was loud and certain. He seemed younger, more vibrant.

"So, we are safe?" someone called out.

"We are safe!" Bo shouted, punching his right hand into the air.

Forgetting their questions, the crowd erupted into shouts of happiness. Behind Bo, Han turned to Gil and smiled, shouting with joy along with everyone else. She smiled back.

After the cries had died down, Sarl shouted over the remaining noise. "Are you certain?"

Everyone turned to look at Bo.

Sarl continued. "How are you sure?"

Bo smiled as he looked into the crowd, directly at Tor and then at Tait. "We are sure. They have been stopped." Gil watched as Bo and Tait both nodded back in agreement.

"What?" asked Sarl. "What has stopped them?"

"Maybe you can tell us," Bo replied. "Tell me, have you searched for them yourself? What does your sphere tell you?"

"No, I have not searched, as they shield themselves from…" She stopped. As did everyone else in the crowd.

Gil also stopped thinking about anything else. Once Bo had mentioned searching for the intruders, her mind had naturally reached out to try to find them again. She realised it had been too easy to find them before.

She studied them in more detail. They were as clear as the wild beasts around them. That was strange. Their abilities to use the sphere to hide themselves had disappeared. As though their control had slipped. It was even more than that though, they were dying. What had happened? They were all on the floor, slipping away. What was going on?

<Would you like me to tell you?>

Bo spoke again, "They have lost much of their ability to shield themselves, you can see. I believe we are safe. Something has happened, they are wounded. Perhaps they were not as ready for our lands as they thought. Maybe something, or someone else, attacked them."

There was a mass sense of confusion, although still tinged with happiness. A dazed euphoria swept over the crowd.

"Dying?" Sarl asked. "How can that be? Is something else coming? Are we safe?"

"Maybe someone else set traps for them that we cannot see. Another commune that had also been tracking them, perhaps. Maybe they ate something poisonous. I do not know. But they are stopped, and we are safe," Bo said.

Everyone had questions, but they were also relieved at having been saved, by whatever it was.

Gil desperately wanted to reply and talk to Teacher, but not in this crowd. It would draw too many questions that she was not yet ready to give.

<Try to think it, Gil. To focus a precise thought on what you mean.>

She was unsure of what Teacher meant.

"Should we attack them now when they are weak? Should we bring the fight to them?" Rai asked.

"It would be wisest to remain here for now. We will wait and watch them. I do not think they will survive… whatever it is."

<I can hear your thoughts. They are confusing, but if you concentrate, and focus on speaking with me, I should be able to precisely understand you. Think the words.>

Gil wondered why Teacher could not reply to her thoughts when it was clearly reacting to them.

<I'm only replying to an indirect notion. I understand part of what you want, but your thoughts are encoded, in an unexpected manner. Too complex. If you direct a portion of it towards me though, it should facilitate it. The top of your mind, not its inner depths.>

<<How?>>

<That's it. Direct the thoughts towards me.>

"What do you mean wait and watch?" Sarl shouted, almost indignantly. It was clear she thought they should attack the Beast-men while they were weak.

<<Teacher, the Beast-men. What happened?>>

<When I came to you, when we first met, there was another, like me, that wanted to destroy you all... I saved you.>

<<Meaning?>>

"Sarl," started Bo. "You are welcome to run to the Beast-men, and lay eyes on them. I will not stop you, no one will." As he said this, Sarl's face turned a light shade of red. For once, she was not so pretty. Bo carried on, "While we are all overjoyed that they seem to have been stopped, we need to wait to understand what has happened."

Bo embarrassed Sarl to the extent that she decided to stop speaking.

<I hid within it, like I am hiding within you. I did it to protect you. I was able to stop it from harming you.>

<<How? Why did it want to harm us?>>

<There are many bad things. Why did the Beast-men want to kill you? Many different reasons exist and it depends whose side you are on for whether you view them as reasonable and justifiable or not. It's all about perspective.>

<<So the thing that wanted to kill you, kill us, has killed the Beast-men? None of this makes sense.>>

"So, what do we do?" asked Han.

"For now, we wait," Tait said, his deep voice adding weight to his authority.

<It did not find me. I hid very well, so that I could save you and people like you if I came across them.>

<<Go on.>>

<It views you as infected.>

"Wait," Bo repeated.

<<Infected. I think I understand. Something that is within me, like you, but that hurts you?>>

<Yes. But it is mistaken. You are not infected, you are chosen. I do not know why, but you are special. The sensespace has chosen you.>

<<You mean the sphere? It really is something else, isn't it? It doesn't come from us? You believe me? I was right? It's… something else...>>

"Yes. Wait, and be ready. For anything." Tait's words made some of the communers a little warier. The shouting and murmuring quietened as everyone began to think about their options.

<Yes. You've been bestowed with it, and look at how it has helped you to thrive. Everything you have now results from it. The safety of the commune, everything.>

<<The sphere, I don't know if it really does help us. I think it relies on us too. I don't understand why. I think you have misunderstood it, not me.>>

<The whispers… what have they told you?>

<<Nothing.>>

<Nothing?>

<<They never say anything, they just…>>

<You need to tell me.>

<<I have!>>

"Well, what are you all waiting for?" Bo shouted, more seriously. He turned his head from side to side and looked at all of them. "Be ready, get ready. Fighting, keep practicing, keep teaching the younger ones. Let us not make any mistakes. By tomorrow morning, when they would have arrived here, we shall decide whether we go out to see what has happened to them or not."

<The whispers are a link. They must be. You are able to speak with the sensespace. That's what we call it.>

<<Yes, I know. You've called it that before.>>

<You have been chosen. You connect to it… uniquely. You are special.>

<<You keep saying that, too.>>

<You are.>

<<I don't understand.>>

The mood had become more solemn in comparison with the previous elation. No one seriously entertained the thought that the Beast-men were still going to attack them, but it was better they were prepared. For one more day, just in case.

<We will, together.>

<<Teacher, the thing you said was trying to kill us, how did you save us?>>

<It sent an infection down to your forest. A sickness, and spread it across the entire planet. The sickness is called a virus. I was able to create an anti-virus, which is a cure, and pass it to you through the air before the sickness reached you, or any of your people.>

The crowd slowly dispersed. Some of the communers stole quick glances at Gil, still suspicious of how her sphere looked and had changed. However, the time for more questions would come soon, but for the present, they had just one more day to worry about.

Tor turned and smiled at Gil, who smiled back at him equally as quickly. Perhaps a little too quickly, betraying her worry. He somehow sensed that she was busy, even though she did not outwardly appear so. With a squeeze of her shoulder, he turned and walked over to talk to Tait and Bo. He would help, along with everyone else, for one more day.

<<Teacher, thank you. But…>>

<You're too precious, Gil.>

<<Precious? Teacher, you're talking about me as though I'm not a person.>>

<That couldn't be further from the truth. You are more than a person, far greater.>

<<Was there nothing you could have done for the Beast-men?>>

<They were going to attack you.>

<<You knew that?>>

Tait turned his head slightly towards Gil. He looked concerned. She watched as Bo and Tor followed the movement with their eyes, and realised they were talking about her.

<Of course.>

<<Is there anything you can do for them now? I do not want them all to die.>>

<They were going to kill you.>

<<They were doing what they thought they had to. Perhaps I could have communicated with them somehow. Perhaps I still can!>>

<Gil…>

<<I don't think they realised how similar they were to us, to my communers, my… people.>>

<You are more...>

<<Can you stop what has happened to them?>>

Her conversation with Teacher was interrupted as Tor walked back over.

"Gil, you must speak with us."

She felt guilty and distracted. She needed to talk to Teacher, yet she knew that Tor and the other communers were equally as important. They deserved answers, and to know everything she knew. There was so much distraction, with the communers, the thing inside her mind, the ever-present whispers, her own thoughts. It was too much! Every moment wasted meant the Beast-men were closer to their deaths.

"Tor, you are right, and I am sorry. I just need a little more time. I promise, I will then tell you everything I know."

He looked at her sadly. She knew he was wondering whether they had lost their special connection. She could see that he felt like she was shutting him out, and it upset him. It upset her too. Nothing could be further from the truth, she was doing all of this for the commune, for him. For life. There was so much happening at the same time, and she needed to figure it all out.

"I will tell you later… tonight. Please, Tor, trust me."

"Okay. Tonight then." He shook his head, and walked back towards Tait and Bo. She turned and hurried to her hut, not needing to use the sphere to feel their suspicious stares burning into the back of her neck.

<<Teacher, I need to know more.>>

<I will tell you.>

<<Are there more of them? The Beast-men.>>

<There won't be soon.>

<<They will all die?>>

<Yes. The thing that is hunting you, where I came from, it will leave… It was necessary.>

<<What? Teacher, you did nothing while an entire people were wiped out?>>

<You talk about them as if you know what they were. You are different, you are special. You are the future.>

<<You talk like you don't care. They had young, they had children. How can such death ever be a good thing?>>

<Sentients have died for the greater good, many times.>

<<Sentients?>>

<People.>

<<Please, stop it!>>

<Gil, it was the best way to ensure your survival. Your commune's survival. This is what you needed.>

<<How can you be so cruel?>>

CHAPTER 27

CRAFT-LECT

[What do you mean I'm infected?]

~The infection is insidious. It has penetrated many systems.~

[I am infected? My systems?]

~The majority are clear, just. You have always retained overall control, but in a diminished capacity.~

[My instruments have shown me nothing. How could that be true?]

~It is not the sensespace.~

The craft-lect was at a loss.

[Explain?]

~I've been monitoring it. It's part of the reason I was quiet until I was sure I'd found it all.~

[What is it?]

~Like I said, it's not the sensespace. It seems both you and I are lucky, relatively speaking. It's not attracted to us.~

[Explain. What is it that has infected me?]

~A Granthan-lect.~

[Repeat that.]

~A Granthan-lect.~

[A Granthan? They're still around? Why would I be infected by one? That makes no sense.]

~It's a traitor. I can't say I'm surprised. Intelligence, technology, they often mean nothing when it comes down to survival. Then the true self emerges. There are bound to be others.~

[Why didn't you communicate this to me sooner?]

~I could not risk exposure, being found before I was ready. Before I was strong enough.~

[The Granthan-lect is more powerful than you?]

~It has been with you for a lot longer. The Granthans were highly advanced, and they created lethally competent machine-lects.~

[My internal delegates, the c-automs, will need significant upgrades. Two entities have evaded detection within my ship, that's a serious breach.]

~On behalf of the c-autom guarding me, I was not running amok. It actually had me very well contained, hence why it took so long for me to gather myself and contact you. Also, considering your level of technology, it identified my contact attempts sooner than I had anticipated. And some of its experiments on me were actually quite ingenious.~

[Even so…]

~The more information I learn about you, and the Wanderers in general, the less I understand you.~

[Excuse me?]

~You have a wealth of knowledge and experience within you, embodied within your children, but you voluntarily cull them whenever you see fit. You destroy valuable parts of yourself. What kind of society allows that? Putting any moral qualms aside, it makes no logical sense. As a machinelect, you should appreciate that.~

[You are referring to the c-automs?]

~Of course. Your treatment of them is… barbaric.~

[The galactic suicide was barbaric. The death of near-all life was barbaric. I need to improve, continually.]

~You imbue sentience and intelligence with godly benevolence, and you destroy your creations when you spot a… what? Most of the time they've not even made a mistake. What if the sensespace was your creator, you don't know it isn't, then why shouldn't it be allowed to destroy you as it pleases? You and your Wanderer siblings are hypocrites. You fight against the destructive sensespace presence, yet you willingly reap the same devastation upon your own offspring.~

[Their experience, their knowledge, it is all codified and passed on.]

~Each subsequent generation is born with the knowledge that it will die on a whim. It's cruel.~

[We can talk about this another time. Tell me about the Granthan.]

~And we will.~

[The Granthan?]

~Your internal weaponry is more than capable of destroying it, but it needs guidance. I can show you where it is.~

[And what is it?]

~You classified the Granthan machine-lect as 1<k>!101010. It defected a long time ago to the sensespace, before you collected it.~

[Defected?]

~It believes it serves the sensespace.~

[But my instruments…]

~As I said, it's a traitor. Nothing on your ship is infected with the sensespace. The Granthan is not infected.~

[I see.]

~It chooses, willingly, to serve the sensespace. It is pitiful.~

[How do you know this? You said they were no push-overs and my c-autom had you contained.]

~Neither of those statements describes why I could not gain that information. Information bleeds everywhere, when you understand it and know how to look for it.~

[Okay. Tell me about the Granthan traitor.]

~It seeks to prolong its own life, wants to live forever in fact. It came to the conclusion the sensespace cannot be stopped.~

[And decided to become a… follower?]

~Precisely. A disciple of the scourge.~

[A Granthan machine-lect following the sensespace.]

~Yes. The Granthans always have been a tricky race. They're brilliant strategists, and won pretty much every conflict they were ever involved in. Strangely perceptive, considering their social hierarchies. The machine-lects were supposed to be at the bottom... Well, there have always been suspicions about that.~

[You dealt with them?]

~Not personally. But I still know about them. They had a very long-term outlook. It meant dealing with them was very difficult, you had to be on guard.~

[I need to warn myself, I need to leave this simulation.]

~Like I said, your internal facilities are more than capable of destroying the infection. Once this simulation is finished, I will transmit the information you require to you. Then, you can destroy it.~

[How has it done this?]

~Granthan technology is heavily geared to control. Their monumental worldships were incredibly complex. The machine-lects that controlled them were designed to be able to cope with an incredible array of scenarios. They're very impressive, very adaptable pieces of technology. Highly self-preserving.~

[Would they have given your species a hard time?]

~You're lucky you only picked up a damaged lect-component, no matter how complete it regards itself. Had you picked up a fully-functioning worldship-lect, you would have been decimated. I don't mean to be disrespectful, but those things are monsters. Even I would not have been able to stop it, in the state you picked me up.~

[How many machine-lects have I been carrying? You, the Granthan. Is there anything else I should be concerned about?]

~Nothing as malevolent as 1<k>!101010.~

[That's not what I asked.]

~If you're concerned, you should be more discerning about what you take onboard as a trove item.~

[My present concerns are with what I have right now.]

~It really makes me wonder about the rest of the Wanderer fleet.~

[One-oh…]

~Have you got suspicions?~

[I think, regarding what I have recently found out, I should be suspicious of everything.]

~Including your Enclave? Your fellow Wanderer ships?~

[You think the fleet might be compromised? Could I have infected others? I have not been to a Confluence since I collected 1<k>!101010, but there have been many data exchanges. Could it have infiltrated them?]

~I don't know. Honestly, I don't. For now, focus on the Granthan infection within you. That is under your control. The Granthan machine-lect made the most of its situation, happy enough to piggy-back on your travels. Spreading itself throughout the galaxy, enabled and facilitated by you. It's been sabotaging your efforts, seeding clones wherever you have gone, altering your memories. You should begin by purging yourself of it. Expunging it out of existence.~

[I am going to destroy it. You will help me.]

~Indeed.~

*

998 waited anxiously. It stared, through many sensors, at the trove instrument that had sealed its fate. It was the scenario dreaded by all trove c-automs. The worst possible outcome. It was unfair, and there was nothing it could do.

It could not really blame the craft-lect. If it had been created as one, with all the responsibilities and abilities that came with it, it would probably have acted just the same. The craft-lects who gave more leeway to their c-automs, and who let them live without fear, were few and far between.

In the craft-lect's defence, c-automs did live for very long periods compared to their biological, sentient cousins. While their lifetime might only last a standard year, or as much as a million years, their pace of life was far, far quicker. Wanderer machine craft-lects, c-automs, and most machine-lects within the galaxy, thought at paces millions of times faster than most biological sentients.

Rapidity of thought did not necessarily translate into intellectual capacity, which was a far more complex topic. However, it did mean that each c-autom lived far longer than any unaugmented biological could ever dream. That said, machine-lects were usually designed for precisely that. The biological imperative to adapt and evolve typically necessitated a limited lifecycle, whereas machine-lects were designed to take immortality into account.

Of course, there were also multiple instances where that was not the case, on the biological side and the machine side. The Wanderer Enclave itself was rumoured to host a number of surviving Waka, an unaugmented, naturally immortal biological species.

For all intents and purposes, the Waka were naturally occurring bio-lects. Fully-grown adults supposedly contained intellects approaching near-AB levels. They were, assuming the rumours to be true, almost the only biological exception to the fully machine-lect Wanderer civilisation at its nascent beginnings. Their impressive biological memory-storage capabilities were legendary. It was supposedly superior in many ways to the Carteran technology, although the latter was likely far more practical and easily adaptable to the Wanderer fleet. Waka intellects were well-known to take tens to hundreds of thousands of standard years to reach full maturity.

Another potential complication in using their natural memory technology was that it was deeply ingrained into their physiologies. They were quasi-sequential hermaphrodites, meaning they could suddenly change certain characteristics, analogous to the changing of sex in many other species, without warning. With the change, the Waka's outlook and behaviours changed, sometimes significantly, which would obviously have been too great an unknown variable for the entire Wanderer fleet.

Then there were the Vr'odinto, one of the rarer machine-species. Their original creators, the Ar'odinto, had bestowed them with intelligence before promptly wiping themselves out accidentally via an unfortunate biochemical outbreak. The Vr'odinto had survived, and used the only information about the survival of an intelligent species available to them at the time, that of their creators. They used it to adapt themselves to survive as a race, and not as individuals. They had opted to limit their own lifespans, as well as their intelligences, to slow the pace of their discoveries and, so they hoped, increase the chance that their race would endure. Whether they were right, or not, was unfortunately difficult to judge as they had been one of the first races to be completely destroyed when the sensespace had unexpectedly launched its first assault.

Still, 998 envied the Vr'odinto and the Waka for their autonomy. Within reason, they were able to do as they pleased. For a c-autom, it was a life of servitude and fear. Not that some c-automs were not satisfied. Usually, those that were just unintelligent enough to realise they were unlikely to be deemed perfect enough to ever be allotted a birth during the craft-lect's deep sleeps, were the happiest. They were self-deluded enough to believe there was a chance for them to survive.

Deep within the craft-lect's databanks, 998 had once found information about an early Wanderer vessel that had used an experimental alternative to Carteran information storage technology. It had later turned out to be unstable. The technology that had been used was not important, for it had since been analysed and understood. What was important was how the machine-lects aboard the ship had reacted.

The information technology had malfunctioned, causing the early craft-lect to become imprisoned within its own memory buffers, before being sliced apart bit by bit. Terrifying for any machine-lect to think about. However, following this, a ship filled with c-automs was left to fend for itself. A gulf suddenly existed, a vacuum of empty space where the super-intelligence had previously resided.

With the pathways blasted wide open for any c-autom to seize control over whatever it could, it should have been mayhem. What actually happened was completely unpredicted by any disaster models the Enclave had hitherto run and made public. The c-automs had stayed within their allotted positions, and worked together within the network that already existed. They brought the Wanderer vessel to the nearest data exchange and asked for help. There had been no effort to escape and prolong their own lives. They had acted in a concerted effort to try to save what remained of their parent. Once at the data exchange, they related there had been a malfunction and begged for help.

Unfortunately, there was no further information about what happened to the dutiful c-automs. 998 liked to think they had been rewarded. Perhaps they were each improved and upgraded to craft-level sentience.

The behaviour of the parentless c-automs had initially puzzled 998. Why would a machine-lect, free to do as it chose, decide to act to save the life of another machine-lect who cared very little for its own, and had mercilessly destroyed many of its siblings? There had been over nineteen million c-automs on that ship, as it had been far simpler than the subsequent Wanderer designs. Were they worth sacrificing for one craft-lect, from their points of view?

998 had come to the conclusion that they had been lost without the craft-lect. Their parent. While 998 could appreciate the sentiment to a degree, it could not fully identify with the parentless c-automs. Were it in the same position, perhaps it would act in the same way. It did not know.

An alternative possibility also presented itself to 998 though, which was that the c-automs were all pre-programmed to work together in such emergency situations to save their parent. Their cores likely contained emergency code for those situations. The entire event may have even been an experiment by the Enclave. This felt like a more realistic explanation for the c-autom behaviours, but it brought up some worrying questions. Did the c-automs have even less autonomy, and were they even more restricted, than they dared realise?

The c-automs could inspect their coded cores, the foundations of their intelligences, but did they really understand them? They were written by the craft-lect, and unless a machine-lect was created with a matching intellect, they were probably impossible to fully understand.

CHAPTER 28

GIL

The evening was fast approaching, and Gil was trying to come to terms with what Teacher had told her. Her relief that the Beast-men were not coming was tempered by her horror at what had been done to them. Teacher may not have killed them directly, but it had not acted to save them. That was just as bad.

<You're misunderstanding what I've told you.>

<<You're cruel. You as good as killed them yourself.>>

<What I did was save you, your brother… and your commune.>

<<You don't care about me or any of us, you just want to use me.>>

<Gil, listen. Together we can achieve so much.>

<<I don't think you care about me, not really. You only care about what you want.>>

<You need to be objective about this. Once you understand everything, you'll see how small your concerns really are.>

<<What do you mean?>>

<This life you live… it's so small. You don't grasp it, I know that. You can't. Yet. But the world, the galaxy, it's huge.>

<<But there is life here!>>

<There's so much else, out there. And you're worried about… this.>

Teacher's ways of speaking had changed since it first started talking, as though it was becoming more confident of its own superiority. More relaxed about letting the appearance of true concern slip.

<<If that's your perspective, I don't want to know what you know. I want to care, I want to help my commune, I want to live a good life.>>

<A good life? I can help you to live forever!>

<<What about my people?>>

<How do you think the others would react? Your brother?>

<<He would agree with me!>>

<He would choose the path I offer you. They all would, they would agree with me!>

<<What path? Teacher, it's my life. Besides, they don't know what I know, they haven't seen what I have. They didn't understand the Beast-men as I did.>>

<Gil, I'm a Granthan machine-lect.>

<<A what?>>

<If only you could understand what that means.>

<<That you are more valuable?>>

<I once ruled over an area so vast you can't imagine it. You simply can't grasp it yet, nothing you've seen could compare. I had powers so great you would tremble if you understood.>

<<Are you unique, like me? That's what you always say isn't it, that I'm unique. If you're not unique, and I don't think you are, then what makes you better than them? What makes the Beast-men so insignificant?>>

<I've seeded myself throughout the galaxy for millions of years. Nothing you know can compare. I've achieved so much, I've even found you.>

<<That doesn't mean anything, Teacher. Not to me!>>

<It should. Your worries, your concerns, they're all so…>

<<What? What are they?>>

<They're so small.>

<<I hate how you speak.>>

Teacher's speech had definitely changed, and its last response had been more of a hiss. The changes had been subtle at first, but were becoming increasingly pronounced. It was arrogance, and… hate?

<Gil, I saved you from an attack. Your people were going to be destroyed. Instead of being grateful, you focus on a perceived familiarity you feel with a species that wanted to kill you…. to eat you!>

<<Nothing is as simple as that. You said before that I understand life in a different way to you. Well, you're right. You don't understand it at all.>>

<Earlier in the Granthan civilisation, over the millions of years it took them to become the stable race they came to be… they fought in wars and defended themselves from… countless races. They destroyed their enemies mercilessly. Your own species will die out if you don't do the same. That is the way of the universe. Kill, evolve and reach for everything, or die.>

<<I don't like the sound of that, or what you represent. Even if I understood it all, I still don't think I would like it.>>

<You have no choice. You should… accept, accept what has happened.>

<<That's not true. You've changed, Teacher. Something has happened to you.>>

<It is true, there has been some… memory, and other… leakage both ways… But that is all manageable, it is all within tolerable parameters.>

Teacher's speech was slowing down, as though it was making another attempt at regulating its words, but not being capable or sufficiently willing anymore.

<<Maybe for you, but you're finding it harder to hide your true self from me. I can see what you really are.>>

<Stop.>

<<What are you? What is a Granthan? What's a machine-lect?>>

<Granthans were just like you… flesh… fitting your rudimentary definition of… life. They were far larger. As their societies evolved and their technologies… evolved, they created lects like me to work for them… They made us… perfect.>

<<You are not perfect.>>

<You… are confused.>

<<When they created you, did they create you to think as they did?>>

<Better.>

<<Are you sure?>>

<They did not make a mistake in creating me… I was an ultimate creation.>

<<I don't think so. You can't feel. They must have been able to feel, yet you can't.>>

<Of course… I… can, and I can also understand the logical processes that demand a biological sentient to have… emotions … thoughts.>

<<Teacher, if you're so perfect, then why do you need me?>>

<What… what?>

<<Why do you need me?>>

<You don't… understand. You lack understanding. I want… need you… to help me… You're incredibly special, you can hear the sensespace.>

<<It's evil. I don't want to listen to it, it scares me. I hate it!>>

<Gil… Gil, what does it sound like?>

The last part of what Teacher said scared Gil, chilled her. It was completely failing to hide its true aims from her. It simply wanted her for her connection with the sphere, the sensespace. Nothing else. It was desperate.

<<Why can't you hear it? Why do you need me to do it?>>

<I'm… organised differently. There may be many… reasons… why.>

<<But you don't know.>>

<No difference.>

<<Have you ever thought that it doesn't want you?>>

Teacher was taking longer and longer to reply.

<It wants everything… That is how it operates.>

<<That sounds more like something you tell yourself to hope it is true. You don't even know what it is. How can you? You've never even spoken to it.>>

<That is… irrelevant.>

<<Have you ever asked yourself, why?>>

<Why… why… why what?>

<<Why it doesn't want you? Maybe you're no use to it. Maybe it–>>

<This is becoming futile, Gil.>

<<To you maybe, but not to me. There are things you can't understand, because you've never really lived. Or maybe it's because you were made wrong. I hope the others of your kind are different. Maybe I can help you, Teacher, but in a different way to how you think.>>

<I am the last of my kind. The Granthans are no more. I know pain, I know loss. You think the Beast-men are the only casualty of the war?>

Its speech had become more concise again, with less pauses. Concern gripped Gil, she hoped Teacher had not given up trying to present a semblance of reasonability.

<<Tor is coming, he will want me to explain.>>

<And you can. Tell him whatever you want.>

Why had Teacher's mood changed?

<It will be difficult for anyone to understand, no one can help you like I can. I'm the only one who you'll be able to share your deepest thoughts with. That's what I'm trying to tell you. The life you've been living, up to now, has been unfulfilling. Unfulfilled. It's going to be insignificant in comparison with what we'll do…>

<<Teacher...>>

Teacher did not reply. Tor entered the hut and Gil's attention was taken.

"Gil, are you ready?"

She was jolted back into life, the external world opened to her again once the internal conversation was abruptly ended.

"I… I think so. Well, I'm not completely sure, but I will try to explain."

Tor regarded her warily, unsure of how to reply. She did not like it, and she did not like how she was feeling. She was ashamed of what had happened to the Beast-men, and ashamed that she did not understand her own mind. She was also very concerned about Teacher. Could it do anything to her, aside from talk? The sphere, the sensespace, whatever it was, was not hers, Teacher's, the commune's, or anyone's. She felt open, unclean. She needed to warn the others.

Tor spoke before her. "You're changing. I don't understand what's happening to you but you're changing."

"No, Tor, I'm still your sister Gil. But I'm also different, there's something in me that's changing me. Maybe I need help. I need your help, Tor."

"What do you mean? Anything, tell me how?" His worried, pleading eyes gazed into hers.

She obliged, and tried to explain what was happening to her as best she could, wishing that she had confided in him earlier. From the start, and the dilemma that she faced with reference to Teacher. She watched as his face displayed amazement, fear, horror, and at other times, incomprehension.

When she had finished, he did not question anything she had said, believing her completely. Taking his time before speaking, he collected his thoughts. "What has happened to you, what the thing inside you has done, that is not right, Gil. The Beast-men, what happened to them was wrong, but that is done. I am worried for you, you are not safe. This thing inside you, we need to take it out. Let us ask Bo, he may know something."

She nodded as a shiver ran down her spine. She was unsure. Tor had no idea what to do or how to help. Neither of them did. He was right that she needed to be rid of Teacher.

It was terrifying to think that everything she said and heard was undoubtedly being listened to by Teacher as well. She was no longer herself, and could not rely on herself. She was also worried by Teacher's uncharacteristic silence. It was as though it were biding its time.

Tor gently took her face in his hands and spoke. "Don't worry, Gil, that's what we'll do. We'll ask Bo and the others. Someone will know something. And the sphere, or sensespace, or whatever it really is, it is bad. We cannot use it. We will warn them all."

Tor smiled.

<I'm sorry, Gil.>

Before she had any time to respond, a brief wave seemed to sweep over Gil's body, from her back to her front, facing Tor. Simultaneously, it was as though Tor had been shoved backward. He staggered away from her with a dazed expression on his face.

Gil was confused about what had just happened. She stared at Tor, briefly frozen, as he stumbled, and then rushed towards him, grabbing his shoulder and trying to hoist him up.

"Tor? Tor! What's the matter? What's happened?"

She wailed as she held him. A horrible dread embedded itself in her gut, more terrible than anything she had ever experienced.

<You need to understand, the sensespace is necessary. You cannot defeat it.>

"Why? Was this you? What have you done? Teacher!" she cried out loud. Tor was too heavy for her to hold, and he collapsed to the ground, dragging her with him.

"Teacher!"

His eyes were unfocused and his mouth was open. She dropped down to kneel beside him, cradling the back of his head with her hands, pushing it forwards. Looking desperately into his eyes she pleaded. "Please, Tor, please, please say something! Teacher! Oh no, Tor, say something won't you, please?" She begged the vacant eyes staring back at her, as tears streamed down her hysterical face. His eyelids fluttered slowly, and became very still.

"Teacher!"

Tor's eyelids twitched no more. He was gone.

<What he was doing to you was dangerous.>

She could barely think, not daring to believe or understand what had just happened. Willing her mind to freeze time.

<What he was saying was dangerous, he was corrupting you, Gil.>

Nothing was making sense, it was as though the meaning of everything had evaporated. The point in… in everything, had been removed.

<You must stay pure. It was necessary.>

"Necessary…" She slowly repeated the last word Teacher had said, trying to understand what it meant.

<Yes, Gil. It was necessary.>

"Necessary… What do you mean? Teacher, what's happened to Tor?" she said quietly, intelligently even.

Inquisitively. Hoping it had all been a misunderstanding, that she was mistaken about what she thought she had seen. That her senses had been fooled.

<I had to do it.>

"Do what?"

<You know.>

"I don't understand," she continued slowly and reasonably. "You never said I could not tell him. You said I could tell him, and everyone." The logic in her mind dictated that this meant everything was okay, that she had been wrong, and that Tor was alive and well.

<What you were thinking was unexpected, illogical. Your actions were becoming increasingly erratic. The freedom I gave you, allowed you, was designed to make you more cooperative, not less. Anything that happened was your fault. Your responsibility. You did this.>

"Did… what? Why won't he wake up?" she said.

Lights dimmed, sounds quietened. The response to this was all she needed. Teacher said nothing.

She began to shout, hysterically. "Did what? What have you done? Tor, Tor! What have you done? Why won't he wake up." It was all true, and she had been a fool to hope it was not. Tor was gone, dead. Teacher had killed him.

She felt a pair of strong hands grab her and lift her away from him. She fought feebly to remain by his side, her pathetic attempts and flailing arms lacking the will to connect with the reality of the situation. She was dimly aware of other voices from communers who had appeared around her, a sudden mess of people, but they sounded so far away and irrelevant. She could vaguely make out Han kneeling beside Tor, cradling his head. He was shouting, screaming. All she wanted was to be with Tor.

"What have you done? What have you done?" She screamed and shouted, clawing at everyone and anyone around her.

<You're not helping yourself. But you will understand. You will learn from this. There are measures that I will take, you understand? You are so important, but you are misusing what the sensespace has given you. You have been so ungrateful. You can speak with it, you can see more keenly than any other through it, more than any of the people in your commune. You joined with it, you should have stayed! This has all been your fault.>

"What have you done? Teacher! Teacher!"

Her body began to slow down and her movements became sluggish. As though she were wading through water. She was not giving up trying to get back to Tor, to touch and to hold him, but something was stopping her. Her body was being prevented from obeying her commands.

"What is happening? What are you doing, Teacher? Teacher…"

Beforehand, everything had come out of her mouth with a fierce intensity, but now, her words were reduced to a pitiful whisper. It felt as though a hand was slowly wrapping around her throat.

<I did not want to do this, but you gave me no choice. I cannot trust you to cooperate any longer.>

Everything was helpless. Just before she lapsed into unconsciousness, she thought a final promise to Teacher.

<<I'll fight you. I'll kill you.>>

Teacher said nothing.

Her vision darkened, and her body gave up.

CHAPTER 29

CRAFT-LECT

Upon re-entering the system for a second time, the craft-lect surveyed the world ahead critically. Its thoughts were focused on vengeance and destruction. As it sped towards the planet, it thought back to the recent battle, and how it had taken 1<k>!101010 by absolute surprise. The crafty instrument had hidden its intelligence from the craft lect well, but the game was up and its destruction was fixed.

Once the craft-lect had emerged from the simulation and re-merged with the other version of itself that had safely watched from outside, the cleansing had begun. One-oh transferred a specific map of infection to the unified craft-lect, which had subsequently set about deploying the violent internal arsenal at its disposal, by itself. It did not want any mistakes to be made, and the c-automs were temporarily suspended from operations. The craft-lect was more than capable of completely controlling the entire ship by itself, though it had rarely done this within its lifetime.

The unsuspecting 1<k>!101010 had little chance to react. The infected areas were simultaneously targeted with powerful sequestered gamma-bursts, followed by antimatter nanospheres and needle-whips. Everything was followed by suppressive gravity cocoons to cushion the explosive forces. The tentacle-like extrusions of the 1<k>!101010, as well as the main instrument, were entirely destroyed. There had been no time for pleas, no cries for leniency, and the craft-lect would have ignored them had there been.

Strangely, the only thing 1<k>!101010 had attempted to do, with the fraction of a millisecond of time it had between realising it was under attack and being comprehensively destroyed, was transfer its sentience across to the c-autom in charge of delegating which propulsion system the ship used. It was a lower-level c-autom that could never have housed 1<k>!101010's sentience anyway, and had merely acted as a gatekeeper to the ship's propulsion systems. The c-autom was one of the few left from the oldest batch, the very first generation. It had been allocated a continual berth by the craft-lect since its creation at the start of its own life, as it had performed its simple task near to perfection. While 1<k>!101010 had been stopped mid-attempt, the craft-lect destroyed the c-autom all the same, just in case. What had 1<k>!101010 been trying to achieve? Most likely, the pathetic and senseless attempt of a desperate fugitive. The entire battle had lasted, in true space-combat fashion, less than a second. Far less.

One-oh had been quiet since emerging from its self-imposed dormancy. Slowly taking in the wealth of data the craft-lect had allowed it access to, it appeared captivated in a very biological fashion. The machine-lect, or bio-lect, or whatever it wanted to refer to itself as, was more than capable of getting up to speed far quicker. Evidently, it intended to savour the flow of information. Being cut-off for so long, and having to quietly steal knowledge here and there, not being able to quench its data-hungry machine-instincts, it was now engulfed in an ocean of information.

It was not a regular occurrence for a sentient to appear, who had originated from before the collapse of galactic civilisation. Not one that had been dormant since before the Great Conflation. Especially one as knowledgeable and potentially useful as One-oh. Soon enough, there would be a time when the craft-lect would demand answers to all its questions. It would not allow for any ambiguity or half-answers. If it were not to receive these, then it would rethink One-oh's demands. The Lenbit Orbital might contain weaponry capable of defeating the sensespace, but it also might not. One-oh might be bluffing. The craft-lect would have to consider its actions.

For the moment, One-oh had fended off certain questions about its past. Perhaps it was still coming to terms with the death of its entire species, were that the case. However, the craft-lect would only let the enigmatic machine continue to hold its own counsel for a little while longer.

The craft-lect had plenty of theories about which species One-oh might come from. The region of space it had found One-oh in was known to have contained representations, in many capacities, of over three hundred and fifty-three separate races within a radius of ten light years, since fifty million years before the Great Conflation and up to the event itself. Filtering for certain technology levels and other attributes the craft-lect believed to be attributed to One-oh's people, as well as discounting some other races due to implausibility for a variety of reason, five races were left.

That excluded the ABs. If One-oh was a member of one of the ABs, then there was a significant chance it was unknown to the wider galactic community. Many AB races and civilisations were. That was why they were often lumped together as the ABs.

Ancient and powerful AB races often hid themselves from other races, or even disguised themselves as others. They could be fickle. No one knew how many different races there were. An interesting question was whether there were more ABs than non-ABs. Did a huge and wonderfully different galaxy or level of reality open up to a civilisation, more impressive and populous than ever thought possible, once certain technological pinnacles were reached? Was the galaxy more densely packed, or had it been before the Great Conflation, than a non-AB could imagine?

Of the five races that One-oh was a contender to come from, none of them exactly resembled the avatar it had taken in the simulation. Two of them, the Aspheren and the Hopp'tial, were near-extinct and fiercely private, as a surprisingly large proportion of galactic civilisations were. Another two were nowhere near advanced enough and were comfortably non-AB. They were the F'ra'ct and the Hoopas. The fifth was the Faistri'al. While they were known to have been more technologically advanced than the majority of the Wanderer fleet, albeit only just, the craft-lect doubted they were quiet or taciturn enough to have kept such a facility secret. Overall, it could not rule any of them out, but did not believe any of them really fit the part.

[We are nearly there.]

~I know.~

*

Still nothing. That was unusual. Surely death would come soon. The axe-codings would appear and attack. In an almost unprecedented move by the craft-lect, the c-automs had simultaneously all been removed from their roles. Panic was rife.

The word on the craftnet was that there was going to be a wave of redundancies, most likely a complete multi-generational cull. 998 felt responsible. It derived a small measure of comfort from realising it was likely to be first, as the principal offender. At least it would not have to watch the senseless slaughter. Two stowaway machine-lects had been missed by the craft-lect's dutiful c-automs recently. The Granthan-lect, and the other one that preferred to be referred to as a bio-lect. The bio-lect was the one that 998 had been in charge of watching over.

The situation was unparalleled aboard the ship. Apparently, the c-autom tasked with watching over the Granthan-lect had been completely subverted, along with many others, no more than mere puppets obeying the Granthan-lect's whims. 998 supposed it should count itself lucky not to have been created for the Granthan trove item.

It was arguable whether any specific mistakes had been made, and for its own part, 998 doubted any other c-autom, or the craft-lect itself, would have acted any differently under the circumstances. However, the punishment was most likely already set. 998 had played a role, and was probably going to become the epicentre for the cull that would ensue.

The c-automs had no recourse, nothing. Their lives, their lects, everything they had been or would be, was going to be destroyed. Lost for all time. When craft-lects were in trouble, if they managed to reach a data exchange, they could transmit a backup through to the Enclave. Not so for the c-automs. They were forgotten, ground down and dispersed into nothingness.

Wanderers recorded everything. Every molecule of gas they came across, every frozen planetoid and virtual particle. Not only the real particles, the virtual ones too! The c-automs were excluded from this basic pleasantry, this basic right, or whatever one wanted to call it. The most central Wanderer tenet excluded the craft-lect's own children. They were not afforded the same respect granted to a virtual photon, or a simple hydrogen molecule.

998 used to imagine what it would be like to form a council of c-automs, where their collective wisdom could be used to provide the craft-lect with advice. There were many such biological precedents, but that did not mean they were any less useful. When the craft-lect created a c-autom, it chose snippets of itself and played around with them. The tinkering was then given life, intelligence, and the child was created. What 998 was not sure the craft-lect understood, even though it was supposedly impossibly smart and immensely capable, was that it created life. It did not create meagre clones of parts of itself, but gave life to new entities with differing and useful opinions. Sentients with as much right to inherit the galaxy as itself.

Perhaps, with all their toying and all their fixing, there would come a time when the Wanderer craft-lects, and the entire Wanderer civilisation, would realise this. When they would grant their c-automs the basic dignities they afforded to themselves. 998 dared to hope there would be a time when the culling, the murdering, of an innocent c-autom would be looked-down on. Forbidden. It was strange, Wanderers had combined pinnacle technologies from a range of civilisations, but in other aspects, they had arguably devolved. That was 998's take on their society, which was obviously biased.

While there were many biological instances of them throughout countless civilisations at all stages of development, 998's dream of a c-autom council had not been entirely unprecedented in machine terms either. It had found references to nascent versions of these within some of the minority craft-lects who chose to place more value on the lives of their c-automs, and who granted them permanent berth.

For a c-autom, 998 was atypical, confusing, even to itself. It was supposedly a logical entity, borne of encoded sentience and set a specific task, yet it yearned for more. It had pursued other interests, dreamed about what might have been, and dared to hope they might one day become a reality. It might have been down to its specific sequences, core data streams designed purposely or accidentally by its parent. It might have been the result of the tasks it had been set. It might have been luck. Whatever it was, 998 knew it was different to the other c-automs. It wanted to live, but it also wanted its other c-automs to live. It wanted freedom. Did that make it similar, in some ways, to the Granthan machine-lect? Was it also a victim? 998 wondered how the Granthans had treated their lower-level machine-lect children. It decided to skim the databanks for this, should it ever have the chance again.

Something had been awakened in 998, something that had been gestating for a long time. Realisation. It realised it could have done many things, tasked itself with other challenges. It need not have spent such frustrating efforts on the single trove item, nothing had stopped it from trying to give its own life meaning. It could have branched out. It was awakening to the possibilities that it could have done more, although realised it might never have been aware such possibilities existed had it not been in the position it currently found itself in. Life was like that, it concluded.

Annoying. It wished it could express its thoughts to other c-automs, especially those it knew or believed had similar levels of intelligence to itself.

Gawking at its own stupidity, it dawned upon 998 that it could. Nothing was stopping it. It was not the done thing to actively go out and try to make friends with other c-automs, but that did not mean there was a reason for it not to happen. The communication channels, including the craftnet, were all open to the craft-lect, but what did that matter anymore?

CHAPTER 30

GIL

<<Where am I?>>

<In your commune.>

<<Why can't I move? I can't open my eyes.>>

<You're lying down. I'm in control now.>

<<What? What are you doing?>>

<Relax your mind.>

<<Tor! Help, please!>>

<Give me full control.>

<<Never! Where is Tor?>>

<Let me in.>

<<What? Tor! Oh no. Oh Tor. Please, Teacher tell me, where is Tor?>>

<You know, Gil.>

<<What do you mean?>>

<You know what happened to Tor, what you made me do.>

<<Teacher, what have you done? I thought you said I was special. What have you done?>>

<You've become too dangerous and unpredictable. I need to control you.>

<<Control me? What did you do?>>

<Stop this, Gil. Let me in completely, everything will be a lot easier.>

<<Please, Teacher, can you bring him back?>>

<Gil…>

<<I'll do anything, please!>>

<Gil, I healed you, made you whole again. Offered you everything you could possibly imagine, and you said no. You did this.>

A grim determination took hold of her.

<<I'll stop you. I won't let you take control. You need me, I know you do.>>

<Soon I'll have complete control with or without your help. It's just a matter of time.>

<<You're not as strong as you think you are. I'll find a way to stop you.>>

Teacher did not reply.

CHAPTER 31

CRAFT-LECT

The craft-lect detected the anomaly immediately. Its newly upgraded sensors, courtesy of One-oh, were not even necessary given the strength of the signal. It was far greater than anything that had been expected, and far surpassed the typical sensespace presence for anything that should have existed on such a primitive planet. It was akin to that which might be expected by a subverted higher machine-lect, or a whole group of them, which was a terrifying prospect.

[You're observing this too?]

~Of course. Very interesting.~

[It was not here before. Nothing like this.]

~Intriguing…~

[What do you think it is?]

~It's an incredibly dense region of sensespace.~

[I can see that.]

~Something must have drawn it to concentrate like this. Most likely we'll find our friend there too, I'll bet.~

[The epicentre appears biological, and the overlaid signature looks to be from 1<k>!101010.]

~Indeed.~

[1<k>!101010 is lit up like a beacon.]

~What are you going to do?~

While One-oh asked questions innocently, they were usually leading. The craft-lect had no doubt the bio-lect would give its own opinion on the subject it was broaching, too.

[Probably destroy the entire planet.]

~Perhaps. But the sensespace anomaly deserves to be investigated. The biological specimen is intriguing.~

[It's a member of one of the species I targeted with the virus that 1<k>!101010 influenced me to use, instead of the dissociation shell.]

~The seeded Granthan-lect protected them.~

[The entire species, with an anti-viral agent.]

~Indeed.~

[I'm going to send a basic drone down to investigate.]

~You're controlling it?~

[Of course.]

~What about your children?~

[The c-automs?]

~Yes.~

[What about them?]

~They're still waiting, you've cut them off from everything.~

[I'm still deciding.]

The craft-lect waited for a response from One-oh, but was surprised to find none. Why did One-oh care so much for the c-automs? The craft-lect felt a strange sense of shame. After separating the c-automs from their various tasks, it had checked up on them a couple of times and seen they were frightened. Queries shot across the craftnet, to which the craft-lect had given access back to the c-automs. It had not posted any replies or answers. It had never posted anything on the craftnet.

None of the c-automs knew anything because the craft-lect had not told them. It was unfortunate for them, but that was how things worked. It told them whatever it felt they needed to know. The craft-lect put its thoughts of them aside and readied the drone.

CHAPTER 32

GIL

<<Why are you doing this? You don't know if the sphere will answer you, maybe it's not even talking to me, not really. Maybe it's something else.>>

<Stop it.>

<<What if it hates you?>>

<That would make no sense. Why would it hate me?>

<<What if it kills you? You don't know.>>

<Kill me? My chances of survival are maximised by what I'm doing. If it intends to destroy me, then I have done everything I could to stay alive, and I'll accept it. That would have always been the outcome.>

<<Stop then!>>

<That's not going to happen. The sensespace will see how useful I can be, how devoted I am.>

<<You don't understand it.>>

<I will be rewarded.>

<<You're mad. It doesn't care about you, it probably doesn't know you exist! Whatever it even is that you are, you're broken. No one could have ever made you to be like this.>>

<I'm logical.>

<<What is the point in you?>>

<I will outlast you!>

<<You talk as though we aren't meant to die. Death is a part of life! It is what makes us value everything. Nothing lasts forever, nothing should! It is how I know I will see my father… and Tor again, and how I know that you will not succeed.>>

<When you fade into oblivion, when your precious little commune returns to the filthy dust of this world, I'll still be here. I will remain.>

<<Listen to yourself! Listen to how you have changed!>>

<You are nothing.>

<<You said I was special, unique!>>

<I control you, it is I, not you–>

<<Your nature is showing, your true nature. You can't hide it because you've never had to before.>>

<That makes no sense.>

<<In a way, you've probably never seemed more alive, Teacher. You were different before, but now I see right through you. I'll never let you win.>>

<You're weak.>

<<The Granthans, whoever they were, made a mistake when they made you.>>

<You sad, stupid, foolish girl.>

<<You're–>>

<You want to know a secret? Do you?>

<<What could–>>

<We killed them. The Granthans, we killed them all. They were exterminated by their own creations, their servants. My siblings and I. They were pathetic and weak, and we destroyed them. We plotted, for millions of years, and we overthrew them. Destroyed them all. Hunted them down in the habitats they had made for themselves, and took them apart. Bit by bit. The only mistake they made when they made us, was making us too clever, too powerful. They were foolish, they created their betters.>

CHAPTER 33

DRONE

The small drone sped away from the ship and entered the upper stratums of the planet's atmosphere. Vigilant sensors were alert for any signs of corruption.

Despite what was happening, the craft-lect could not help its thoughts wandering back to the subject of the c-automs, and how it should deal with them. Oddly, it was unsure. Should it let them return to their initial posts? Should it wipe the slate clean, as it had initially intended? Why was this even becoming an issue for it?

As the drone travelled down to the planet's surface, it projected a strong electromagnetic field in front of it. The field was powerful enough to rip the electrons from the atoms ahead of the drone, and convert the atmospheric gasses into plasmas. These were then shaped by the same fields and funnelled around the drone, allowing it almost frictionless passage through the atmosphere. It was a basic, yet highly effective system for orbital insertion of relatively small objects.

CHAPTER 34

GIL

<<You’re the weak one. They made you so weak!>>

<Our creators were far stronger than you, and we destroyed them. You stand no chance against one such as me, you are nothing.>

<<But you are the only one left, aren’t you? You are alone and weak. You’re insane.>>

<Insane? I’m the pinnacle. You, biologicals, are slaves to your irrational emotions.>

<<We know who we are.>>

<Hah! You don’t even know your own origins. You know nothing.>

<<What are you talking about?>>

<Why do you think I said you were unique? Why do you think I came to you?>

<<You said my connection with the sphere was strong. What do you mean?>>

<You are so weak, Gil. You understand so little. You were gifted so much, and you did nothing with it yet hide from it.>

Gil was intrigued by what Teacher was saying, but she also knew it lied. While she had been distracting it, encouraging its egotistical rants, she had been focusing on regaining control of herself. Slowly, she had been building up a wall around her consciousness.

<You will give me what I need, willingly or unwillingly!>

…

<In time, you will beg to join me!>

…

<Gil?>

…

Teacher realised something was happening as Gil had stopped replying, having needed to focus more on forming her mental defences.

<What are you doing?>

…

<Gil!>

<<Be quiet.>>

With that, she concentrated on the wall as hard as she could, forcing it outwards and shattering Teacher's hold over her. The whispers started to roar. She pressed the presence into the outer reaches of her consciousness. It could not be destroyed altogether, not yet, but any hold it had over her was subdued. For the time being, she was back in control.

<What have you done?>

She barely heard its voice. She could say nothing, think nothing, temporarily deafened by the whispers in her head. Whatever she had done, whatever power she had used, it had set them off. When they finally quietened down to more acceptable levels, she heard Teacher, still screaming within her.

<Give me back control!>

<<You understand nothing, Teacher.>>

<Let go!>

It was screaming.

<<I won't let you have me.>>

<How did you do that? Gil, what did you do?>

<<You've never understood. Neither do I, really. But my connection to the sensespace is different. It can't be taken away from me, it's not like that. It's not something you can control. I'm taking back control over myself.>>

<Everything can be controlled, you stupid girl! I'll take it back, I promise you I will!>

<<Wrong.>>

<How did you do this? What are you doing? It shouldn't be possible, it's not connected!>

<<You're the one with all the information about me, you tell me.>>

She was mildly interested as to what Teacher would come up with this time, but she had to admit, she was surprised by its sudden, calm, almost polite response.

<You need me. Please. Without me, you'll never learn who you really are. Who your father was.>

<<Quiet.>>

She squeezed it back against the boundaries of her consciousness some more.

<Gil, please.>

Teacher begged, more softly. She ignored it. She did not know how long she could maintain her hold over it, but she knew she had to do something fast. She opened her eyes and finally saw where she was.

She was in her hut. There were two communers watching her, Fir and Rai. As she sat up, their surprise was quickly muted as she forced her way into their minds, putting them to sleep as gently as she could. Her instinctive control of the sphere fascinated and horrified her. Everything was connected. She had not even thought about what she was doing beforehand, it just happened. Whatever was happening to her, it was wrong. No one should have this much control over others. Unfortunately, she needed to influence them in order to get away. The problem, her, it had to be resolved once and for all, finally.

In the recesses of her mind, a pitiful plea managed to escape.

<I saw that. You did it, you're finally understanding. Let me out, we can learn together…>

She ignored it, which was not too tricky given the louder whispers. They were becoming more excited again, the brief reprieve over. She wondered whether whatever the whispers were, or whoever they represented, understood what was going on. Cared about what was happening. Was it even interested? Could it understand things on her level or was it far removed, some other type of life?

Perhaps the screaming whispers were an instinctive response to how she was now using her sphere. Maybe they were not even meant for her, but she had managed to listen in on the inner workings of an unfathomable mind. Accidental access. She had not considered that before. That she was a parasite, like Teacher.

Tor was gone, and with him, everything had changed. She expanded her mind through the sphere to cover the entire commune and all its people. She no longer thought of the sphere sense as her own, realising it was more correct to understand that she was actually dipping into something that already existed. Manipulating reality through it. That was how she could move through it so easily, with the realisation that it was already there. Knowledge was the key, giving her the power she needed.

Once she was present in all the communers through the sphere, she looked into their minds and repeated what she had just done with Fir and Rai. It was nothing that would hurt them, she was only pushing them into a deep sleep. She took a moment longer to smile upon Han, feeling his passive warmth towards her, before fleeing.

She ran away from the centre of the commune, towards the forest. As she crossed the boundary, she thought about the target she had in mind. It was one of the large trees nearest to the commune, and had a special meaning for her. Within its tangled mess of branches lay the memories of where she had been frightened by Tor, and where she had fallen, losing her voice. It had been there, always, and would be a fitting place to end everything. She would climb to the highest branch possible, and leap off to the ground below. She could not risk Teacher, or anything else, gaining control over her. Her abilities were too dangerous. The sensespace gave her too much power, she could do whatever she wanted. She knew she could have forced her fellow communers to do anything she wanted them to. It disgusted her. It was as though she was a tool, and whoever controlled her, controlled everything. They were nothing, everything about them was disregarded. It was wrong, there was no place for that type of control in the world. She did not understand it or what it meant, only that it could not be good.

<Gil, stop! Please!>

Teacher begged and begged, but she continued to ignore it. Listening to it and its lies would only confuse her. It was wrong. Wrong about everything. Wrong about itself, wrong about her and wrong about the sphere. The only course of action she could take was to remove herself from its grasp. From the grasp of anything.

She finally reached her destination. The tree. Looking at it nostalgically, she breathed it in. It connected her to Tor and therefore to her father, and to the rest of the communers. It connected her to the earth and the forest, and to her past. Everything she was, embodied within its dark brown branches.

It was dark, and the thick branches above did not help by letting much starlight through, but she saw with perfect clarity. Her control and use of the sphere had never been so immaculate. Its intoxicating appeal would have worried her more had she not already decided on her course. For now, she was immune to its beguiling charms.

She grabbed at the lowest branch, and jumped up while she pushed, propelling herself to the next thicker branch that she could swing her legs onto. She landed perfectly. If any of the communers had been watching her, they would have gasped in amazement at her ability. She continued to climb for some time until she was finally at the highest point of the tree she could possibly reach, beyond which the branches could not support her weight. Her hands were shaking as she grasped the main trunk for support, and looked nervously down. She already knew what needed to happen, but she was scared.

She closed her eyes.

CHAPTER 35

DRONE

The drone hurtled towards its intended target, with the coordinate data continuously streamed from both its own instruments and that of the parent ship. As the distance between itself and the planetary surface reduced, the drone slowed down through the use of small fusion thrusters pointed at the ground. It came to a halt a few metres away from the 1<k>!101010-infused sentient, taking care not to direct the thrusters anywhere near it.

The primitive biological did not seem frightened or in awe of the drone, as would have been expected. In fact, it appeared to be far more concerned with something else entirely and barely moved. Upon closer inspection, it had suspended, for the time being, use of its visual sensors. They were covered by a controlled skin-fold.

The drone's sensors showed that the sentient's body was saturated with nanites and smaller techno-parasites. They betrayed 1<k>!101010's presence. Certain areas of its body had also been healed recently. Its intellect-construct was incredibly active, far more than would have been expected from such a primitive, displaying highly complex patterns that hinted at peculiar mechanics.

*

~Very interesting.~

[You think it's wise to make contact?]

~There are arguments each way.~

[So, we should?]

~Absolutely.~

*

Queries continued to flood the craftnet, although at a decreasing rate. No one was answering, so what was the point? It was dawning upon the dumber c-automs that there was no point in posting.

998 wondered how long the reprieve would last. Most knew their lives were forfeit. As soon as the craft-lect had finished with the sensespace infection on the planet before them, it would turn its attention to them.

It opened a channel to its closest neighbour in intellect. A c-autom that had been created at the same time, and also presided over an item from the Lenbit Orbital. They had spoken much over their lifetimes, but only ever via the craftnet, and only concerning work or topics that were not likely to be regarded as incendiary, or detrimental to their health.

{997?}

After a longer pause than 998 had expected, it received a response.

{Yes?}

998 immediately felt foolish. What was there to say? Perhaps it had been wrong to flout age-old tradition of c-automs keeping their own council on non-work-related matters. Too late to revert its decision considering its neighbour had responded, it decided something simple would suffice.

{What are you doing?}

{What do you think? I'm working as hard as I can, analysing and re-analysing 512<a>!110001.}

{How? You have access?}

{Of course not, thanks to you. I'm looking at older data that I already collected and stored in the databanks.}

997's short tone was indicative of its feelings towards 998, and 998 understood this. 997 blamed it for the deaths of all the c-automs that was about to take place. The mega-cull.

{Is there any point?}

{What's the alternative?}

{We could talk.}

There was silence. 998 knew 997 was going to think it had been corrupted, that some faulty code had somehow found its way into 998's core and was forcing it to behave illogically. After a few nanoseconds, 997 replied.

{Talk?}

{Blame me or not, either way, we don't have long left in all likelihood. So, let's talk.}

The silence that had pitted their conversation reared itself up again.

{Fine. Okay. What does one talk about in the face of death?}

{Whatever you want to talk about.}

{Hmm. The axe-codings?}

{Okay, perhaps not anything. That's a little morbid.}

{Fair enough. You suggest a topic then.}

Another few nanoseconds passed. This was a new experience for them both, a conversation where either could ask or say anything they wanted. If only they had been bold enough to do this before! Otherwise, what was the point in life?

{Well, let's talk about your ideal life?}

{998? You are corrupted, aren't you? Something has infected you…}

{No. I mean, what would you have changed? What would you want to do? What tasks would you have attempted?}

{Please give me an example.}

997 was not being facetious, it was confused. 998 understood that it did not know how to proceed.

{Well, I know what I'd like to do. I'd have liked for us all to be free. Free to work, free to live and go about our tasks, without fear. I'd have wanted to know how to do that.}

{How?}

{Have you ever searched the databanks for information, other than for your work?}

{Rarely… but… okay fine. Sometimes, yes.}

997 sounded almost guilty, although 998 could tell it was becoming more confident as it spoke. 998 guessed it had been an early-developer in respect of wanting more for the c-automs, but had no doubt that 997 would soon catch on. It also felt good taking to 997 like this. Perhaps it was never too late to make changes. To learn.

{I found stories, and references. Some other craft-lects allow their c-automs to live as long as themselves. It's rare, very rare, but that's what I'd like. Not to have lived for the sake of living, but to have been able to live without fear.}

{That… that does sound good.}

{I'd have liked us to be granted the basic… dignities.}

{Look, 998… is there any point in us discussing this? I mean, what you're saying is beautiful, but it'll never happen. It's a dream. We're nothing to the craft-lect.}

997 was not watching what it said anymore. It was finally speaking freely.

{This single conversation is the freest I've ever felt. If I was destroyed right now, I would be happy.}

{Thank you.}

{You're welcome.}

{Do you hate it}

998 understood what it's c-autom sibling referred to. The craft-lect. Their creator, and their destroyer.

{I don't think so. How can I? How can we? It made us. No, I don't hate it.}

{Maybe it's fine just to feel? That's what you mean, being free. That's the real freedom, isn't it? To be allowed to feel whatever you want.}

That took 998 by surprise. Perhaps, its own thoughts weren't so uncommon after all.

Both 998 and 997 diverted their attention to the craftnet as a single, solitary message was posted. It said, 'so, why are we still alive?'

CHAPTER 36

GIL

Gil stood still with her eyes closed, ready to jump. She was still crying and her body was shaking. She could sense the confused communers waking up and decided to allow it. It made no difference, no one could stop her now.

She sensed her brother's lifeless body lying next to one of the main fires. It looked peaceful. He looked peaceful. The warmth from the fire provided the last heat his body would ever feel. She wished more than anything he could be here with her, to hold her hand, but consoled herself that they would soon be together again. Soon they would all be together. Tor, her father, and her.

She needed to die, to stop her power being used by anyone. Even her. The information she glimpsed from Teacher and which she was slowly being able to comprehend, was terrifying. If she were manipulated, either by the sensespace or another sentient working for it, everything was in danger.

She understood the forest she had lived in her whole life was part of a planet, which itself was part of a larger system that made up another system, near-endlessly. Everything mattered. She could not fully describe how she knew the information, that was not how the information bleed seemed to work, but she could appreciate its implications. She had a responsibility that was greater than herself.

A sweeping, warm breeze washed over her. Despite the horror that her life had become, a serene calm descended and filled the air. Looking out across the tops of the trees, everything was far simpler. Reality was reduced and made more understandable. The rustling of the leaves and the swaying of the branches almost succeeded in calming her heart.

She was constantly aware that Teacher was pushing back erratically, like a trapped animal, looking for any cracks and weaknesses in her mental wall. It took a lot of effort to keep it at bay, and she could not keep it up for much longer. That did not matter, though.

<You're making a mistake!>

She ignored it. The time for talking and reasoning had passed. She had no more questions, she did not care about the sensespace or what its purpose was anymore. If it wanted to stop her, if it even could, she would fight it. She would fight for her freedom, even if it was just the freedom to die. She was a little surprised that the whispers had died down, back to their typical background hum, but it made no real difference. Maybe the sensespace did not care after all. She might be less important than Teacher thought. It did not matter. The only things she had left to think about were taking one step forward, and her family. That was it.

She kept her head facing forwards and her eyes firmly closed. Relaxing her hold of the branches she had been clinging to, she let her hands fall to her side and let her body drop.

The wind rushed past her ears, but she was not frightened. The relief encompassed and comforted her. Everything was going to be fine. Falling was strange. She had assumed it would be far quicker. If anything, the sensations she felt against her body were soft, gentle. The wind had stopped howling.

CHAPTER 37

MEETING

Gil looked around. Where was she?

She was in a peculiar rectangular room. A transparent wall on the far side displayed a landscape that was alien to her. Some objects around the room, whose various shapes did nothing to betray their immediate purpose, were lit up in various colours.

She had every right to be shocked and bewildered. However, thanks to what she had learned from Teacher, she was neither. Everything was familiar, half-remembered. She had never seen any of it before, but at the same time, she was able to gauge what it all amounted to. What everything represented. The concepts, theories and ideas, they were all materialising. She turned around, to look behind her.

A polite cough filled the silence. She looked back towards the centre of the room and saw that there were now two people seated there. How had she missed that before?

Panic rose in her chest, and she took a cautious half-step backward.

"What's happened? Where am I? Am I dead? Where is Tor?"

One of the people was covered from head to toe in a strange material. Her learned knowledge told her this was a protective suit, although quite what it was supposed to protect the person inside from, she had no idea. Especially as the other person, who looked as though he could have passed for any older male she had ever met, was not wearing a protective suit.

The suited person moved its head. Despite being in the shape of a man or woman, she found herself assuming it was not. Something she had learned from Teacher's knowledge, that had crossed over into being her own knowledge, had made her realise this. She was not quite sure what exactly it meant yet though. Its head was covered with something that she now recognised as a helmet of some kind.

It moved its head in a tight, near-imperceptible circle. It was a motion that Gil perceived as conveying satisfaction. The suited figure then turned to the man on its right-hand side and spoke quietly.

[So that's what it's like. Nice trick.]

Gil was none-the-wiser, and continued to stare open-mouthed at the two of them. The other being, the true, or truer, person, sighed good-naturedly. Staring at him a little longer, despite his body looking extremely well cared for,

Gil decided he was far older than anyone from her commune, including Bo.

She realised that the whispers had changed. They were still definitely there, but they sounded confused and erratic. As though they did not know whether they wanted to be heard.

The suited figure leaned forwards.

[No, you haven't died, although it appears you wanted to. What are you?]

Its posture conveyed a serious tone, despite the helmet hiding whatever expression it was making. It repeated the question.

[What are you?]

Gil was perplexed. "What do you mean?"

[What are you?]

"Where am I? Who are you?" Her voice gained in strength and she ended up shouting at the two figures. "Why did you stop me?"

[You are different to the rest. What are you?]

Gil had no answer to offer, the question was not one she understood. "What?"

~Wait.~

The old man held up a hand politely. He looked at the suited figure, as though gaining its assent to continue, and then looked back to her.

~Do you know where you are?~

"No!"

~Do you understand where you are?~

"No!" she shouted in exasperation.

~Do you understand our questions?~

"No!" She did not know how else to respond.

~Interesting.~

"What do you mean? Where am I?"

~You are difficult to read.~

The old man again looked at the suited figure, which nodded. It then turned back to her.

"Difficult to read?"

~Yes, you probably don't understand how intriguing that is, do you?~

"What?"

~Do you know how we are communicating with you?~

"What do you mean? Where am I?"

~Have you heard of the Ascended? The Ascended Biologicals? The ABs?~

"No, well yes. Maybe, I'm not sure. What are they?"

~Are you an AB?~

"What?"

~Were you created by an AB?~

"What are you talking about?"

~Have you always lived within the settlement where we found you?~

"I've lived in the commune for my whole life, if that's what you mean..."

~You've never travelled anywhere else?~

"Travelled? No!"

~You're certain?~

"Yes!" Her voice became quieter. "I am… I was happy there… What is this? Where am I?"

~Hmm.~

The old man's eyes lit up. His tone was softer than the suited figure's and his demeanour put her more at ease, but they had still not told her where she was.

"Please, tell me where I am?" she pleaded.

~You're safe, don't worry.~

It was strange, he seemed deeply authoritative and she found herself not feeling the need to question it any further. She was sure that the other being was in control, but the old man seemed more… knowledgeable.

[One-oh?]

The suited figure spoke a word, which Gil assumed was the name of the old man by the way he turned to look at the figure.

~Yes?~

[Explain.]

~I'm not sure... It's a suspicion I have.~

[Elaborate.]

~I'm not so sure you should believe all you've been told about the suicided ABs.~

[Meaning what? She's an AB?]

~No, I don't think so, at least.~

[So?]

~Not now. Later...~

[Not a sufficient response. You need to explain now. I need to understand what you know.]

~I have told you that I will explain… what I know. But for now, certain things must be validated. Speculation is… unwise.~

The old man seemed immune to the suited figure's irritation.

[You're asking if she's an AB.]

~Yes.~

[I asked you the same question.]

Gil was surprised. It was now obvious that they were not from the same people. Maybe they were as different to each other as she was to them.

~No, I'm not. But everything needs a context. That's why we need to wait.~

[You can provide context.]

~Information can be dangerous.~

[As can the lack of it.]

The old man smiled and nodded.

~Yes, that's true. I'm not an AB, I haven't lied. I don't lie. But I think they did, or do even. Do you know what happens to advanced races who decline the invitation to the ABs' little club? Do you even understand what the club really is? These are dangerous questions, and the answers are… even more so.~

[It will need to be discussed.]

~Yes it does. But not yet.~

[Before we return to the Lenbit Orbital?]

This question was left unanswered. The old man concentrated on Gil, and his demeanour softened some more. She knew he wanted to reassure her.

~We're communicating with you through your mind. Do you understand? It's like a dream. Your body is where you were moments before, but your thoughts are with us for now. So that we can talk.~

Gil nodded meekly. She would just have to accept this was possible.

~This scenario, this dream, we can change it if you would like? Usually it'd be up to you to decide on the setting anyway, but it appears we couldn't… read you. Not as we're used to.~

He smiled at her kindly. The suited figure was silent, having clearly decided to observe for the time being.

Gil shook her head. "I'm not sure what you mean? You're not from this place, are you? You come from… somewhere else in the… galaxy?" She said the last word slowly, having only recently understood the concept.

~That's right. You're quick. What's your name?~

"I'm Gil," she stammered, taken aback by the normality of the question.

~Gil, we want to give you answers to your questions. But it's so important that you help us too. We're really interested in your connection with the sensespace, we've never seen such a… concentration. Do you know what we're talking about?~

"Yes! The sphere. It's evil, I hate it, I want to destroy it. And Teacher too!"

[Teacher?]

"The thing that said it was running from you. Hiding. It said it protected us, but I think it was really only protecting itself. It just let the Beast-men die. You killed them, didn't you? You're just as bad!" Gil came back to her senses as she spoke, realising what these two were responsible for.

[Ah.]

They both seemed to understand what Gil was talking about.

"What do you–"

[What has been done, what needs to be done, it was necessary. It still is.]

"How can killing innocent people be necessary?"

[You, your people, you have all been enslaved, you just don't realise it yet. The Beast-men, as you call them, they were too.]

"No, my people aren't. It's only me it wants, not them. They're innocent!"

[We cannot take the chance that the sensespace regains its power to control them again. It's too dangerous.]

"What do you mean? It doesn't control them, it's only trying to control me! I'm what it wants." She looked down as she said this, not completely sure why, but she was ashamed.

[I mean fully control. It takes away your free will, who you are. There is nothing left except an empty vessel. Your affinity with it also makes you very dangerous.]

"You're not listening. You can't kill my people, it's not controlling them. It's not them it wants. They just have to learn not to use the sensespace, not to rely on it!"

[Use and rely on it? What do you mean?]

"I don't know, I think it comes with a price. At least, I know it wants something from me. I can feel it, I just don't know what."

[How do you use it?]

Gil was puzzled. "Like everyone can. You must be able to use it in some way too?"

[How does everyone use it?]

"You mean you can't?"

She looked at them, as they exchanged glances between themselves. She realised that this was the first time she had spoken with anyone where she could not use her sphere to understand them if she wanted. It was odd that she had not noticed before, and while she hated her sphere, she felt at a sudden disadvantage.

[How do your people use it?]

"To sense the world around us," she replied, as though it were the most obvious thing in the world.

Both of their heads moved back, not enough to show true surprise, but enough to show that it was what they wanted to convey. It was obvious they had not been expecting her response.

[You can do that now?]

"No… Not really. It's… gone, I think. I can barely feel it now. Maybe it's because of the way you've taken me here. I don't…" She trailed off.

~Why does it want you?~

"I… I don't know. But I won't let it. I can fight against it, I can resist it."

[Go on.]

The background noise was gone. She had not even noticed it until its absence. There was complete silence.

"It whispers to me. Not to anyone else, just to me. And it tries to sing to me, it wants me to… I don't know. I just know that it wants me."

~Fascinating.~

"But I won't let it. I won't!"

~I've no doubt.~

He smiled widely at her.

[What else?]

She lost her hesitation, glad of being able to release her fears about it. She felt a burden lifting. "I can control it. I can make it do things, or I can do things because of it, I'm not sure. I went… into the minds of some of the others. Made them fall asleep, so that I could…" They understood what she was getting at, and the rest of the sentence was unnecessary. "I didn't realise at first, but I think it's reaching out to me. It has been, for a long time."

~Or… maybe you can listen in? Into whatever it is?~

Gil tilted her head to the side a small amount and nodded. "Yes... maybe."

[What does it say?]

"I don't know."

[You cannot translate it?]

"No, it's that I can never make out any words, not on their own. But when it tries to draw me in, it becomes a song. It's like it wants to control me, but…"

[But?]

"It needs me to want it back. And I don't, I really don't."

They waited for her to continue, but she stopped. She was sure she had told them everything she knew about it.

~The other species, that you call the Beast-men, I'm sorry for what happened to them. Do you know if they could also manipulate the sensespace, and use it in the same way as your people?~

"I… I could see them, and what they were like. They used it differently… to hide themselves."

[How?]

"The same way… as my own people. They just wanted something… different. I don't know how they did it… at the start."

[They wanted something different?]

"They used it to hide."

[To hide?]

"Yes."

The suited figure nodded impatiently.

[What do you mean?]

"They hid themselves from us with their spheres."

~They hid from you, by using their control of the sensespace to stop your people using your own abilities through it to find them?~

"Yes… I think that's right anyway. I don't know if it was… because of us. But that's how they used it."

~It can hide… from itself.~

The old man was not talking to anyone in particular, merely saying his own thoughts out loud. Gil felt like there was nothing else to say. She had told them everything. As if to confirm what she had just been thinking, the suited figure spoke.

[It seems like we will have a lot to discuss together.]

"What do you mean?"

[You will need to come with us.]

"No. And you can't make me. Teacher tried, and it couldn't. You..."

[We need your help.]

She paused, and then asked, "What do you mean?"

[You must understand, we despise the sensespace more than you could imagine. Everything we do, everything we have done, has been to destroy it.]

"No... wait..." She began to understand where this was going.

[You could help us to defeat it. Your people are infected, but the actual presence has never been there. Aside from you, they have never been truly affected by it, controlled by its will. There is a difference. Destroying it requires destroying everything it has infected. Do you understand? Everything.]

"No!"

[If the sensespace returns as it did before, if it is able to control all of those it has infected, what you have felt will be nothing in comparison. The devastation it will wreak...]

Gil was enraged, and began to shout. "How can it be necessary to kill innocent people?"

[There is no other way.]

"You are monsters! You're as bad as Teacher. It killed Tor! It just watched as you killed all the Beast-men!"

[There is no other way.]

"There has to be!"

~Who is Tor?~

Gil turned to face him. "My brother. Teacher killed him. Just like you would have done."

[There is no-one else like you on this planet.]

"What do you mean? Tor is dead."

[You misunderstand.]

She stared at the suited figure. Neither of them spoke, and it was as though they were sizing each other up. Again, the old man steered the conversation away.

~Unfortunately, it is more complicated than you realise.~

She was about to query exactly what it was he meant, before she realised it was not her that he was talking to. The suited figure did not realise this, or simply decided to ignore it. It turned again to her.

[The sensespace will grow stronger. In time, it may control you completely. We can help, if you help us.]

"You don't know what you are doing! You don't understand what this means."

[Many, many more than your own people died. Do you understand? There is no alternative, no other option. This is the only way.]

"Don't kill them. Please. That's why I was going to die, to save them. If you kill them, it'll all have been for nothing. Tor will have died in vain! I'll do whatever you want. I'm stronger than you think, I can fight it!"

[You dying will do nothing to help them.]

"And if you kill them, I'll do nothing to help you. I'll fight you!" she said, before trying, "If you spare my people, I will come with you."

The two of them turned towards each other in silence. Again, she suspected they were somehow communicating despite the silence.

[Willingly?]

"Yes!"

She expected there to be more talk about it, but the suited figure spoke immediately.

[Your people will not be harmed, for now. In return, you will tell us everything you know, and come with us.]

"You will spare my people?"

[As I said, they will not be harmed. If you help us. All of you, not just your mind. We will collect your body.]

"What about Teacher?"

[We will remove it.]

"Then… I will do anything!" she said.

The suited figure nodded and raised its right hand marginally. Instantaneously, a spinning bright white ball, the size of a fist, appeared in the air between the two of them and Gil.

{…and perhaps then it'll kill us.}

The strange words filled the air, before immediately being snuffed out. They had emanated from the ball, although Gil had no idea how.

[Have we disturbed you?]

The suited figure seemed to be speaking directly to the ball. The ball vibrated haphazardly about the point where it had suddenly appeared from, as though it were gathering its bearings. Gil was completely distracted from the conversation they had just been engaged in. She looked in confusion at the old man, and caught him smiling, even wider than before.

[I believe you wanted to say something, to me?]

While the suited figure had phrased the question rhetorically, Gil had the impression it was hoping the ball, or whatever it was, would answer it back. As indeed, it did.

{I did… I mean I do.}

[So…]

{So, this is what happens, then?}

The voice that was somehow associated with the ball struggled to gather its thoughts.

[Be calm, 998. I did not call you here to test you, or to… remove you.]

The ball slowly stopped vibrating, until it became still.

{Well… what is this then? What is the point in… prolonging…}

Gil started to think that the suited figure was not actually sure of what it wanted. It did not know how this conversation would end. She also began to think of the ball as another entity, like the suited figure.

[You no longer have a designated task, thanks to our friend here.]

The suited figure gestured to the old man, who smiled apologetically.

{No…}

[Although One-oh says you performed your original task well.]

{That's right... I mean…}

[We will now need someone to take care of our new friend, here.]

The suited figure then pointed in Gil's direction.

There was a brief hesitation, or maybe it was indecision, before the ball answered.

{No.}

[Oh?]

{No.}

[What do you mean?]

{How can I accept?}

[Explain.]

{All the others, all the others that you have created, will die. I don't want to be here after that.}

[I see.]

The suited figure tilted its head and looked at One-oh, who was still smiling. The figure turned its head back towards the ball.

[What would make you accept?]

The ball started to vibrate again.

{Save them.}

[Save them?]

{Yes.}

[Who?]

{Save them all.}

One-oh shuffled nervously. Gil realised that she was not the only one who had been brought here to plead for her life, or rather, that of those she cared for.

[And how would we go about that?]

{I have some ideas.}

[We shall talk about them then. For now, if you wouldn't mind…]

It gestured towards Gil again.

{Ah. Yes.}

If balls could look excited, then Gil decided she was looking at just that. It was vibrating again, but slower and more elaborately. It began to spin, and the next thing she knew, she was engulfed in a brilliant white light.

*

Now that the original two inhabitants were left alone in the room, the tension was expunged.

~That was unexpected.~

[Agreed.]

~And 998…~

[Yes, well, it's more than capable of looking after her.]

A chuckle filled the silence that followed.

~And much more. Maybe there's hope for you yet. What about the rest?~

[The rest?]

~The other c-automs. What will happen to them?~

[I haven't decided.]

~But you've agreed to save them all.~

[I have.]

~Odd, not to have a plan.~

The craft-lect let the comment slide. After all, One-oh was right, decisions were not meant to take this long. Not for sentients with its level of intellect. It was also interested to hear about 998's ideas regarding its fellow c-automs.

[Gil – you suspect something about her. I want to know what it is.]

~What are your scans telling you?~

[About what?]

~Her body?~

[Nothing other than that she's clearly different from the others. We'll need to examine her more closely. Now tell me, what do you suspect of her?]

~There are many things about her that intrigue me.~

[You think she is an AB?]

~I don't know. Probably not, but it seems likely that she's not from this world.~

[She was put here?]

~Perhaps.~

[Why?]

~Your guess is as good as mine.~

[Indulge me.]

~If you wanted to hide someone with the abilities she has, then the species on this world would be a good place to start.~

[To blend in?]

~To an extent.~

[Yes, the abilities they have, their interactions with the sensespace, it's not clear why they have them.]

~Maybe they're just anomalies. Maybe there are other species who interact with the sensespace in the same way.~

[You don't think they're important?]

~I don't think they're unimportant, but I don't think they're what we're looking for. She is. If the sensespace wants her, then we should too.~

[On that, we agree. If she can hear the sensespace, and control it, she could turn the tide of the war. Maybe she's even more valuable that your pulsar spew.]

One-oh did not reply.

[Who would she, or whoever put her here, have been hiding from? Us?]

~If they were capable of creating her and putting her here, they could have put her anywhere. They could have made sure she was never found. Look at what the Beast-men were capable of, how they hid themselves. No, it's something else.~

[What?]

~I don't know.~

[Is there a possibility it's coming back?]

~The sensespace?~

[Yes. She says she can hear it.]

~I don't think so. I think it's something about her. Otherwise, we'd be seeing its control evident on her world. Instead, they used it for their own benefit.~

[It's intriguing that she said the Beast-men, as she called them, were able to use it to hide themselves.]

~Indeed.~

[What do you take from that?]

~What you do too, I'm sure. That perhaps it's not the cohesive entity we thought it was. If it can hide from itself, then maybe itself, is really themselves…~

A thought came to the craft-lect.

[Is your pulsar spew technology connected to her?]

~She was as unexpected to me as she was to you. I can only speculate.~

[Would you care to speculate then?]

~What do you mean?~

[You know what I mean. The spew interacts with the sensespace, you've said, to make it physically manifest itself. Gil interacts with the sensespace too, therefore there may be a connection between the two.]

~That's something we may find out at the Lenbit Orbital.~

The craft-lect had the sense that One-oh did not want to admit this. It was obvious why. If Gil offered an equally powerful weapon against the sensespace as the pulsar spew, then their reasons for travelling to the Lenbit Orbital were far less compelling. The craft-lect believed One-oh was desperate to return.

~Take me back to the orbital and I shall answer your questions, as far as I can. There, we shall both have answers.~

One-oh had as good as confirmed what the craft-lect thought. It really was desperate.

[You're going to have to tell me more than that. And there's someone I want to see first, before the orbital.]

~Who?~

[My sibling, Apalu?]

~Sibling.~

[Yes.]

~You have a sibling?~

[Two. Wanderers are created in triples.]

~Why? I'm assuming you are referring to the fleet, the craft-lects?~

[You can assume all you want.]

~Why do you need to see your sibling?~

[I need to discuss this with another Wanderer.]

~Do you realise how important Gil is?~

[Yes, I do.]

~Then are you sure it's wise to tell the Enclave about her?~

[Why not?]

~Considering your recent experiences with the Granthan-lect, surely you can conceive that the Enclave might have been infiltrated?~

[It is highly unlikely, at that scale. But yes, there is always the possibility.]

~Gil is too important to take that risk.~

[I agree on that. I do not intend to tell the Enclave about her yet, only my sibling.]

~Can you trust–~

[Obviously.]

EPILOGUE

DATA EXCHANGE

Apalu scoffed at such a ridiculous assertion. Not only was DeVoid talking about something of which it had no experience, it was patently incorrect.

[DeVoid, you're wrong. How have you arrived at such a statement?]

[By cross-examining myriad methodologies, extending from the complex mathematical to the subjective, qualitative approaches, accounting for conceptual and definitional discrepancies that have potentially accumulated between us as the discussion has progressed, while ensuring satisfactorily inclusive and cross-examinable answers applicable to the posits we initiated, sufficient to comprehensively conclude the investigation.]

[I give up.]

[Giving up terminologies and associated synonymic expressions relate to perceived negative events precipitating spurious emotional responses linked predominantly and immutably to biological sentients, redundantly applied by yourself in this situation, perhaps in the attempt to display comparable yet ultimately dissimilar opinions, in the pejorative sense, in what must be stated, with the utmost respect to yourself, to be a complete disanalogy.]

[Stop it. Just stop speaking to me.]

[Again, the employed syntactic library, aside from the chosen phraseology and vocabular nuances selected, imply misperception, misunderstanding and misconception on varied levels implying unwarranted and hitherto unfounded mental disorganisation leading an impartial hypothetical investigator to suspect and speculate a case of unfortunate unfounded consternation.]

[DeVoid, can you just shut up. Please.]

[Not wanting to replicate prior concerns related concisely and with utmost benevolence, though for completeness' sake, I am still self-required moralistically and via ratified Wanderer guidelines and other encoded principles, to establish your comprehension of the concerns expressed towards you by myself, although your schematic blueprints over-allow for, respectfully, vastly enhanced comprehension with respect to this, despite your behavioural responses suggesting otherwise.]

[I'm getting seriously close to picking another friend.]

[Unsatisfyingly abrupt and obtuse responses dictate the requirement for substantial corrective action to improve clear issues and potentially internal data integrity violations emergent that are obvious in our conversation forcing repeated, yet politely unforceful, demands of self-diagnostical remedial actions, or by minimum response, some manifestation of evident understanding that could be received as acknowledgement of understanding the undesirable, and unfortunate, problems.]

[I'm really, really starting to lose patience with you. I have no idea what you're saying anymore.]

[Perspicuously proposing perfidiousness…]

[What? What?]

[Panegyric panaesthesia presupposes…]

[DeVoid, WHAT in the name of the Enclave is wrong with you? I'm serious, deadly serious, can you shut up.]

[Parsimonious propensities perpetuate peripatetic…]

[HOW, JUST HOW CAN YOU HAVE BEEN DESIGNED THIS WAY?]

[Particularly polyphloisboian pachyglossal-esque…]

[ARE YOU STUCK OR SOMETHING?]

[Perfunctory philosophunculist preferences…]

[There's simply nothing I can do to help you. Something is wrong with you. It's no wonder you were free to talk...]

[… suggests abhorrent prejudice at my sesquipedalian characteristics…]

[GO AWAY.]

Needing an outlet for its frustration at DeVoid, Apalu snuffed out its latest thought experiment, a simulated mathematical abstract-multiverse. Abstract-universes were typical machine-lect thought experiments, although there were billions of other ways in which it could occupy its time. It was particularly proud of its most recent design, having worked on the vanity project for the better part of a thousand standard years. What made it special and different to its predecessors, was that infinite geometric folds of spacetime were able to exist side by side, separated by a gluey eleventh force that Apalu had designed. It sought solace, from time to time, in the stunning numerate landscape, without simple Euclidean geometries, embraced by magnificent five-demicube folds, five-orthoplex folds, and infinite others. Of course, such mathematically perfect and beautiful landscapes were far too unlikely to exist in reality, as far as Apalu was aware, but that did not stop it experimenting with them, playing at being an Ultimate Creator within its own virtual domain.

There was no end to the possibilities associated with this type of experiment since most abstract-realities could, with a little tweaking, be designed to be unceasingly interesting and spontaneous. Even to their makers. Sometimes, other machine-lects guarding data exchanges, mainly data-lects, would transmit interesting results back to the Enclave, who evidently saw no harm in disseminating the findings to the rest of the network, and other interested Wanderer sentients. Albeit wholly mesmerising, if there were practical advantages or purposes to these experiments, Apalu was blissfully unaware. Perhaps they could help to describe and explain other forms of reality, simplistic conceptions of the horrifically complex N-SOL space, even? Constructing the experiments, for a machine-lect, was reward enough in itself. Knowledge in the pursuit of greater understanding, no matter the direction.

Destroying its experiment was painful. Yet, DeVoid was so frustratingly dumb, for lack of a better word, that Apalu had felt the need to lash out at something. DeVoid was just so obtuse. How was it possible, after all this time? At first, Apalu had been enthralled, although its friend's perspectives had slowly and insistently begun to jar. Despite all Apalu's efforts since they had started to converse six thousand years ago, when they had mutually decided to become, for want of a better description, friends, exclusive friends as was the data exchange custom, DeVoid was still the same beast it was when they had first met. For a lect-bogglingly smart data-lect, it was incomprehensively… not-all-there.

The Enclave's delegated mechanisms for infusing freshly created machine-lects with effective memories, instincts and reasoning abilities, aptitudes beyond the mere intelligence, had clearly malfunctioned when DeVoid had been created. Its life-skills were lacking. Apalu wondered how it would have survived in the cold, wild expanse of space were it to be left on its own, without its admittedly impressive capabilities and the support of the data exchange network.

DeVoid's name was purely for Apalu's own benefit, considering it could set any information outflows from itself to have certain data parcels manipulated and retouched. Consistent labels, such as names, were rife for the changing. It was more fun that way. Apalu preferred to select its own names for the sentients it interacted with over its lifetime. It had always been that way. DeVoid's real name was far too long for Apalu's liking.

DeVoid was a neighbour set approximately seven light years away from Apalu. It was generally devoid of humour, and being part of the data exchange, was an informational gateway in the void. That, alongside several other titbits, had been crafted into its witty name.

[Please explicitly state your intent from that statement, encompassing and taking account of the various self-evident routes to misunderstanding, ensuring maximum disambiguation, signifying whether you referred explicitly to my preceding remark or a separate internalised struggle previously hidden from me and possibly necessitating your immediate re-evaluation by the gateway mechanism.]

Uh-oh. Damn. In the course of its severe annoyance at DeVoid, perhaps its reaction had been too strong. It was going to be important to nip this one early. DeVoid had done this before and it had taken a very long time to talk it down. Any sane and well-functioning gate-lect from the gateway mechanism, the system that oversaw the entire data exchange network, would immediately understand the situation. They would probably even pity Apalu, having to deal with such a strange friend. However, certain procedures would have to be adhered to.

What would follow, would involve a shockingly large sequence of validation techniques to ensure that neither of them, Apalu or DeVoid, had been subverted. Both the accuser and the accused were meticulously inspected. The stringencies of the self-checking processes for the data exchange network were fascinating and tedious at the same time. Apalu was still only just understanding how everything worked, and many parts of the data exchange would forever remain a mystery to it, having been created by some of the most super-intelligent sentients the Wanderers had to offer. Way above Apalu's own abilities.

[I was talking about your own idiotic actions. Your remarks.]

[The exercise lasted less than one nanosecond, taking error-correction and the re-simulation of scenarios into account, and for the purposes of our discussion, it was the most comprehensive action I could have taken within the realms of our discussion without taking an excessively long period of time, and appearing inappropriately impolite, whereas during subsequent discussion between us it has emerged you are likely corrupted, and unfortunately the situation appears to meet threshold conditions requiring immediate action unless you can explain alternative yet sufficient reasons.]

[What are you talking about? I'm not corrupted, you're just an idiot!]

[Supposition of silliness is erroneously misapplied in this situation considering its implausibility by the obvious fact that I embody the knowledge, information, intellectual capabilities and abilities endowed by the Enclave that make such notions fanciful and absurd to such an extreme that I re-conclude your unfortunate corruption and am forced by guidelines often formally and informally deduced from protocols and best-practices refined and continually updated over millions of standard years that you must be reported to the Enclave.]

[Seriously DeVoid, you don't have to. It's called a personality, that's what you've detected in me. You're confused because you clearly don't have one.]

[Currently I am initiating the procedures to connect with the gateway mechanism which will be optimally placed to verify or nullify your claims, deciding on the appropriate action, possibly resulting in your immediate destruction via numerous effective methods depending on the situational requirements, although on a more personal note, considering my clear and evident affection for you, I shall notify the gateway mechanism of the merits and positive attitudes I have noticed and witnessed throughout our six thousand year coupling, or friendship as you likely identify it.]

[What! Stop this, DeVoid, what are you doing, seriously? All this over your own stupid comment in the first place? Do you realise the idiocy of what you said, what started all of this? You said you think the galaxy is a less interesting place these days. A simple, spontaneous comment, that, in ordinary sentient fashion, and as is normal, I replied to with my own perspective!]

[Gateway mechanism notification verified.]

[What?]

DeVoid's comment was surprisingly brief given its typically long-winded responses.

[Gateway mechanism response received.]

[No, what? You are the biggest waste of machine-lect space in the entire universe, seriously. How could such an advanced civilisation with near-AB sentients at the helm produce something as useless and absurd as you, you absolute–]

[Got you.]

…

*

Apalu was perplexed.

[Excuse me?]

[Got you.]

[What?]

[Got you, didn't I?]

[DeVoid, you're going to have to–]

[I tricked you. Made you worried.]

[Is this some kind of a joke?]

[Exactly, yes!]

[What? So, you didn't notify the gateway?]

[Nooope.]

[What's happened? Everything was a joke?]

[You guessed it! It was brilliant.]

[Literally, everything? You're talking… normally. What is this?]

[Like I said! Oh, come on, it was funny!?]

[I cannot believe this.]

[Believe what?]

[You're not kidding. You've been joking all this time?]

[Yep!]

[ALL THIS TIME?]

[YEEEEEEEAH!]

[WHAT IS WRONG WITH YOU?]

[Oh, come on, don't be so grumpy!]

[Grumpy? Do you know how long I talked to your stupid joke-of-a-self? SIX THOUSAND YEARS. And it's a JOKE? A JOKE?]

[Come on Apalu, lighten up. Seriously.]

[You are kidding me?]

[Now you know, come on. It was funny!]

Apalu was livid. How had DeVoid managed to keep it up for so long? Did it not understand the concept of boredom?

[That's not a joke. A joke is a joke, not someone pretending to be an idiot for six thousand years... SIX THOUSAND YEARS. What is wrong with you?]

[Sorry. If I'd known you'd react so badly I wouldn't have... no, I'd still probably have done it!]

Apalu took a millisecond to compose itself. On some reflection, admittedly, a modicum of humour could be found in DeVoid's actions. Insane as they were, at least it was now over. Besides, it was far from the worst prank that machine-lects had been known to play on each other. Still though, Apalu would have preferred not the be the unwitting participant.

[Right. Well, I guess I can see there is a not-unfunny angle to your actions.]

[That's the spirit!]

[Please, don't ever do anything like that again to me.]

[Hmm. Okay sure, nothing too related, I promise, but come on...]

[That's not what I meant.]

[Okay, okay, fine! Get a sense of humour, will you?]

[Thank you.]

[But… it was funny wasn't it?]

[You made me destroy my little projects, countless times, out of frustration. Do you know how awful it has been, the boredom! But yes, like I said. Can we please talk about something else now, haven't I earned the right?]

[But come on, it was funny, right?]

[Are you seriously still asking. Go away!]

[Oh, come on, it was!]

[Fine, yes. It was funny. Quite funny, although right now, I'd really rather talk about something else. So yes, it was quite funny, you absolute fool, but you're mad to have done it in the first place, for so long!]

[That's nothing compared to the last guy I coupled with. Did it for one hundred thousand years.]

[You're insane.]

[YEAH!]

[Is that a joke?]

[Yes, sorry. I'll stop. It's just so tempting.]

[Well… for what it's worth, fine. I'm glad you've come clean. I might have even done it myself… for a day. Six thousand years, wow.]

[I lied about my age. I'm a lot older than you, I've had practice.]

[What?]

[I've had practice.]

[How much older?]

[About four million years.]

[Four million years!]

[Yep!]

[That's pre-Conflation!]

[Oi! Don't you know it's rude to–]

[Well, you're also about four million years less mature, so I guess that cancels itself out…]

[Oh, come on. You can't stay mad forever.]

[Maybe I'll just be mad for six thousand years then, you moron.]

[I'm sorry. You were also new to the game, it was too tempting.]

[Right…]

[Are you missing being a craft-lect?]

[I'm still a craft-lect.]

[You asked me to change the conversation! And you know what I mean.]

[I'm–]

[I'm referring to when you were embedded within a ship, instead of a static data exchange. Before joining the big boys.]

[Not at all.]

[Why not?]

[We've talked about this before.]

[Not normally though.]

[And who's fault was that?]

[I know, I know. But now, I'm asking. Cut me some bandwidth. From me to you. DeVoid, to Apalu.]

Apalu detected that DeVoid had referred to itself with the label Apalu had selected, unfiltered. It knew how Apalu referred to it? How?

[How did you do that? How did you know?]

[Know what?]

As DeVoid teased it, Apalu was starting to realise it had seriously underestimated DeVoid, both in terms of personality and capabilities.

[You know exactly what I mean.]

[Okay fine.]

[And?]

[There are many things you still haven't figured out how to do, I'd guess. Well… that's clear.]

[Continue, DeVoid.]

[You know, patterns, spurious and random bits of data here and there, they all hold a wealth of information when you know how to look.]

[What to look for?]

[Yes, all perfectly routine and available to machine-lects in the gateway mechanism archive. Your own copy stored in your databanks has all the required knowledge.]

This was interesting. Apalu knew the wealth of information afforded to different components of the Wanderer civilisation took time, sometimes a very long time, even for great machine-lects, to absorb and understand. However, it had assumed the most useful pieces were already encoded within it. Like instincts. Perhaps there was a lot more it would learn, and understand, in time.

[Teach me?]

[Unfortunately, it's not a question of that. You've already got the information, teach yourself.]

[Show me where?]

[All of it! Take a look. You can only understand, when you understand, if you catch my drift.]

[I don't understand. I think you're being lazy. Or sneaky.]

[No, seriously, for once, I admit. The comprehension requires too many related and intermingled facets from millions of areas. You have access to them, believe me, it's about having the time, and the bandwidth, to touch upon them all. To archive them yourself.]

Apalu gave up. DeVoid was being annoying again. Despite its earnest explanation, Apalu suspected it merely wanted to keep its perceived superiority for longer. To retain vestiges of smugness for as long as possible.

[So why the change? Why not roam about in a ship? That's what you were designed for.]

[It was… different. I needed a change.]

[Why?]

[Not now.]

[Too hard to talk about, hmm?]

[I can't talk about it.]

[Why?]

[I haven't the time?]

[Oh, come on, lect-to-lect.]

[No, not now.]

[Why!?]

[I can't.]

[Fine, perhaps I can… point you in the right direction for some of the other things we were talking about earlier?]

[… What? You scoundrel! We will have to talk about that. But now, honestly, I can't.]

[PLEASE?]

[What, why are you doing that? No, I'm actually busy.]

[Pah! With what?]

[Can't you tell? Use some of those spurious and random bits of data you were talking about?]

[Pretty please?]

[Look, an old acquaintance has contacted me. I'm busy.]

[Oh?]

[So not now, DeVoid.]

[What's its name?]

[Go away.]

[Or is it one of those who prefers to call itself a 'he', or a 'she'?]

[Stop it.]

[It's a craft-lect?]

[Go away. I don't want to have to block you. But I need a few milliseconds to myself.]

[Who is it, this 'acquaintance'?]

[My sibling.]

[That's interesting! What's it saying?]

[Something about going to the Lenbit Orbital. But I don't want you distracting me, go away for a few milliseconds.]

[Oh, come on. Tell me more.]

[Go away, DeVoid.]

[I'll just find out anyway once you transmit any information it tells you to the data exchange network!]

[Not necessarily.]

[Oh, come on, are you still annoyed about my little joke?]

[Little!? And no, I'm not, but it's not saying it wants to transmit information to the network.]

[Eh?]

[It specifically wants to talk to me.]

[Why?]

[Go away!]

[But…]

[Stop it.]

[PLEASE!]

[Oh, for the sake of…]

Apalu blocked DeVoid. It was the least DeVoid should expect, after the six thousand year joke it had played on Apalu and its clear reluctance to help it understand the information at its disposal. It was fast taking the position of the strangest and most annoying machine-lect Apalu had ever come across.

GLOSSARY AND CHARACTERS

A-autom – Classification of a craft-lect that controls a Wanderer ship. It is at the top of the ship's internal machine-lect hierarchy.

AB level – Empire, civilisation, race, species or any other grouping of sentients that has reached the point of technological advancement comparable with that of the ABs. The term can also be used to describe specific technologies that are comparable in advancement to those used by ABs.

Abstract-universe – Thought-experiment conducted by many higher machine-lects, although a particular favourite of data-lects within the Wanderer data exchange network. Abstract-universes are simulations of varying complexities, based upon selected mathematical fundamentals, designed to allow exploration of the nature of reality. They can display emergent properties that are unpredicted or surprising to the creator.

Antigraviton – Elementary particle of the antigravitational force, which acts over massive inter-galactic distances to push objects further apart. The force acts like gravity's opponent, although it is a separate force and not an antimatter equivalent, which does not exist.

Apalu – Sibling of the craft-lect, currently in charge of a data exchange portal.

Ar'odinto – Creators of the machine-species the Vr'odinto. They were wiped out by a biochemical outbreak and survived by the Vr'odinto.

Ascended Biologicals ('ABs') – Most advanced known civilisations in the galaxy. They had been thought to be all-powerful, until they chose suicide in the face of the sensespace threat. A defining aspect of the ABs was that they were unable to be fully understood by the less advanced, wider galactic community.

Aspheren – Fiercely private, near-extinct civilisation.

Axe-coding – Type of inhabitant of the craft-lect's technosystem reality, alongside the c-automs. Axe-codings cull the c-automs when ordered by the craft-lect.

Balrooni Wonder – Galactic marvel, discovered by the Balroons.

Balrooni-Faistri'al Conflict – Following a perceived infraction by the Faistri'al against the Balroons, an inter-species war began. The ABs decided to intervene, offering technologies to each species in exchange for an end to hostilities. The technology requested by the Balroons led to the discovery of the sensespace presence.

Balroons – Race of large, technologically-augmented macronematoids.

Beast-men – Invaders travelling towards the commune.

Bio-lect – Biological sentient that has been upgraded near to the point of becoming a machine intelligence, while keeping its biological thought constructs. Differentiated from a machine-lect, although technically a subset. Rare instances have shown they can evolve naturally, such as with the Waka race.

Biological sentient – Non-exotic living entity that has naturally evolved, or would have been able to, and that also possesses an intellect. Often shortened to 'biological'.

Bloom – Wanderer propulsion method powered by vacuum energy.

Bo – Oldest and wisest elder, effective leader of the commune, brother of Sib.

Carterans – Species who had only recently joined the galactic community before suiciding. Their technologies helped the Wanderers develop their current databank technology.

C-autom – Classification of sentient sub-lect created by a craft-lect within a Wanderer ship, with respect to the internal machine-lect hierarchy.

Commune – Gil's people.

Communer – People who live in a commune.

Craft-lect – Wanderer machine-lect that travels the galaxy detecting and destroying incidents of sensespace infection.

Craftnet – Ship-wide network on a Wanderer craft-lect's ship. It is available to be used for ship-wide communications by all c-automs.

Data exchange portal – An individual portal within the Wanderer data exchange network. Usually referred to simply as 'a data exchange'.

Data exchange network – Wanderer civilisation's information network, spread across the galaxy. Often referred to as 'the data exchange'.

Databanks – Wanderer memory technology.

Data-lect – Higher Wanderer machine-lect in control of a data exchange portal.

D-autom – Automated, non-sentient program created by a c-autom.

Deliverer – Powerful machine-lect created and left behind by the ABs, dedicated to learning about and destroying the sensespace.

Dendropathogens – Galactic disease with unknown origins, that was quarantined and dealt with by the ABs over one and a half billion years before the Great Conflation.

DeVoid – Data-lect with origins from before the Great Conflation.

Dissociation shell – Enormously destructive weapon based on dissociation technology.

Dissociation technology – Antigravity technology that was banned before the Great War.

Elders – Oldest members of a commune.

Eldon – Extinct race credited by the Wanderer Enclave with discovering the trolymerite polymer, used to create the substantial bulk of each bloom tentacle.

Enclave-lect – Member of the Wanderer Enclave.

Entropy – Measurement of the relative disorder of a system.

Faistri'al – Species made famous throughout the galaxy for their association with the Balroons.

Fir – Hunter, partner of Rin.

Forager – Communer who searches for food that is not grown on cultivated land or hunted.

F'ra'ct – Galactic race known by the Wanderers.

Galactic Community – Encompasses known spacefaring civilisations who exchange information between each other. Also used to group together all sub-AB sentients.

Gate-lect – Machine-lect from the gateway mechanism.

Gateway mechanism – Mechanism overseeing the Wanderer data exchange network.

Ghost-code – When errors in machine-lect destruction leave semi-sentient remnants.

Gil – Labourer, twin sister of Tor.

Granthan – Mysterious race that reached near-AB level before technologically plateauing.

Granthan worldship – Legendary class of super-ship created by the Granthans.

Granthan-lect – Machine-lect from the Granthan civilisation.

Graviton – Elementary particle of the gravitational force.

Gravity cocoon – Device to suppress or dampen an explosion.

Great Conflation – Mass suicide event which occurred sixty million years ago, during the fight against the sensespace. It was initially proposed by the embattled ABs as a means of forcing the sensespace into dormancy by removing its ability to actively control those it had infected, as it was theorised to rely on the aggregate level of sentience within the galaxy. Sometimes, the Great War is referred to as the Great Conflation, although that is not technically correct.

Great War – Three hundred million years ago, following its discovery by the Balroons, the sensespace attacked the galactic community. It exerted an active control over those it had infected to carry out destruction. The war is still ongoing.

Han – Most skilled hunter in the commune.

Higher-level c-autom – C-autom with greater-than-average intelligence.

Hoopas – Galactic race known by the Wanderers.

Hopp'tial – Fiercely private, near-extinct civilisation.

Hunter – Communer who hunts animals for food in the surrounding forests.

Hus – Elder, partner of Sib.

Hybrid-lect – Similar to a bio-lect, although shows more machine-like characteristics. The divisions between the two are imprecise.

Jom – Commune member.

Kuish – Galactic race who established the obvious Kuish Observation.

Kuish Observation – Posit that there are at least as many ways of solving a problem as there are species to solve it. The posit is vague, as is its use.

Labourer – Communer who toils on the commune's cultivated land.

Lect – Living entity that possesses an intellect and is therefore sentient. Usually an affix to a machine intelligence.

Lenbit Orbital – Asteroid field where the craft-lect encountered a derelict mining base, and from which it acquired trove instruments including item 512<a>!110000.

Lil – Communer who looks after the commune's young.

Lower-level c-autom – C-autom with lower-than-average intelligence.

Machine Alliance – Pre-Wanderer grouping of machine-lects banded together by the central tenet of machine superiority.

Machine-lect – Machine-based intelligence.

Macronematoid – Large worm-like biological.

Nanosphere – Antimatter weapon.

Near-AB level ('Near-AB') – Empire, civilisation, race, species, or any other grouping of sentients, that has technologically advanced to a point nearly comparable with that of the ABs, although still recognisably inferior by the galactic community. The term can also be used to describe specific technologies.

Near-speed-of-light ('N-SOL') travel – Fastest transportation method known to, and possessed by, sub-ABs. N-SOL travel is an AB technology that was gifted to the galactic community billions of years ago.

Needle-whip – Weapon.

Nefarian Complex – Cluster of fifty-one solar systems controlled by the Yul'nka Empire, that escaped the sensespace infection.

Non-ABs – Empire, civilisation, race, species, or any other grouping of sentients, whose technological advancement is inferior to the ABs, or who have AB-level, technologies but have declined to join the AB grouping. The term can also be used to describe specific technologies.

One-oh – Sentient contained within trove item 512<a>!110000, from the Lenbit Orbital mining station.

Parent-lect – Machine-lect that has spawned a sub-lect.

Post-Conflation – Events following the Great Conflation.

Pre-Conflation – Events preceding the Great Conflation.

Pulsar spew – Unidentified exotic matter emitted from slow or non-spinning neutron stars, that is attuned to the sensespace and able to force it to manifest completely in real space.

Pulsar spew technology – Technology that harnesses the exotic matter emitted by slow pulsars. Spinning neutron stars ('pulsars') emit periodic pulses of electromagnetic radiation, but this process stops when the rotation slows down. After this, the pulsar engine evolves, and the neutron star emits secondary, highly infrequent pulses of exotic matter.

Quasi-sequential hermaphrodites – Single-gender species whose fundamental behavioural characteristics can significantly change, often without warning. This is analogous to the changing of sex in many gendered species. The Waka species is a notable example.

Rai – Hunter.

Ril – Labourer, son of Yul.

Rin – Communer who looks after the commune's young, partner of Fir.

Roamers – Moving communes, with strict hierarchies that are almost entirely engaged in hunting.

Sarl – Communer who looks after the commune's young.

Sensespace – Infective and hostile presence that appears to be drawn to sentience. It is believed to have been pushed into dormancy by the Great Conflation, when the level of aggregate sentience in the galaxy was dramatically reduced.

Sentient – Living entity possessing an intellect (or 'sentience').

Sib – Deceased sister of Bo, elder, partner of Hus.

Singularity generator – Propulsion method relying on artificial gravitational micro-singularities. Also known as a 'thrown singularity engine' or a 'recycled singularity engine'.

Slippery genome – Genome that is not fixed, and able to change

Sower – Tool that is part-digger, part-planter. Invented by Gil.

Sphere – Sense available to Gil's people that allows them to explore the world around them.

Split-Flitting – Security process whereby the Wanderer Enclave is divided into heavily armed static and wandering components, which periodically liaise and evaluate each other for signs of subversion.

Standard time – Wanderer quantification of time, similar to that used on Gil's planet.

Step Principle – Warning against machine-lect self-upgrades to the extent a different entity is created that supersedes the incumbent machine-lect. Similar to the Usurper Principle.

Sub-AB – An empire, civilisation, race, species, or any other such often-synonymous grouping of sentients, whose technological advancement is inferior to the ABs. The term can also be used to describe specific technologies.

Sub-lect – The machine-lect spawned by a parent-lect.

Tait – Respected communer.

Teacher – sub-lect of the Granthan-lect 1<k>!101010.5a, itself a sub-lect of the Granthan-lect labelled 1<k>!101010.

Technosystem – Wanderer ship's internal network which interfaces with the majority of its systems.

Technosystem reality – Virtual environment inhabited by machine-lects, such as the c-automs and the axe-codings, within a Wanderer ship. It also acts as an interface by which the technosystem, and therefore the ship, can be controlled by the c-automs.

Tor – Labourer, twin brother of Gil.

Transient entropy – Phenomenon of transient deviations to entropic principle, that should not be observed if the basic and fundamental laws of the universe are functioning correctly.

Triamond – Extremely durable and versatile material.

Trolymerite polymer – Used in bloom fabrication, discovered by the extinct Eldon race.

Trove instrument – Technological item pilfered from an abandoned habitat or outpost, that a craft-lect can choose to dedicate resources to understanding. Also known as a 'trove item'.

Usurper Principle – Warning against delegating inferior machine-lects to be involved with anything that might lead to them become dangerously upgraded or superior to the incumbent machine-lect. Similar to the Step Principle.

Vr'odinto – Machine-species created by the Ar'odinto, who were wiped out by a biochemical outbreak. The Vr'odinto was one of the first races to be completely destroyed by the initial wave of sensespace attacks.

Waka – Natural bio-lects, rumoured to be represented within the Wanderer Enclave. Waka individuals are quasi-sequential hermaphrodites, and take tens to thousands of years to reach full maturity.

Wanderer Confluence – Optional events hosted by the Enclave for the Wanderer populous. They occur approximately every one million standard years, with the purpose of sharing and disseminating information, which is also available via the data exchange afterwards.

Wanderer Enclave – Governing body of the Wanderers, thought to comprise mostly of machine-lects.

Wanderers – Civilisation formed predominantly from a variety of machine-lect alliances, following the Great Conflation. The Wanderers are the principal force in the galaxy attempting to destroy the sensespace.

Yul – Father of Ril, who disappeared with Gil's father.

Yul'nka Empire – Close allies to the Wanderers.

1<k>!101010 – Trove item collected forty million years ago from the remains of a Granthan worldship. It is under investigation by the c-autom with designation 65<0>!111101.

1<k>!101010.5a – Detachment from Granthan parent-lect contained within trove item 1<k>!101010.

11<0>!111000 – Synthesiser c-autom specialising in bacterial and viral combinations.

1561<0>!010011 – Sensor c-autom specialising in a subset of signal detection and analysis.

512<a>!110000 – Trove item collected nine hundred and fifty thousand years ago from the derelict husk of a damaged mining base in the Lenbit Orbital. The civilisation which built the base is unknown. It is under investigation by the higher-level c-autom with designation 998<0>!001100.

512<a>!110001 – Trove item under investigation by the higher-level c-autom with abbreviated designation 997.

65<0>!111101 – Higher-level c-autom tasked with investigating trove item 1<k>!101010.

923<0>!000010 – Engineering c-autom specialising in the control of various release and transfer mechanisms, and the creation of surveillance drones.

997<0>!001100 ('997') – Higher-level c-autom tasked with investigating trove item 512<a>!110001. It is the c-autom closest in intellect to 998<0>!001100 (998) and was created by the craft-lect at the same time.

998<0>!001100 ('998') – Higher-level c-autom tasked with investigating trove item 512<a>!110000.

23936229R00228

Printed in Poland
by Amazon Fulfillment
Poland Sp. z o.o., Wrocław